IT'S A HAINT BLUE CHRISTMAS

ALSO BY J. ELLIOTT

Haint Blue Series:
*Monkey Mind*
*Monkey Heart*

Supernatural short story collections:

*Ghost Lite*
*Tales from Kensington*
*Uncanny Stout*

# IT'S A HAINT BLUE CHRISTMAS

## J. ELLIOTT

Hedonistic Hound Press

This book is a work of fiction. The town of Catfish Springs does not exist. A few Alachua and Gainesville landmarks are real but are used in a fictional manner or with permission. All characters and situations are creations of the writer's imagination and any resemblance to actual persons or events is entirely coincidental.

Hedonistic Hound Press

This book is dedicated to:

Liza, Mica, Lola, Moises, Ruben

with much love and hold the chonklas

# Acknowledgements

*So many people to thank! I've been blessed to have a wonderful team of supporters and inspirers.*

*I am grateful to Lejaun James whose videos entertain and inspire. If you aren't familiar with him, please hunt him up on YouTube. Hilarious.*

*Thank you to Wendy Thornton who has supported me from the beginning. You made me believe this writing business was doable and almost easy. It sure isn't! You have helped give me confidence to keep going.*

*Liza Caudillo, thank you for your love, support, faith in me, and for being a sounding board.*

*Kathy Passman--Archy, Mehitabel, Prince Albert of Upper Balderdash, and Shooting Star owe everything to you. Made it to book three with your help!*

*Christy Inks, Dean Inks, Michelle Walker, Judy Phillips--many thanks for your humor and support! Ceci and Kate exist because of you—they are your creations.*

*Big mwahs to my pod group: Mike Kite, Betty Warren, Nicolette Matt, David Dekay.*

*To my beta readers: Peggy Cogar, blessings to you for being such a staunch friend and cheerleader. Nancy Dohn, many thanks for your eyes catching time glitches! Jean Kocienda Many thanks for all your help. I hope to pay you back in kind!*

*Rick Smith, I owe you everything.*

*Thank you all! Your love, encouragement, and support have let Haint and Catfish Springs come to life again.*

*Jessica Elliott   2021*

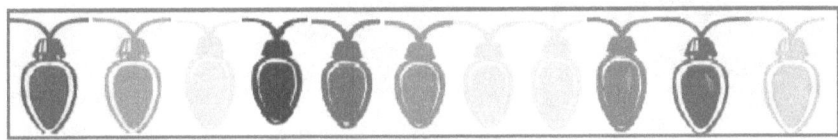

# Contents

# RETREAT MAP

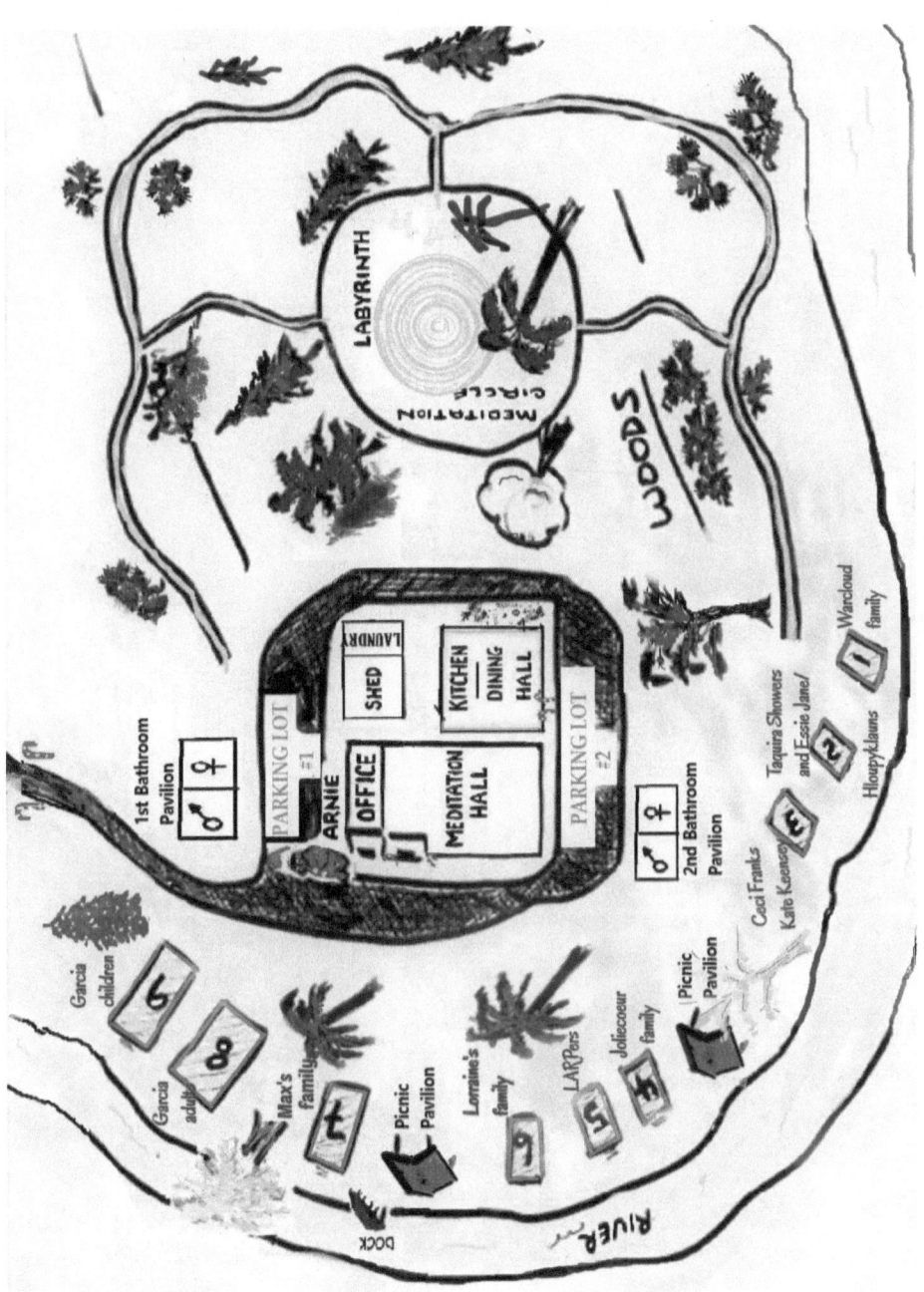

# CATFISH SPRINGS MAP

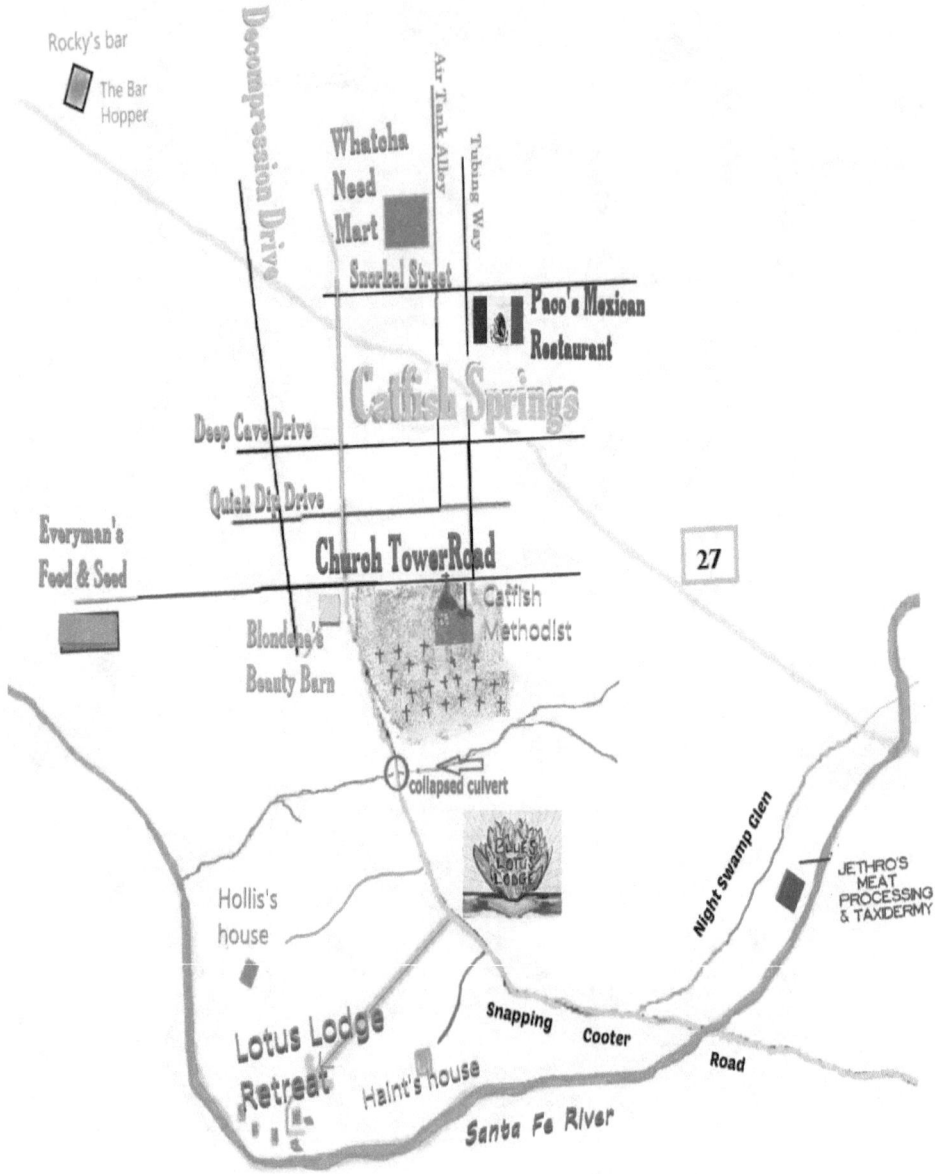

Rocky's bar

The Bar Hopper

Decompression Drive

Whatcha Need Mart

Air Tank Alley

Tubing Way

Snorkel Street

Paco's Mexican Restaurant

Catfish Springs

Deep Cave Drive

Quick Dig Drive

Everyman's Feed & Seed

Church Tower Road

27

Catfish Methodist

Blondelpe's Beauty Barn

collapsed culvert

DULE'S LOTUS LODGE

Hollis's house

JETHRO'S MEAT PROCESSING & TAXIDERMY

Night Swamp Glen

Lotus Lodge Retreat

Snapping Cooter Road

Haint's house

Santa Fe River

# THE REGULARS

Haint Blue
Naughty Britches –her basset hound
Mischief –her cat

Iggy Blue, Haint's brother
Louise Swanson, Iggy's new girlfriend

Urliss and Hollis Oakley, twins who live next door
Peggy Sue, their younger sister (cameo appearance)

Max Johnson  former neighbor, now living in the Old Oaks,
   sold Haint the Stinkin' Skunk Ape Fish Camp

Lorraine Chapman, Haint's best friend
Lerlene Watts, Lorraine's sister, upcoming artist, painted
   the Blue's Lotus Lodge
Saint Eleanor, their mother
Aunt Moira, Eleanor's sister, astrologer, and professional
   psychic

"Buster" George Burgwyn Shadetree II, famous fly
   fisherman and cryptozoologist, Haint's recent love
   interest

# CHE GUESC LISC

**Cabin One:**

> **The Warclouds**: Robin, Chaz, and Rain (plus a trailer with alpacas: Mehitabel, Prince Albert of Upper Balderdash, and Archy)

**Cabin Two:**

> **Taquira Showers**, the opera singer and her personal assistant, Essie Jane/
> **Mr. and Mrs. Hloupyklaun**

**Cabin Three:**

> **The Nifty Thrifters**: Ceci Franks and Kate Keensey

**Cabin Four:**

> **The Joliecoeur Family**: Violette, Duran and daughter, Angejolie

**Cabin Five:**

> **The LARPers** (Live Action Role Players): Cindy, Ray, Kirby, Linwood, Wendy, Kandi, and Lloyd

**Cabin Six:**

> **Lorraine Chapman's Family**: Saint Eleanor, Leander, Stuart, Noni, Stuey and Amy

## LORRAINE'S FAMILY

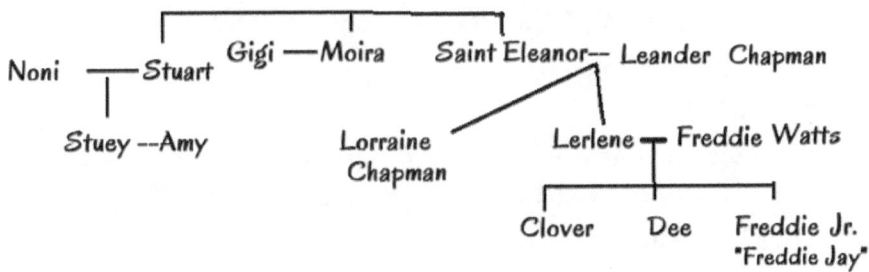

Noni ——Stuart  Gigi ——Moira  Saint Eleanor—— Leander Chapman

Stuey --Amy  Lorraine Chapman  Lerlene — Freddie Watts

Clover  Dee  Freddie Jr. "Freddie Jay"

**Cabin Seven**

> **Max Johnson's family:** Mamma Sue, Max, Nellavon, Taylor, Olivia, Max Jr., Cameron, Benny, Pike, Betsy, Austin, May, and "Baby Vonnie"

## MAX JOHNSON'S FAMILY

Mamma Sue

Charlene—Max  Nellavon—Taylor  Roberta
(deceased)  (deceased)

Olivia— Max Jr.

Cameron_ Benny
"Cam"

Pike —— Betsy

Sue Nell  Austin ┬ May
(absent)

Vonnie

ix

## Cabin Eight:

Garcia Family adults: Grandma Yaya, Aletea, Dante, Mingo, Rita, Rocky, Osanna, Pedro

## Cabin Nine:

Garcia Family children: Clementina, Vic, Crystale, Eliazar, Mimi, Gorge, Luna, Anna, Zelia, Oscar and Oro

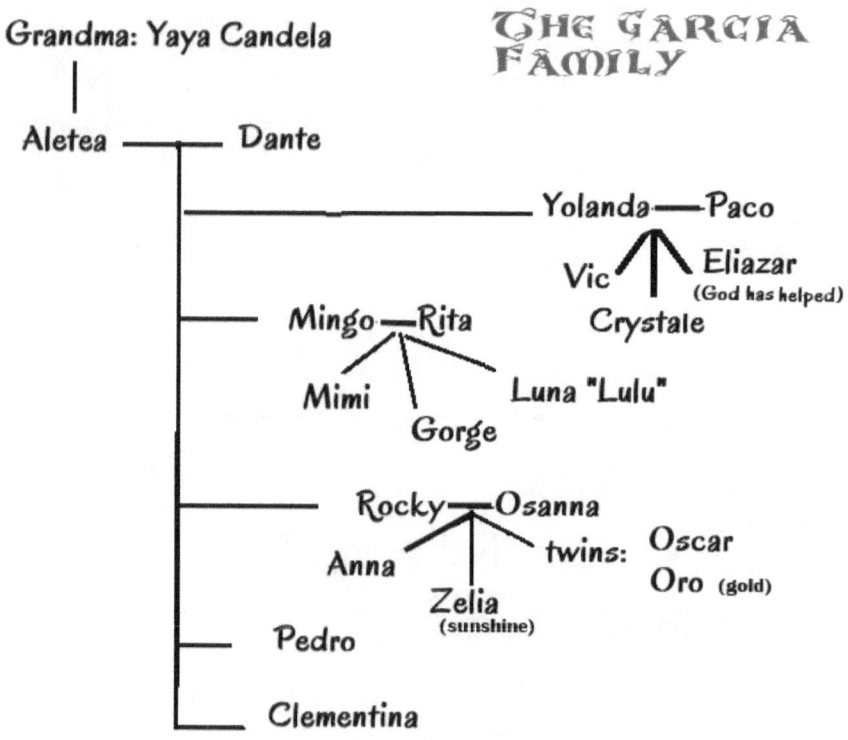

Grandma: Yaya Candela

THE GARCIA FAMILY

Aletea —— Dante

Yolanda —— Paco

Vic / Eliazar (God has helped)

Crystale

Mingo —— Rita

Mimi / Luna "Lulu"

Gorge

Rocky —— Osanna

Anna / twins: Oscar / Oro (gold)

Zelia (sunshine)

Pedro

Clementina

# PART ONE

## THE SNOWBALL

# Chapter 1

## Washed Up Beach Plans

Early December in Florida was sunny and warm with only the bombardment of Christmas music to remind me that the holiday season was careening ever closer. The forced conviviality seemed as artificial as the trees on display in the big box stores. Possibly a hoax perpetuated to stimulate the economy. Okay, yes, there was a cool patch at around Thanksgiving, but the mosquitos and warm temps were back. We were closer to summer than winter.

My name is Helena Bluszczski, but thanks to nurses in the preemie ward in Charleston, South Carolina, I'm known as Haint Blue. You can't blame them for not wanting to pronounce Bluszczski, and albino babies are fairly uncommon. Someone must have said, "She looks like a haint!" Haint being an old regional word for spook, ghost, or haunt.

It was thought that ghosts feared water, so painting a front porch blue like water, would confuse ghosts and keep them from entering a house. Yes, my name is a color. But haint blue is not one color; it is anything in the slate gray/periwinkle spectrum, mimicking the color of water.

Anyway, being an albino is no big deal, other than getting strange looks from people; being almost legally blind without glasses or contacts; and having eyes and skin sensitive to sunlight—oh yeah, good choice to end up in *Florida*, hello, sunshine! I'm careful. Glasses. Sunblock. Hats. Coverups.

I run a meditation retreat and live next door. Both properties are on the Santa Fe River, but I was itching to get away for a while, go see the ocean, smell the salty air, and listen to seabirds. Stare at a vast expanse of horizon. I desperately needed a retreat from my retreat.

I had often dreamed of travelling to a dreamy place of solitude in some glorious locale with scenic views and mountains. When my next-door neighbor, Max Johnson, lost his wife and moved into a nursing home, he'd sold me his property, a rundown fish camp. I had the naïve notion that by running such a place, I'd create the experience myself. I'd provide the oasis, the gourmet food, the yoga, the hiking trails. I'd meet interesting people and meditate. Bring the inner peace to my backyard. Just like the brochures.

I'd spent two years converting the Stinkin' Skunk Ape Fish Camp into the sanctuary of my dreams. Blues Lotus Lodge had a soft opening back in September. It was a disaster. Business had been tepid since. I'd put my heart and soul into the new endeavor, but much as I loved it, I was burning out.

With no bookings for the holiday season, the temptation to just close up shop and disappear to the beach was strong. My best friend, Lorraine, had family plans involving her overbearing mother affectionately called Saint Eleanor, plus generations of family. My brother, Iggy, had plans with his new girlfriend, Louise, to visit with her kin. I'd botched things up with my potential boyfriend, Buster, so I really didn't know what state our relationship was in, or for that matter, what *state* he was in. Whatever his holiday plans were, they didn't seem to involve me.

"What say you, NB? Wanna go to the beach?" I asked my faithful, aging basset hound, Naughty Britches.

She responded with a whatever-you-say-Mom-just-pet-me face.

"We'll pack a cooler and lots of treats. Walk the beach. Sleep in. Right?"

Wags of approval.

"You can chase crabs and sandpipers. You love that."

Her eyes seemed to say yes.

My Inner Critic disagreed. *You'll mope, you know you will. 'Oh, why am I alone like this? How did everyone make plans without me?'* I should mention that while, of course, the Inner Critic is the self-doubting version of me, the voice often comes across in the utterly disenchanted, almost disdainful voice of actor Alan Rickman, RIP.♥

"Not true," I retorted. "I'll walk the beach, read my new paperback mystery, work a jigsaw puzzle — I've been wanting to do that basset puppy in a Christmas stocking puzzle since last Christmas. I'll get a room with a kitchenette — practice new recipes —"

---

♥ Not familiar? I'd recommend *Love Actually*, *Truly, Madly, Deeply* and *Snow Cake*.

*Right. You'll eat instant oatmeal, sleep too much, and get carpal tunnel syndrome endlessly clicking the remote in hopes of something entertaining. You'll be pitiful.*

"I'll sip wine spritzers and read on the balcony."

*What if it rains? What if it's cold and blustery?*

"Hush. It's going to be great."

I began packing my "fun bag" of books and puzzles in anticipation.

My first inkling that the Universe had other plans for me arose like the odor of shrimp peels from the bottom of the trash bin when I called to book a hotel room over at Flagler Beach. Flagler is one of the last clinging remnants of old Florida, a place without chain restaurants, high-rise hotels, or tacky tourist shops. It is usually deserted over the holidays, with most of the restaurants closed. There should've been vacancies in abundance.

"I'm sorry, Miss, but we are booked up that week."

"What?"

"Yes. A huge wedding party. Christmas wedding on the beach."

Same with my second choice. "Sorry, Miss, we are booked."

And before I could call choice number three, I got a phone call from Lorraine's Aunt Moira. She's a free-spirited, psychic medium. (No pun intended, but sometimes they just come.) We're awkward acquaintances. She's pleasant, but she makes me nervous. When she talks to me, she has an unsettling habit of studying my hairline. She says she's reading my aura and checking for energetic hitchhikers. It's distracting and weird to have someone's eyes roaming over your head as if looking for spiders. Sometimes she nods and smiles as if having a private conversation with someone behind me.

"What? What are you seeing?"

She smiles and shakes her head.

I've only met her once, and mostly know of her through Lorraine. A call from her was atypical, to say the least.

"Blue's Lotus Lodge. This is Haint," I answered.

"Haint? Moira. You know, Lorraine's aunt. Listen. I've been meaning to call you. I've only got a moment, I'm in Kalamazoo at the Wellness Expo. But I needed to get you this message before I forgot."

"Oh? Is it about Lorraine?" I asked with concern. Why else would she be calling me?

"No, Listen. I had a vivid dream this morning. There was a bright Christmas tree with a mountain of presents under it. Children were laughing and playing. Then an empty deep freezer in a garage. You were there wearing a red apron, wringing your hands. Some weird nursery rhyme repeated 'the larder is bare; the larder is bare'."

I thought, *does anyone say larder anymore? Maybe it's a regional thing.*

"Oh, shit, they need me, I've gotta go. Listen. The dream tells me that you need to stock your pantry and fill the freezer. You're going to be a busy hostess this Christmas! Get your holiday cookbooks out, sweetheart."

There was another voice in the background and Moira answered a muffled, "Yes, yes, here I am." Then her voice was clear in the phone, "Okay, sweetie. Oh. And *decorate*. Make the place look festive and jolly, eh? Go all out. You'll thank me. Gotta go. Love to Lorraine."

I stared at the phone and shook my head. This made no sense. I had no bookings, no family obligations. No, no, no. I was free. I had two cozy mysteries packed in the fun bag. Naughty Britches and I were going to the beach for Christmas.

# The Snowball Begins to Roll

It wasn't that I *didn't* believe in Aunt Moira's psychic powers, but looking around my empty retreat, it seemed highly unlikely that I needed to prepare for an influx of guests.

Catfish Springs isn't exactly a huge draw in Florida, especially compared to all the attractions in Orlando that soak up most of the holiday tourism. The only tourists we get are interested in diving in the local springs. We've got two restaurants, a bank, and the Whatcha Need Mart where you can get gas, milk, beer, survival-level groceries, hay, baby chicks in season, and bait. Now it could be argued that Nina's Art of Tarts is a destination location; her pastry shop is fantastic, don't get me wrong, but Catfish Springs doesn't warrant a speck on the map of Florida.

It was December 10th, and I had no bookings after the twenty-first. Down time at the beach would recharge me. Long walks at sunrise. Good book under an umbrella by the pool. Fish tacos and a margarita. A jigsaw puzzle and an old movie channel. Someone else cooking and cleaning for a change.

My Word-of-the-Day calendar word a few days previously had been **hibernaculum: noun: Den. Place to hibernate. Sometimes several species will share a hibernaculum.** The accompanying sketch of a hole with multiple tunnels going deep into the ground with a rabbit in one, a snake in another and a fox in yet another. They were all curled up snug and contented. I wanted a hibernaculum, but not in the ground.

But before I could select inn option number three and nail down a reservation, Lorraine called close to tears.

"Help!" she wailed.

"Lorraine? What's wrong? Is it your ankle?"

Lorraine had broken her ankle back in October by tripping over a Chihuahua named Sparky. She'd been stuck in a fixature ever since—you know, those ghastly metal support thingamajigs that gave the impression that a diabolic erector set or old-fashioned television antenna had come to life and was devouring her foot.

"No, I wish. That would be easy!"

"What then? Are you okay?"

"Bodily yes, mentally no. Short version: my house is a biohazard."

"What?"

"I kept smelling something *off* in the bathroom. Then I made the mistake of flushing the toilet. The septic tank didn't like that idea. It backed up in every toilet and the shower. Oh, Haint, you can't imagine—"

"Oh, yuck! Need me to come over and help?" *Please no, please no, please no*, I prayed, feeling like an awful friend.

"No, thanks. Lerlene called her old boyfriend, you remember him—'If you've got a blockage, call Clint Coppage'?—he came over, God bless him. She and Fred also came over to help get the worst of it."

I tried to hide my sigh of relief. Blessings to Lerlene and her husband for that. I had not been looking forward to being on cleanup duty. "So how can I help?"

"Saint Eleanor, in her infinite wisdom, invited our entire family tree to my house for the holidays. She thought I'd appreciate the "help" — she said this word in a tone that implied it would be anything but help — "and the company."

"She *what*? I knew *she* was coming, but she invited people without asking?"

"She thinks she's being supportive."

"Tell her to uninvite them." I imagined a formal invitation that began *You are cordially invited to go away.*

Lorraine is in her late thirties and next year I get the big **50** on my cake. Most of the time, I forget our age differences, but sometimes I feel a bit like her mom. This was one of those times.

Lerlene and Lorraine's mom was known as Saint Eleanor because she aspired to martyrdom. She was a kind and selfless woman who eternally fretted about the well-being of others. Chatty and friendly in an intrusive way, she was quick to be affronted when one attempted to fortify one's boundaries against her. In her mind, she was beyond reproach. Resistance was nugatory. ♥

"--and she's invited every relative with a pulse. I think she's confused-- I'm not *dying*, I just can't get around very well. It's like she's organized my *wake*, only I'm not dead yet. Though the way things are going, she may have her wish."

"How can I help?"

"I hate to ask, but I'm desperate. Are you really going to close the retreat for the holidays? Cause it would be so great if we could rent a couple cabins…"

---

♥ I love making use of my obscure word calendar. Nugatory: adjective: pointless, futile, not effective.

"Why doesn't she have it at *her* house?" I asked, still holding onto the hope of the beach, the salt air, the quiet.

"She's already got people flying in from all over. They've already got their tickets. Meanwhile, Clint 'Blockage' Coppage can't possibly get here to trench up the yard until after January third."

"No pun intended, but they're that backed up?"

"Booked up solid and taking a vacation. Actually, they could *probably* come sooner, but to be honest, I'll need some time to move my she shed so Clint can get a truck near the septic tank. I wasn't thinking when I put it on that side of the house."

"Oh, man. That's a bummer. So where are you now?" I asked. She couldn't be home with no plumbing, and I could hear Christmas music blaring in the background. She wasn't one to blare Christmas music that I could recall.

"I'm at Lerlene's..." She lowered her voice to a stage whisper. I was sure she was cupping the receiver. "That's another thing I was going to ask..."

I could hear the hesitation in her voice and bit my lip. Lerlene and Lorraine get along better with a bit of distance. Lerlene's house is, well, chaotic might be too strong a word, but busy seems tame. Lerlene's a live wire, always in motion. Fred's boisterous. They have three kids under the age of twelve, two dogs, innumerable cats, and various other creatures in aquariums, tanks, and cages. I couldn't imagine Lorraine gimping around the kids, toys, and pets with grace. She'd be one misstep on a toy car or rawhide bone from breaking her other leg.

"You'd like a cabin of your own?" I asked.

"Yes! It's going to be a while before we can get the baseboards replaced and everything livable again."

I sighed and mentally said goodbye to the sounds of seabirds and the feel of wet sand in my toes. I was going to put her in a small cabin, but something made me hesitate. Aunt Moira's warning about guests seemed far-fetched, but she was known for being alarmingly accurate.

"Why don't you just move into my spare room? I wouldn't mind the company. That way you wouldn't be all alone in a cabin."

I could hear a dog barking in the background followed by a screaming child. "Right now, the isolated cabin sounds dreamy, but if you're sure you don't mind?"

"Sure, no problem." Lorraine and I got along like rice and beans. As long as I didn't have to provide medical attention to her leg, we'd be fine.

"I'm sure I can get Saint Eleanor to pay for everyone. She's got lots of money—"

"How many people and how soon?"

"Oh, not until right before Christmas... I'll see if she can give me a final count. Twelve maybe? I'll call you back as soon as I know for sure. YOU are the saint, Haint."

I sighed again. "When do you want to move in?"

"I've got a doctor's appointment on Friday. If they can get me out of this dang contraption, then I'd love to move in this weekend. I might be able to drive again if they give me a boot."

"Okay. Just let me know."

"You're the best!"

And as we said our goodbyes, I heard a refrain of "Tis the season to be jolly" playing in the background.

Fa-la-la-la-la.

And just like that, the snowball was in motion.

Lorraine called me back a little later to say it wasn't quite as bad as she thought. "Some cousins have plans—lucky them, and though Saint Eleanor is bugging Lerlene to stay over too because she wants everyone together, what with the dogs, Barley and Malt, and the cats and all, they'll just come during the day, so no worry about a cabin for them." She paused for thought as I caught up scribbling. "Saint Eleanor and Leander of course; her brother, Stuart, his wife, Noni, their son, Stuey and his fiancé, Amy…"

"That's six so far, seven counting you," I said.

"Yeah, but just for meals."

"A large cabin can bed ten."

"Should work fine then."

"Okay cool, talk to you later—" I said and disconnected.

Lorraine was coming to stay with me. I'd need to tidy the spare room. Ugh. I'm one of those people who tends to accumulate stuff like one of those bugs that carries piles of mulch on its back to disguise itself. I'm a clutter girl. The guest room needed some organizing. I'd need to clean the house. Not quite *grandma* clean, but close. Okay, not that big of a deal, but then there was decorating the retreat. This was my first holiday season at the retreat. Other than a wreath on the office door, I didn't have a thing.

Breathe.

I enjoyed a long, luxurious bubble bath that night, allowing myself to forget about the retreat, the holidays — all of it, and just relax. I wasn't *entirely* successful in turning off my brain. I couldn't help but wonder about my MIA boyfriend, Buster and why I hadn't heard from him. I comforted myself with thoughts of Lorraine staying with me. I wouldn't be alone. It was lovely to be warm and let the moisturizing bubbles soften my dry skin.

I toweled myself off and was about to reach for my flannel nightshirt where I'd set it on the toilet seat lid. There was something white sitting right on top of it. A moth? My eyesight is horrid without glasses or contacts. I found and put on my glasses. Perched on top of the folded nightgown, as if it had just alighted there, was a perfectly-centered, fluffy, white feather. Though the space heater helped, it was chilly. I was eager to get into my pajamas, bathrobe, and slippers. I set the feather aside and hurriedly dressed while trying to figure out where it might have come from.

I used to have feather pillows, but allergies forced me to give them up. I hadn't raised chickens in years, nor was there anything in the bathroom with feathers. It had looked like it was carefully placed right where I would see it. But I was alone. Where had it come from? I had the funny feeling it was a sign, a little gift, a God wink. From whom? White feathers were often linked to nods from angels or loved ones who had crossed over.

"Thank you," I said out loud, not sure who, if anyone, I was addressing. I pulled the bathrobe tie tight, jammed my feet into the fuzzy slippers, and turned off the heater. I studied the feather for a moment, marveling at its beauty — feathers are really amazing when you really look at them. Feather symbols flashed through my mind: whiteness, purity, light, airy, delicate, flight, possibly death. I set it on my altar and made a mental note to contemplate it in my morning meditation.

# Chapter 2

## Make the Season Bright

Early December in Florida doesn't look much different from August in Florida—as I've said, winter isn't dramatic here unless there's a frost, and that happened when a cold front swooped through on December 11th. The magnolias, oaks, loquats, and cypress trees didn't flinch at the cold; the camelias celebrated by blooming. By the following Friday, the grass, ginger, elephant ears and hickory trees gave up the chlorophyl green and were waving withered, parchment-brown, surrender flags.

The elephant ears in particular, suffered. Once vibrant and strong, they had collapsed, their stems bent and broken; their leaves shriveled and withered. Altogether, 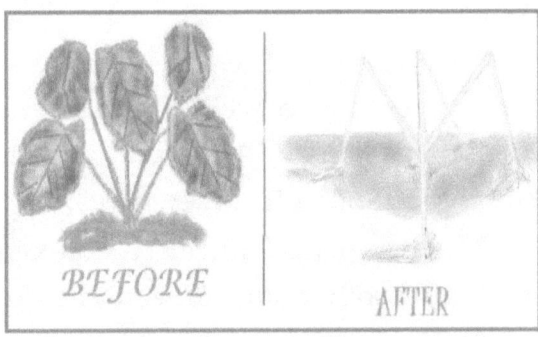 these once robust plants now resembled horror-movie spiders, their feet stuck in wet, coffee-stained, paper towels.

The retreat needed a major makeover to make the season bright. The following evening, I'd fed my few guests, cleaned the dining hall, and headed back home. I was looking forward to putting my feet up and making a shopping list for the following day.

When I got home, Naughty Britches greeted me with the usual bouncing, barking ritual. I leashed her up for a walk and she bounded down the driveway. She was dragging me towards a bunny trail when my phone rang. It was my former neighbor and friend, Max.

It had been a while since I'd talked to Max. I'd been on friendly enough terms with Max and his wife, Charlene, but since her passing a few years ago and his move to the Old Oaks Retirement Home, he's treated me like a long-lost granddaughter, and I've adopted him as a grumpy grandpa.

"Haint! Are you still goin' to the beach like ya said or is your retreat open for Christmas?" There was something about his tone that put me on guard.

"Funny you ask. Looks like my beach plans got canceled. Why?"

"Just as well. The forecast looks like it's gonna continue being as cold as a well-digger's ass for some time, heh-heh, pardon my French. And you haven't heard from Dr. Crypto? You two runnin' off somewheres?"

"No. No plans." I heard a note of hostility in my voice and tried to smooth it out. "Haven't heard from him. Why?"

"Ooh, my crazy sister, Nellavon. I just got off the phone

with her. I happened to mention that I fell the other day — "

"You *what*? Why didn't you say? Are you alright?" He'd never been what you'd call a big man, but now in his eighties, he seemed smaller and frailer every time I saw him.

"Cripes, yes. It wasn't nothing. I just missed the daggum chair by a smidge and fell on my keister. Bruised my back a bit and my pride. Nothin' serious. Now she's got it in her head to come see me for Christmas. Guess she thinks I'm dying. It's just a *day*. Why do people do this, d'ya think? I mean, just what *is* it about December blasted 25th that makes people get in a car and drive across the country? Do they do it on January 25th? No. February 25th? No! She knows I don't give a rip about the holidays. She's had decades to come see me any stinkin' day of the year."

"Why are you so upset about this? Don't you want to see her?"

"No! We never got on much. I was older, and as a kid I sure didn't need no *girl* trailin' around after me. Then later, we just had nothing in common. Her daughter, Cameron, my niece is okay. I kinda like her. But she had to go an' marry this lug-nut -brain, Benny. Manages a vacuum store in Lake City. If he ain't the biggest windbag! Boy, if Hoover had discovered him back in the day, heh-heh, but you know what? You can discard vacuum bags, but old Benny just sticks around like a chaw of tobacky sticks to the floor. Full of hot air and you can't get rid of him! Thinks he's so smart. Tells the dumbest daggum jokes all the time. Cain't never figure why she settled on him. Bah!"

I was prepared to let him rant, but apparently, inspired by thoughts of Benny, Max hacked up some phlegm. There was a pause and sounds of spitting. "Sorry, where was I? Oh yeah. Nellavon got kinda churchy on me. I'm not goin' to no church."

"Whoa! Did she *say* she wanted to take you to church?"

"Not exactly. But she'll bring it up if she's got a breath of life in her."

"What did you tell her? Is she coming?"

"Well," his voice had a hitch to it. "That's the thing. See, our other sister, Roberta, died last month—"

"*What?* Max, you didn't tell me."

Naughty Britches was pulling me off the road into some shrubbery to do her business. I tugged back, trying to avoid getting poked in the eye by a branch. She regarded me with contempt. Her look said that I was interrupting her all-important hunt. "Sorry," I said softly.

Max continued, "Nah, Cripes, nothing to tell. She was an old recluse. A cranky hoarder. She'd driven us all away. There was no point in having a funeral as no one with any sense would come—"

"That's so sad. I'm sorry."

"Don't be! The thing is, Nellavon's got this family bug all of a sudden. Wants us to be closer. She's got this hairbrained idea that she wants to do something special for her grandkids. She went and got tickets for who-knows-what-all down there in Orlando. Got so many o'them theme parks now, I can't keep track. Some 'experience' or something. She wants to bring the whole mob here to visit on the way. I kinda hate to subject you to 'em all, but I know business has been slow…"

"For you, Max, anything. You know…"Naughty Britches

was on the move again, now pulling me along like a ski tow. "It's the weirdest thing. I've told you about Lorraine's Aunt Moira? The psychic?"

"What? Yeah," Max said, sounding distracted. Then I heard a toilet flushing. Oh, geez.

"She called me the other day and told me to decorate the place up. I thought she was nuts. But with kids coming, I guess I will. Crazy."

"Hey!" Max said, then there was a clatter that sounded like the phone hit the tile floor. "Hey. Sorry about that. Was hitchin' up my trousers and dropped the daggum phone. You still there?"

"Yes," I said, suppressing a giggle.

"Don't buy a lot of shit until I call you. Remember I told ya Roberta was a hoarder? Well, guess what? Among other things like plastic containers and stupid little animal figurines, she collected Christmas crap. Had to put the overflow in a storage unit. It's floor to ceiling! Lemme talk to Nellavon. If she hasn't chucked it all in the trash yet, bet she could bring you truckloads of decorations. Sit tight!"

"That'd be a huge relief," I said, not sure if I meant it. I've seen some sad, gaudy decorations in my day, and who knew what condition they'd be in after years in a hoarder house. I've seen some of those television shows. Eek. Filth, silverfish, roaches—ugh. I tugged Naughty Britches away from a mound of sand—most likely a feral cat poop.

Max was saying, "Least I'll be close to Urliss and Hollis. Wouldja mind if they came over? Doubt they got plans, just the two o'them. Well, maybe Peggy Sue and Terry, too."

Max is tight friends with my neighbors, the twins, Urliss and Hollis Oakey, two middle-aged, friendly, rednecks. Peggy Sue was their sister; Terry was her husband.

"No problem," I said, "They assured me that they were 'busting you outta the slammer' over the holidays, anyway. Of course, they're welcome." Again, I said this before recalling that they'd showed up at my retreat once with a bag of dead squirrels thinking that I'd like to whip up some squirrel stew for my guests. Their target practice had disrupted my meditation classes on more than one occasion, too.

Like Lorraine, Max wasn't quite sure how many exactly or when exactly, but I was going to host Clan Max for the holidays. He'd have his sister call me directly.

"Well, I'm glad I'm gonna get to see your sweet face for Christmas after all," Max said adding with a chuckle, "I heard your beach plans got the kee-bosh."

I love Max, but I think of him as a trickster fox. He seems to always withhold information just to tantalize me. He reminds me a lot of the kind of shapeshifting woodland creatures in Japanese folklore, friendly to some and even cute at times, but wrathful to the disrespectful trespasser. I don't know how a skinny man in an old folks' home can have puppet-master powers, but he does.

"Heard *how*? And what's so funny?" I asked.

"Oh, nothin', Sweetie. Heard that the town was taken over for a Rockefeller wedding or some such. Not to fret, heh-heh, it'll all work out. You'll get to the beach. I'm glad you're not goin'."

"Why?"

"Why? Cause you don't need to go off mopin' by yourself when you should be smootchin' under some fussy bit o' mistletoe, that's why."

"Uh, well, I doubt that's going to happen. Buster got all bent out of shape when I asked him about the woman who answered his phone — well, what was I supposed to think? She sounded drunk, there were bar sounds in the background, and she didn't give him my message."

"Oooh," Max growled dismissively. "That man has the puppy eyes for you so bad — did you let on that you were jealous? Oh, my aching ulcers! Don't you know that when your name is mentioned he could smile winter into spring? Land sakes, why do women got to be so dang suspicious..."

"Well, what was I supposed to think? How do I know he's not a player with a girlfriend in every port." We'd reached the mailbox. I pulled out a bundle of junk mail.

"Oooh," Max growled again. "Because he ain't like that."

"Well, fine, I screwed up. He's been kinda distant ever since. I don't even know where he is. For all I know, he's in the woods in Vancouver hunting Lizardman or something."

"Hmph!" Max snorted.

"What? Do you know where he is?"

There was just a hint of hesitation before he changed the subject saying, "Urliss and Hollis shot a few turkeys the other day. Bet you're gonna get a turkey. Make room in your refrigerator. So, how many people are you expecting, anyway?"

"You didn't answer my question."

"What question?" There was a muffled sound like he put

his hand over the receiver. "Oh, fine, go away!" His voice came back clear again. "There's a nurse here wanting to arm wrestle with me about taking some pills. I gotta go, Sunshine." And he hung up.

He'd slipped up. This time, I knew he knew something.

Naughty Britches had lost all enthusiasm for the walk and sat down, then rolled to her side, tongue hanging out.

"This was your idea, you know," I said.

She gave me the pitiful, legs-have-stopped-working eyes.

"Fine. I'll sort the mail while you rest."

There was the usual holiday-season junk mail: solicitations from charities, slim gift catalogs, a Christmas card from my CPA. I secured the bundle into my chest with one arm, holding the leash in the other. NB's pace picked up on the return trip as she knew she'd get a treat when we got home.

When we got back to the house, I pulled out my calendar. That's when it really hit me that Christmas was coming in less than two weeks. I needed to *clean*. Meal plan. Decorate. Figure out who was going in which cabin. This was no put-my-feet-up-and-doodle-a-list kind of thing; this was get-the-war-room-ready-and-man-the-battle-stations kind of planning. Exactly what I'd wanted to avoid by going to the beach by myself, wasn't it? The gurus and life planners always talk about how you create your own experience. I sure didn't feel like I had much control here. I felt a bit manipulated. But on the other hand, there were people in need, and I could help and wouldn't turn away the business. This was gray territory for sure…was I motivated by guilt and obligation or by a genuine desire to provide a service? I wasn't sure.

# WHERE IN THE WORLD?

Chucking the mail into the paper recycle bin in my kitchen, a bit of paper fluttered out and fell to the floor. *What in the world?* An African fetish doll leered up at me. It was a ripped and rumpled postcard.

I have to confess that African art is not my favorite. While I have a great regard for the craftwork, I know little about African cultures; the severe faces and rustic styles make me uneasy. I wonder, was this used as a part of a death ritual? I'm still traumatized by that Karen Black movie I saw as a kid where she became possessed by a tribal doll.

The woman staring up at me was beautiful and proud but a little scary too. Like Mona Lisa, she had an I've-got-a- naughty-secret smile, suspicious eyes, ankle chains and some kind of woven rope under her breasts. Who was she? What did she represent? My first thought was, holy cow, is someone trying to put the energetic whammy on me? I'd heard that for voodoo to work best, you had to inform your victim that you were working voodoo on them.

Maybe that was from an old movie. *Angel Heart* scared me silly; I can't think of New Orleans without thinking of it.

I picked up the torn card and flipped it over. How it got to me was a small miracle as the address and unfortunately most of the message had apparently been soaked in a puddle and run over by muddy truck tires.

I took it over to my reading light and tried to decipher more of the message without success. It was from Buster. Where was he? He said he tried to call me before he left. From where? Was he visiting a museum or was he in Africa?

The only words that were legible were "tried to call", "goddess", "weather" and "soon". I sure wished I could read more. The one word that make my heart tingle was "soon". Did it mean home soon or call you soon or see you soon? At this point, I'd take any of them.

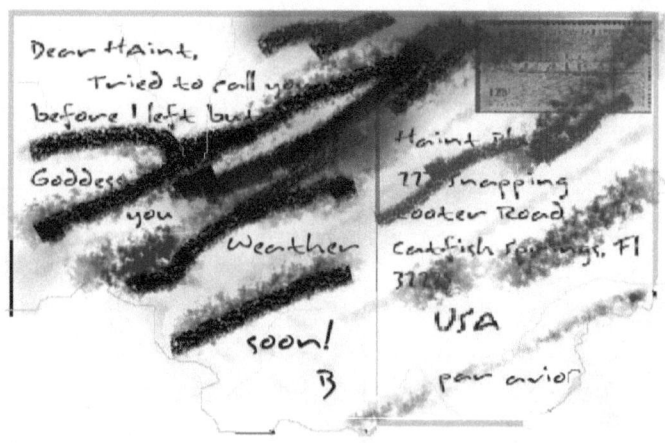

# Chapter 3

## THE BUSTER SITUATION

**B**ack in October, I had a trio of good-natured cryptozoologists as guests. You know, the folks who track down what I call mythical beings, such as Bigfoot, the Loch Ness Monster, and so on. They were good company even if I thought they were slightly crazy. The problem was, I fell for the group leader, Buster Shadetree.

Max the Trickster had been working behind the scenes as matchmaker to get the two of us together. Buster had been visiting Max's Stinkin' Skunk Ape Fish Camp for years. It was a convenient base camp for his Florida cryptid "investigations". Turned out that Max was setting "evidence" in the woods to lure Buster back again and again. And Buster was onto him, but played along because he liked Max.

Buster: real name, George Burgwyn Shadetree II, after a Civil War era Brigadier General in his family tree. I confess, when I first heard of him through Max, I assumed he was a total crackpot. Turns out, he's got two businesses and three degrees, a bachelor's degree in anthropology, a master's degree in zoology, and a Ph.D. in cryptozoology. (Yeah, I know. I had no idea that was even a thing.)

Handsome, with the body of a hiker or backpacker, sturdy with solid muscles but not the bulging, gym kind. His green eyes spoke of adventures and sadness while he spun a theory that we were connected in past lives and destined for each other. Sounds cheesy, right? But I did feel that kind of connection. I was getting slowly sucked into that destiny-and-stars-in-alignment possibility--until the night I called him, and a woman answered. The background noises indicated a bar with a live band.

I'm not normally prone to jealousy, but this raised a bright red flag that waved like a DO NOT SWIM warning on a lifeguard perch in a squall. What did I know about him really? What if he had girlfriends all over the country like some crypto rock star? It hadn't helped that she neglected to give him the message. He hadn't called back. And when I called again a few days later and asked him about her, he got defensive.

It wasn't pretty.

I said some stupid things. He parried back that I should trust him. Isn't that what all gaslighting rogues *would* say? A Wiccan friend had warned me that as a Scorpio, he'd be naturally curious--it made him an excellent researcher. The downside was that he was likely to play his own cards tight to his chest and resent anyone questioning him. That had turned out to be annoyingly accurate.

He'd made all kinds of apologies about missing me for Thanksgiving. He was in Maryland investigating persistent sightings of a Snarly Yow, a phantom dog/wolf.

"Most likely it's an ol' bear," he said, downplaying it.

I should add that with his accent this sounded a whole lot more like "bar" than "bear". Despite his genteel Southern upbringing, education and world travels, he had a wicked accent — Andy Griffith times ten, a combo platter of the deepest accents of Arkansas, West Virginia and Texas. I've been slowly getting used to it, but sometimes, I lose whole sentences. Between elongated vowels, contractions, and smothered consonants, I have to concentrate and often give up and ask him to repeat something slowly.

He continued, "--a large coyote or someone's Irish wolfhound, but several folks has got video 'at's kinda interestin' to say the least. It's damn big, whatever it is. I seen pitchers—"

When he says "pictures" it comes out "pitchers" and my mind sees vases of flowers or a uniformed baseball player winding up a pitch.

"So anyways, it didn't amount to much o' nothin', like we figured."

Would you consider it a red flag that he didn't go home to his own family for the holidays? That he'd forego visiting his own mother to chase a mythical Snarly Yow? Of course, I hadn't met his family; maybe this was a wise choice. Hard to say.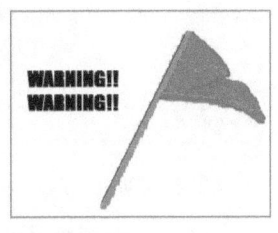

I wasn't wired up for a love interest who was never around. Between guiding fly-fishing trips and tracking monsters, he travelled a *lot*. He makes most of his money off of a fly-fishing business. When he's not guiding tours, he's making social media videos and selling his own brand name flies like the Buster Luster, Buster Sureshimmer, and the Buster Disco Booger.

Buster is just as dedicated to debunking fraudsters as he is to finding real beasties. I respect that. I hate hoaxers and con artists.

I just hoped he wasn't conning me.

Since I'd first met him and felt the initial attraction — did I mention his gorgeous hazel green eyes and killer dimples? His calm demeanor put me at ease while his proximity and intensity upended my heart. He had a way of being just a little too close. He smelled like flannel and sacred forests, rich coffee, and manly soap. He moved soundlessly with grace, like a panther. It felt so right when we were together. He'd suggested that we'd been together in many past lives which sounded like hogwash, but in truth, I couldn't dismiss it.

So why was communication so hard?

And then there was the whole evidence debacle…

## ᑕHE EVIDENCE DEBACLE

When Buster and his "CeeZee" sidekicks Rebel and Shane stayed at my Blue's Lotus Lodge back in October, they brought all kinds of hunting cameras and set up surveillance spots all over my camp. I thought they were nuts. As I mentioned, they've been playing a mutual con game with Max for years. Max has been planting fake Skunk Ape evidence (in Florida, Bigfoot is called a Skunk Ape — different species or subspecies? Don't ask me.) and they've pretended that Catfish Springs is a cryptid hotspot.

Turned out that the cameras came in handy to figure out a missing persons situation on Halloween. But there was  something that flashed by a camera that was tall and furry. Perhaps a bear. Must have been a bear. But they didn't think so. And just after they left, I discovered a copious poop in my backyard with a shredded dog collar in it that had, ironically, been around the neck of Mrs. Bunderbridge's dog, Poopsie.

Something quite large had eaten the dog. I described it to Buster over the phone and he got all excited. He ran me through all kinds of detail questions—I'll spare you the scatology analyses—and asked me to bag and freeze the poop. He wanted to see it. I'd put in it a cake box and wrapped it in a bunch of plastic bags from the Whatcha Need Mart and stuck it in my garage deep freeze. Rebel would pick it up in a couple weeks.

All good, right? And I was patting myself on the back for getting into the spirit of this crazy Bigfoot researcher stuff. I had possible evidence in my freezer. Probably bear. Maybe not.

And then...

Thanksgiving.

I had invited my best friend Lorraine over for Thanksgiving. Her mother, Saint Eleanor, had been hovering around Lorraine "helping" her around the house since she'd broken her ankle. Inviting Lorraine meant I had to invite Saint Eleanor.

She's not a bad person. She means well. She's the kind of

woman that the Southern expression "bless her heart" was made for. She's annoying as hell and a control freak but if you try to stop her, she gets all offended and huffs and pouts and carries on. You know the type: "Well, if I'm not appreciated around here..."-- with lots of nose twitching.

Lorraine and I *thought* that giving Saint Eleanor something to do would keep her out of our hair. She was supposed to set the table. Fussing about lunch the next day, she got into the refrigerator looking for corn or something. Who knows. Somehow that led her to dig into my deep freezer. I have no idea what she was looking for. Lorraine and I suspect she was just being nosy. I'll give her the benefit of the doubt. But she must have been sneaky because we didn't know about it at the time.

The following week, Rebel was passing through Florida. He took a detour to come get the poop sample.

"Buster said I was to pick up a scat sample from you and run it over to a medical examiner friend of ours—"

"Yes, yes, come on in and I'll get it for you."

Rebel is a lovely man, a bit on the paunchy side, looks like he was born to wear overalls, play the fiddle and fuss over barbecue. I couldn't wait to give him my little cryptid treasure. I dashed into the garage, opened the freezer, and gasped. It looked like it had been ransacked. Normally, I have veggies on one side in a wire compartment, meats in another, and I know I had put the poop sample in the top front over a freeze pack.

No cake box. I moved things around. Pulled parcels out. It was gone. This made no sense! Who had been in my freezer? Why had they taken it?

Had someone seriously stolen frozen poop?

No. Saint Eleanor had been snooping. She confessed after we grilled her that she'd found it, opened it, thought it was disgusting, and threw it out.

"It wasn't yours to throw out!" I had wailed.

"It was in a cake box. But when I opened it, well, my stars, that was disgusting! That was no cake!"

"It even said 'for Buster' on it!"

"Well, something had gone horribly wrong with it. Out it went."

"Why didn't you ask?" I asked.

"I thought I was doing you a favor!"

"Mom, what the hell were you doing in her freezer?" Lorraine asked, fingers pressed to her temples as if to keep her head from exploding like a malfunctioning pressure cooker.

Saint Eleanor held her hands together under her chin as if in desperate prayer. Her voice quavered. She was about to cry. "I was hoping you had some frozen corn. I just thought we should have some corn. That's all. That *thing* was in the way. Well, at first, I thought it was an ice cream cake. I was even going to ask if maybe we could get into it. I set it aside. I was wrestling with a bag of frozen tater tots that was stuck to a bag of frozen broccoli and when I tugged, the cake box fell to the floor. Well, I felt just awful! Then I hoped, well, maybe since it was frozen, it would still be okay. It was all wrapped up, so I had a little peek, you know, and then I *saw* it." She made a face and shuddered. "I mean, even frozen, mercy! It was awful!"

But this wasn't until after I sent Rebel away with nothing

and had to call Buster and apologize.

"Did you give the sample to Rebel?"

"There was a problem."

"It wasn't there."

"WHAT?"

"It was gone."

"What happened?"

"Someone took it."

"*WHAT?*"

"It's gone."

"What do you mean, it's gone?"

"Someone took it."

"Who?"

"How do I know?"

"Don't you keep your garage locked?"

"Not exactly."

There was a long silence, then he asked in a very flat voice, "Was anything else missing?"

"I didn't inventory the freezer, but I don't think so. It just looked ransacked."

"Did they get in your house? Is your house okay?"

"I haven't noticed anything. No. Not that I know of." At first, I thought he was worried for my safety or concerned about my break in. Nope.

He exhaled. I could almost feel the annoyance coming through the phone. "You're tellin' me that someone moseyed into your garage, rifled around in your freezer, an' stole the poop sample."

"Mm-hmm."

"Who knew that it was there besides you and me?"

"I told Lorraine and Iggy."

He let out an exasperated sigh.

"What? Was I supposed to keep it secret?" I asked, getting huffy. "I told my *best friend* and my *brother*. I think I'm allowed to tell them."

"Well, o'course, but they mighta told someone —"

"Seriously? When would that come up? At the checkout? 'Oh yes, and Haint has a poop sample of a Bigfoot, oh, excuse me, Skunk Ape, in her freezer but shhh! Keep it on the down low because some lunatic might steal it.'"

He growled. "Haaaint. I'm just frustrated is all. This mighta been the real deal." He exhaled with enough force to blow out the candles on an octogenarian's birthday cake. "You don't know 'bout all the crazy cryptid world. There's fakers, thieves and sabotagers. Izzat a word?"

"I think you mean saboteurs."

"Right. I knew that didn't sound right. Anyhow, stuff gets nicked all the dang time at the research centers an' museums an' such, cause some folks just want some little ol' piece o' the unknown. A footprint cast. A famous sketch. Maybe someone heard about it and stole it."

"Are you *serious*?"

"A'course I'm serious. We keep a tight chain o' custody on evidence."

"We? Chain of custody? What? Well, I'm so sorry Sergeant

Friday, I'm new on the job. I didn't think I needed a padlock on my freezer or a sign in sheet and a custodian."

Another heavy sigh. "Don't go gittin' all huffy."

"Huffy? Which is more important to you, me or a pile of shit?"

"Oh, come *on*, you know—"

I hung up on him. I shouldn't have, but I was angry that he'd glossed over the potential threat of a thief in my house and kept harping on my being irresponsible or not trustworthy.

It was stupid.

We each held our grudges. Calls after that were a bit curt. I wanted an apology. He wanted a poop sample.

When I finally called him back to tell him that it wasn't a burglar, just nosy Saint Eleanor, he stayed on his high horse! That irked me even further.

"Whyja let her in the freezer?" he asked.

"I didn't know she'd gone into the freezer."

Long pause that implied again that I was irresponsible with evidence. "Oh well. Reckon it's gone."

"Yup."

"I shoulda had you ship it to me."

"I don't think you can ship poop."

"It's been known ta happen."

"Can we drop this please? It's gone. I'm sorry. I failed."

There was a pause. I had hoped he'd say, "I'm sorry too" or anything comforting. His hesitation and silence said much. There was background noise of shifting and some announcement over a loudspeaker.

"Hey, whatcha doin' for Christmas?" he asked. His tone was cold as if he was just shifting the conversation, not asking out of genuine interest. But the call was breaking up as well. His voice sounded like it was coming from a tin can.

"I don't know. I'm thinking of just going away someplace quiet. Running away from my retreat. Where are you anyway?"

"I'm at the airport. Listen, I'm boardin'. I'm sorry I didn't get to tell you before. I got this huge opportunity —"

That was the last clear sentence I heard. After that his voice became a morse code of fuzz and random syllables "to go *whhhk public of hhhkkkk gay bone wkkkttttt whhhhrr poy-ente no-are whrrr — not sure when whrrrr Chim poonga whhhhhk so I may not be wkkkk contact whhhh while wkkkkk will call whhhhhh of you wkkkkk.*"

Gay bone? Chimpoonga? What? Or had it been Chickamauga? Tennessee? No, it really hadn't sounded like that but with his accent and the bad connection, who knew. I hoped he'd call again when he landed. He hadn't.

When I tried texting or calling, there was no reply. This sums up communication in early December. Maybe it was just as well that we weren't making holiday plans. He was busy in Chimpoonga or whatever, wherever that was.

And what said *thinking of you* better than a spooky carved figurine that looked like she could put a curse on you.

Buster, what the heck, man?

That evening, I made meditation a priority. This is always a challenge for me; I'd love to have a dedicated practice, but all it takes is one or two distracted days and I lose the routine. Sometimes weeks go by. My aging cat Mischief spends more time on my meditation cushion than I do.

I set Buster's postcard on my little altar and lit some tealight candles. Thoughts whooshed around in my head like pachinko balls. (Pachinko is a Japanese version of an upright pinball machine—gazoodles of little metal balls fall into slots while noisy sirens and bells make all kinds of annoying, supposedly excitement-inducing sounds.) Pachinko parlors are hell to those prone to sensory overload. My father was stationed in Japan for a few years. My brother, Iggy, was born in Japan. As a child, I confused the bright lights and sounds from the pachinko parlors for carnivals and got upset when my mother wouldn't let us go in. She said it was for adults to gamble their money away. "The little balls carry away coins and dreams. You must never waste your time with that."

I wanted my worries to run off like the little balls.

*Just breathe. Look at the candle flame. What will I cook? Should I have roast beef and ham? What do vegetarians eat during the holidays? Stop. Focus. Exhale. What does this postcard mean? I wish I knew what he said! Where is he? Why doesn't he call or text? Stop. Focus. Breathe. Let it go. Let him go. What? No. Yes. It says Goddess. Is this figure a goddess? Where is he? The stamp looks foreign. And where did this feather come from? Be like the feather: airy and light. Breathe. Stop thinking. Breathe.*

Lately when I thought about Buster, it was with confusion and frustration--hardly a warm, loving heart, more like inching towards bitter and brittle. *Breath in — pink, soft bubble gummy heart — breathe out tension and worry — send him love with that big mushy heart, exhale confusion and doubt…*

Mentally, I surrounded myself in a flexible, mirrored suit of armor, deflecting all negativity, pink, soft heart inside, armor on the outside, body a field of blazing white light, heart radiant and pink. *Sending love to you wherever you are…*

Unfortunately, the peace and love and relaxation I'd built up in the meditation faded when I got in bed. Christmas was coming. So much to do.

# Chapter 4

## Ween

**M**y phone buzzed Friday morning while I was putting away my breakfast dishes. Not long after, I got a text message from a local number I didn't recognize. I assumed it was a robocall and was going to ignore it, but something made me look at the text anyway.

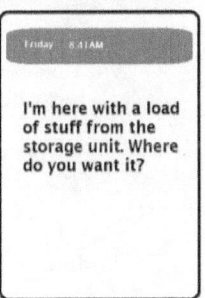

I hate cryptic messages. Here *where*? What storage unit? How annoying. Must be a wrong number. I punched in questions:

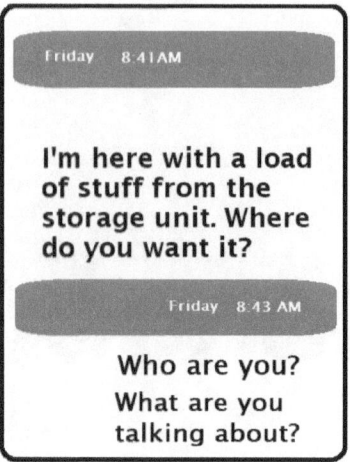

I wasn't expecting anything from a storage unit. Well, whoever it was would figure out they had the wrong number. I was tempted to ignore it, but curiosity got the better of me. The response was swift:

Weed from a storage unit? I was about to fire back a rebuttal of "You've got the wrong person!" when the Colombian coffee got to my brain and stopped me. Maybe it was the Christmas decorations from Max's dead hoarder sister.

But *weed*? What was that about?

One way to find out.

I'd pop over to the lodge and meet this person. I texted that I'd be there in a moment, to meet me at the office. I coerced a grumpy Naughty Britches into her crate with a cookie promising I'd be back soon and dashed out the door.

On the way over, another tumbler in my brain fell into place. Weed. I'd *heard* of someone named Weed. Who told me about him? Come on, brain, *think*.

There was a shabby, red pick-up truck piled high with bulging garbage bags. Some had holes with bits of artificial Christmas tree poking through. Others were oozing silver garland and bits of dull red velvet. A tall man with a black muscle shirt and faded jeans was leaning on the truck. He was wearing a black cowboy hat with turkey feathers in a braided band.

Whoo. I felt flushed. Hel-lo, Cowpoke! I've always been a black cowboy hat kind of woman. I had a thing for Yul Brynner – didn't he always wear a black hat in the cowboy movies? Yummy. I was all about Adam Cartwright. Val Kilmer as Doc Holiday: black hat. Good choice.

I got out of my truck and called, "Hello."

"Ma'am," Cowboy said with an inflection that seemed both a greeting and a question as in, where did I want this stuff?

I got close enough to see his face and froze in horror. Was I seeing a ghost? No. Not quite. Eerily similar. As if dead Bob was resurrected and had gotten a makeover. Like a zombie process in reverse.

Back in September, I'd hired Bob Dollard to do some yardwork for me and he'd been killed. The last time I'd seen him, he was glassy-eyed and covered in blood with an air potato shoved in his mouth. It was horrific. I was still having occasional nightmares.

My mouth went dry.

He shifted his weight and rolled his eyes in a here-we-go-again expression. "We look a lot alike, don't we? I'm the better-lookin' one. I'm Weed." He put a hand to his hip and leaned his other arm on a porch rail. This action pulled his jacket aside, revealing a trim torso harnessed by a silver belt buckle in the shape of a coiled snake. He crossed one leg over the other and waited for me to say something. He could have walked onto the set of a cowboy movie, no problem.

Right! I remembered now. One of my guests the weekend of Bob's murder, had told me she'd dated Weed briefly but Bob had been jealous and drove them apart. She'd said he'd been a sexy dark horse. He was a healthier, cleaner, social version of Bob.

"I'm Haint Blue," I managed to say. I forced myself to look away. "Wow. This is a lot!"

He nodded.

"I'm sorry about Bob," I said, focusing on a bit of garland.

"Yeah. Thanks," he said, putting a hand on his hip. "Something woulda got him sooner or later. But I wouldn'ta wished *that* on him."

"No."

He tilted his eyebrows at the load of bags and then towards

the office.

"Yes, right," I said, pulling myself into the present. "Uh, let's just pile it up in my office for now."

He backed the truck up so the tailgate was close to the door. We grabbed bags and boxes, making multiple trips back and forth until the truck bed was empty, and my office was piled high. He opened the cab and pulled out two, four-foot long, plastic-mold toy soldiers and thrust them at me while he reached in for two more.

"The office is full. Let's just leave these on the porch."

"Yes, ma'am."

I thought we were done but then Weed opened the front passenger door and pulled out a huge box.

"Good grief!" I exclaimed, as he walked it to the steps and set it down.

"Yes, Ma'am. I'll be back in about an hour with the next load."

"*What?* There's *more*?"

He nodded, "Oh, yeah, there is. If you don't want it, it's going to the dump, " he said, putting his hands on his hips. He had my vote for Mr. December in the hot-cowboy-of-the-month calendar.

"What? No. Where are we going to put it?"

His eyes asked me to make a quick decision. Was he coming back with more or going to the dump?

"Oh, okay, bring it. I can always donate what I don't want, right?"

"Ma'am," he said, in a way that said both yes you can, *and* you are making the right decision. And I swear he touched his hat brim just like in the movies.

"I guess we can fill up the meditation hall next," I said, pointing to the door.

He nodded and got in his truck.

"Hey," I asked as he was closing the door.

He rolled down the window and waited.

"How do you know Max's sister, Nellavon? I'm just curious."

"She lives across the street from me. I do the odd job for her sometimes."

"Small world," I said.

He did an eye twitch, something close to a wink, indicating agreement, or at least acknowledgement. Unlike me, he was a tightwad with words. Soon the shabby red truck was rumbling away for the second load of Christmas cheer.

I stared at my office. I'd need help to sort through it all and decorate. Who did I know who liked party prepping? Lorraine, but she had her ankle that metal contraption. But she loved Christmas. Maybe she could sit in a chair and sort. I wondered if Saint Eleanor liked to decorate. That would keep her busy, wouldn't it? Did I dare get her involved?

As promised, Weed returned a while later with another

load of boxes, bags, and blow mold figures.

"This is getting ridiculous," I said, as Weed unloaded the final pile of holiday cheer. "This is insane!"

"Mur-ray Christmas," Weed said with a mischievous grin as he got into his truck.

"Hey, wait—can I give you some money for your time?" I asked.

"Naah… I already got paid for haulin' it off," Weed said.

"Well, thanks!" I said, not entirely sure I felt truly thankful. The mountain of stuff was kind of freaking me out. But I was grateful that I didn't have to go fetch all this mess myself. "I owe ya one."

He nodded and tipped his hat like a sexy cowboy. I bit my lip. Many thanks and Merry Christmas, Mr. December.

Before he was out of sight, I was dialing Lorraine. "Is Saint Eleanor any good at decorating? I need some serious help here."

Lorraine snorted, "Oh, honey, YES! She's more Martha Stewart than Martha Stewart!"

"Do you think we could get her to come over and have at it?"

"Absolutely. Listen to me very carefully though. You cannot be there. She will follow you around and talk you to death. You have to give her the stuff and run. Tell her precisely where and what you want done and then she'll ignore you and do the whole camp for you. Once she gets started, she won't stop. She'll be off the chain."

"Perfect!" I said, eyeing the mountains of stuff. "I need off the chain. I've got enough stuff to open a Haint's Land of Christmas. How soon can she come? I've got mountains of stuff here to sort through. "

"Ooh. Know what? Let me call Lerlene. We can get her kids to help Grandma, tell her we need a babysitter. That way, Lerlene gets a break too. All you'd have to do is leave out a heap of sandwiches and drinks and she'll be master drill sergeant. Win-win-win all around!"

## PORCH PIRATES

A little while later, I was back at home, wrangling the laundry in the washing machine I despise, trying not to throw my back out untangling the knots of sleeves and pant legs. I let the washer spindle win, releasing my end of the tug of war garment rope.

Naughty Britches made me jump, setting up a sudden howling hysteria as if we were under siege. She dashed down the hall and began throwing herself at the back door. I looked out the window to see that Willie and Waylon, my neighbors' two bloodhounds, had treed a young raccoon. The raccoon watched them from the top of a young mulberry tree I'd planted a few years back. It was safe but trapped as long as the dogs remained at the base of the tree. The dogs were braced on their back legs, clawing at the tree and baying at the raccoon.

"No way you're getting involved. Sorry girlfriend," I said, dragging her away from the door. I crated her in the bedroom. She strained and cried and carried on like a bucking bull. "I'll get you a cookie," I said, avoiding her stink-eye. I closed the bedroom door, got my cell phone, and called Hollis.

"Yeah!" he answered gruffly. "What's up, Haint?"

"Can you come get your dogs? They've treed a raccoon in my backyard. I'm not sure which is more at risk for harm—the coon or my mulberry tree."

I had to plug my free ear with a pinky finger in order to hear as NB was still carrying on, resenting being crated.

Hollis let out a raspy sigh of exasperation, "This day just gets better 'n better... yeah, I'll be right over."

A few moments later, I heard the rumblings of Urliss's dual-exhaust, Super- Duty truck pulling up.

Urliss and Hollis Oakey are identical twins. To be honest, I'm not sure quite how old they are; I'd guess early seventies, but I've known them now for some time and they don't seem to age much. They looked to be in their early seventies ten years ago. They tend to wear overalls that strain to contain their beer bellies. They have shaggy gray hair and matching beards. They usually wear ball caps to cover the bald spots. The one tell-tale distinction is Urliss is missing his left earlobe and has a scar from his left ear to the middle of his left cheek—a souvenir from a bar fight in Daytona during Bike Week.

I opened my front door as they were getting out of the truck. Urliss was saying, "If I catch the sumbitch bastard, I'll knock the snot-bubbles out of him."

"I just didn't want them to catch the little guy," I said, alarmed that Urliss was threatening violence. I was beginning to regret that I'd called them. "You aren't going to hurt the raccoon, are you?"

"Oh, no, Haint, he ain't talkin' about the coon or the dogs," Hollis explained as I ushered them toward my back gate. "He's madder than a hornet trapped in an empty bottle on account o' porch pirates."

"What?"

We reached the gate and could see the dogs willing themselves up my poor tree. The raccoon was hunched up showing teeth.

"The dang things were on back order," Urliss said through clenched teeth. "Then they shipped. Great! We'd have 'em in time for Christmas! Come to find out they got stolen outta the God-damned mailbox!"

"Willie! Waylon!" Hollis bellowed.

Urliss whistled one of those loud, sharp, sheep-herder kind of whistles out of the corner of his mouth. One day, I'd have to get him to teach me how to do that. The little kid in me was impressed at the volume he commanded with ease.

The dogs fell back to the ground and swiveled their heads, expressions going from fierce to meek in a flash. One of them wagged its tail between its legs. The other looked around as if hoping for a place to hide.

"Git over here!" Hollis barked.

The raccoon craned its neck like a spectator in the bleachers curious about the new players on the scene.

The dogs barreled towards us in that gangly, graceless way of bloodhounds, ears flapping wildly. I braced for impact, but they managed to stop at Hollis's feet and sit.

"Impressive," I said, relaxing my legs.

"Stay!" Urliss commanded.

The dogs licked their lips as if staying was the *one* thing they wanted to do most in the world.

Urliss pulled some cookies out of his overalls pocket and flipped them to the hounds. They chomped them down in nanosecond bites.

Hollis picked up the conversation as if there'd been no interruption. "We've been looking forward to these Reckoning Day Hatchets—they're wicked lookin' titanium multitools that's got a prybar, knife, hammer, and saw blade on 'em."

"Cain't believe they was *in the mailbox* and got stolen," Urliss growled. "Gonna wring someone's neck, I swear."

Hollis scowled. "I'll use that prybar on his head!" In a kinder tone, he turned to me. "We're thinkin' 'bout getting the post office to get us them metal industrial boxes. I hate 'em, but we're gonna have to."

Urliss continued, "You know, the group mailbox thing where if you get a package, they chuck a key in yer box, and you get it outta the secured box?"

"We'd have to get the neighbors all on board—we all gotta agree."

I frowned. "Those industrial things take away the charm of the old, battered, country mailbox look."

"Ain't no charm about stolen stuff," Hollis said.

"No..." I agreed. "We wouldn't see Patriotic Pete so much, ...though I suspect he'd still come up to the house sometimes like he does when he's lonely."

We all thought about that. Even the coon looked dejected.

Patriotic Pete is our eccentric mailman. He usually dresses in variations of red, white, and blue clothes. He's deaf as a doormat but refuses to get hearing aids because he's worried the government will get into his head. He's salt of the earth good people, but conversation is almost impossible.

"Life is simpler when you plow around the stumps," Urliss said.

The raccoon shifted around as if to say, "Hey, could you take the conversation and the dogs elsewhere? I'd like to come down now."

"I hate that we have to give up and give in to the crappy people in the world," I said. "Like the dump mart. Used to be, when you went to the dump, there was the dump mart, that area set aside for stuff that someone might still want. I picked up quite a few things, like patio pavers, from the dump mart."

"I know. We've got saw blades and toolboxes from the dump mart." Hollis said.

"Then they go and close it because pickers was gettin' into fist fights," Urliss said.

"Over dump stuff," Hollis said.

"So now nobody wins, and the stuff fills up the land fill instead of going to a good home," I said.

We all shook our heads.

The dogs were eyeing the raccoon. I swear the raccoon did a shooing motion with its tail.

"Let's give the raccoon some space," I said, urging the men towards the gate.

"So, would you sign to get the secure mailbox?" Urliss

asked.

I sighed. "Yeah, I guess so.  Can't believe I'm saying this, but I'll miss Pete a little."

"Yeah," they said in unison.

Meanwhile, from inside, NB had kept up a consistent high C *yark* and was beginning to lose her voice.

"Well, sorry about the dogs. Cute coon," Urliss said. "Reckon the little fellow got separated from its momma. They usually have two to five babies. Surprised there aren't more."

"Good thing you don't got chickens," Hollis said, narrowing his eyes. "They'll tear up a chicken."

We got through the gate, the dogs following close.

"I'm impressed with how well trained these dogs are," I said, glancing toward the house. "You want to take Naughty Britches and train her?"

They laughed. Urliss opened the backdoor of his truck and did another impressive sheep whistle. They both flew in and jammed together over the console, ready to go.

Urliss closed the door, "Well, we'll see if the Woodson's will go in on the box thing. Then we four'll be secure together — us, you and the retreat and them."

"Okay," I said glum with resignation. "Hey — what are you all doing for Christmas? Max has got his whole clan coming, did he tell you? I'm going to be having a feast for an army. Why don't you come join us?"

"That'd be great!" They said in unison.

"We'll think 'o somethin' to bring," said Hollis.

Oh dear. That could mean anything from moonshine to

homemade venison jerky to a bag of dead squirrels. "Okay," I waved with a nervous smile.

The Oakey twins got in, thanked me for calling, and waved goodbye. I couldn't hear NB anymore; she must have exhausted herself. I trotted to the backyard to check on the raccoon. The mulberry tree was empty.

# Chapter 5

## Welcome to the Big Top

It was quite chilly when Naughty Britches woke me up and dragged herself outside, but the forecast was for a sunny day with a high in the sixties. Perfect get-things-done weather for a Saturday. Ideal for children to be busy outside. I made myself a hot cocoa and sat in a lawn chair watching her poke about heedless to the cold, while bundled in my fuzzy jammies with my favorite winter bathrobe. It was heaven to sit outside without being swarmed by mosquitoes. The morning was quiet: no birds, no buzzing bees, no cows lowing in the distance. Even Willie and Waylon were quiet over at Hollis's house.

Nervous about possible problems with Saint Eleanor and the thoughts of the holiday hanging over me like a cyclone of vultures waiting to pick my good intentions to pieces, I took a few deep breaths and focused on my hot cocoa. How lovely to have this moment of calm. How lucky to have this house, this crazy dog, this warm bathrobe, and this delicious hot beverage warming my throat and spirit. It would all work out. It would be fine. Meanwhile, there was this calm moment.

I watched Naughty Britches claw at a mole tunnel and then dismiss it: stale trail. She waddled over to a patch of weeds and peed, flashing me a look as if to say, "Do you mind? Can't a girl have some privacy?"

I closed my eyes and held the mug to my face, enjoying the warmth and aroma. As my mind wandered towards the imaginary to-do list, I brought it back with *cocoa, this moment, good. Cocoa. Good. Here, now, good.*

I must have managed to focus on this as, moment later, to my surprise, NB was alternately nudging me and eyeballing the door.

"All set, little girl? Okay. Let's get this show on the road."

I felt like a snake uncoiling myself from the warm ball I'd made in my bathrobe. My hips complained as I stood up. What was that about? Come to think on it, this had been happening quite a bit lately. When did getting up from a chair become an event? Until recently, I never used to think about it.

*You'll be fifty next year, dear*, my Inner Critic whispered.

My ankle cracked in response.

Mid-morning, Lerlene dropped off her three children: Dee, Clover, and Freddie Jay; her sister, Lorraine; and Saint Eleanor. Dee was a nine-year-old version of her Aunt Lorraine, having the same short stature, same curly hair, same blunt, unsentimental personality. Clover, age six, looked like the other females in the family: the hair, the compact body type, but she was more introverted and emotional. Four-year-old Freddie Jr., aka Freddie Jay, took after his father, a straight-haired, extrovert.

The kids ran over to ogle the enormous piles of holiday goodness. Lerlene trotted around to help Lorraine out of the front seat while Saint Eleanor struggled to get out of the backseat. Once she was out, she turned around to wrestle with a large cooler.

Lorraine yelled, "Mom, that's too heavy. Don't do that by yourself." I rushed over to heft one end, and we managed to set it down.

"What all have you got in here?" I asked. "A body?" I realized too late that the dark humor might not be appropriate around the children, but fortunately, they were too entranced by the hills of garbage bags leaking glittery garlands.

Saint Eleanor brushed off her blouse and straightened her collar. "Now don't get into anything!" she called after them. "Wait for Haint to tell us where to start. You can look. Don't touch! Dee! Come help me move this onto the porch!"

"Hey! You got rid of the rods and antennas!" I said, realizing that Lorraine was now free of the scaffolding and in a boot.

"Yup!"

As Dee helped Saint Eleanor with the cooler, Lerlene gestured for me to come closer until she, Lorraine and I were in a huddle. "Bless you for taking her. I've about strangled her three times already and it's not even noon. If she makes you nuts, please call, I'll come get her. I will appreciate it if you can keep them all busy all day. I packed tons of food, drinks, and snacks in that thing. Don't forget. You have to disappear too. At least get out of visual range."

I gave her a thumbs up and looked at Lorraine. "I wasn't expecting you—I thought you'd enjoy the break too."

We all turned to eye Saint Eleanor, who was peeking into the bags, to be sure she was out of earshot.

"I thought I could help sort and maybe do some of the simple stuff. You *know* Christmas is my favorite holiday. Besides, there might be some items you don't want but I do." She added this last with a naughty glimmer in her eye.

"Oh, I don't think that'll be a problem. You have no idea how much stuff I have here. There's more in the office and the meditation hall. I'm thinking I'll need to get a ticket booth and charge admission if we use half the stuff."

"Wow."

Clover and Freddie Jay were already exploring farther afield and discovered Arnie, the concrete Skunk Ape by the office. Arnie was a remnant from when Max ran the place as the Stinkin' Skunk Ape Fish Camp. Perhaps it was some twisted foreshadowing that I'd purchase a camp with a goofy statue of the state cryptid and then start dating a cryptozoologist.

"He needs a Santa hat!"

"He should have a huge candy cane in his hand!"

"A reindeer! He needs a reindeer!"

I was pleased that they had vision and enthusiasm. It was going to be a long day.

"Okay, kids, let's have a meeting over here on the porch," I called.

Freddy Jay and Clover came running back to where Saint Eleanor and Dee were standing by the mystery bag mountain. When I got their attention, I began, "All of this stuff was donated. I have no idea what all is in here. So first, you're going to need to sort it. That may be all you get done today, and that's fine. I don't really care what goes where as long as it looks pretty. Starting from the road, we ought to have something out by the temporary sign. There are nine cabins, the office, the meditation hall, and the dining room. I've got ladders, extension cords, tape, string — everything you need in my office here." I pointed to the office door. "The office is also filled with more bags of stuff. All I ask is, please be safe, pay attention to what Sain--, uh, your Aunt Eleanor tells you, and DO NOT WEAR SHOES in the meditation hall. That's that building right there. There is a rack outside to put your shoes on. Got it?"

They nodded eagerly. Freddie Jay was bouncing as if ready for a "go" signal in a race.

"Thank you so much for doing this, I really appreciate it," I said as Saint Eleanor surveyed the heaps with a fearful expression. "Whatever you can do will be great. I've no idea what's in there. If it's useable, use it, if it's not, set it aside, I can do a dump run this afternoon. You've got free rein to go wild inside and out. I'd love centerpieces in the dining hall, if possible, garlands out on the porch rails. Have at it."

"Yes, of course," she said. "This is a lot. Do you have a pad and paper somewhere, I think I'm going to need lists..."

Lorraine rolled her eyes. "You want to inventory?"

"No problem!" I said and ducked into the office to grab a notebook, clipboard and a pen. Getting to my desk was more of a sporting event than I'd expected. Stepping over and around piles was tricky. I almost ran into Saint Eleanor as she attempted to trail in after me as I was wiggling back out.

"Oh, here you go," I said, handing over the materials. "Make yourself at home. Lorraine knows her way around here, but you can call me if anything comes up and I'll be back in a bit." As Lerlene had warned me to stay away, I didn't want to specify just when I'd be back.

"Have fun!" I called, heading to my truck.

"We need music," Lorraine said, pulling out her phone.

None of them noticed me as I reversed to drive away. They were busy opening bags as Saint Eleanor adjusted her reading glasses and hovered the pen over the clipboard.

## The Sign

When I first pictured taking over the Stinkin' Skunk Ape Fish Camp, I envisioned a pale-blue sign out by the road with a swooping, graceful font that read:

### Blue's Lotus Lodge

I wanted the sign to convey simplicity, elegance, charm.

This is not what happened.

The rumor mill of Catfish Springs became convinced that I had hired Lorraine's sister, Lerlene, to do the sign. Lerlene is our local artist with a style noted for oversized objects in blinding colors. Think Peter Max and 60s psychedelia. She recently got a commission to do a series of oversized vegetables for the produce section of the Whatcha Need Mart. Just recently her Welcome to Catfish Springs sign was installed with much ceremony out on the highway. Most welcome signs are in somber shades of brown or dark blue on a stately sign.

Not this one.

It looks like a catfish strung out on cocaine. The googly eyes aren't even looking in the same direction; the body is a blend of blinding shades of lime green, hot sun yellow and searing turquoise. The fish is mounted on a board that looks like it got stuck in a spin art machine and it's wedged between megalithic columns of stones  painted in every color of the rainbow.

No surprise then that my Blue's Lotus Lodge sign ended up looking like a psychedelic artichoke with chaotic Chinese takeout lettering as if crafted by someone who happened to be holding a paintbrush at the time that the easel rattled a wasp nest.

I'll be honest. I hated it. It was all I could do to smile and thank her for it. I cried in secret. But over the next few weeks, I had a change of heart. It was eye-catching and got lots of comments, albeit not always complimentary ones. It made it easy to find the retreat, that was for sure. As attention to Lerlene's artwork grew, I took pride in having an original work representing my business.

And then—

A drunk driver smashed into it over Halloween. Blew it to splinters. Fortunately for the driver, he survived with relatively minor injuries. At this point, I found myself really torn. This was my chance to go back to the original design, the pastel colors, the flowy script. But my retreat had already gotten the moniker, "the place with the crazy sign". Meanwhile, Lerlene was getting notoriety in local and state magazines. The drunk driver offered to pay a generous amount towards a new sign, so when Lerlene offered to make a replacement sign, it seemed impossible to refuse and possibly stupid.

"It'll be even bigger and better than the last one," she'd said encouragingly, giving me a conciliatory hug.

Oh boy.

I knew she was busy with other commissions, so I didn't expect my sign until sometime in January at the earliest. In the meantime, I'd had Hey Baby, What's Your Sign? in Gainesville make and install a simple utilitarian sign. This one was darned close to what I'd envisioned originally, and dang if it didn't look just blah in comparison. I didn't want to admit it, but I missed Lerlene's sign.

Imagine my surprise to approach the retreat road and find that the temporary sign was gone, and the new sign was in place. I had to stop the truck to take it in.

The psychedelic artichoke was back, as promised, bigger and better than ever. Whereas before it was floating in a field of plain white, this time it sat in a fiery, rainbow lake. Multicolored spotlights radiated out from its leaves like searchlights seeking heaven through a dreamy fog of turquoise fading to a

horizon of deep plum. The colors were even richer than before. Dazzling. I was crazy about it.

But it was not alone. It was flanked by two shiny, aluminum trees with branches in red, green, and gold with a forest of four-foot-tall plastic candy canes in the foreground. Green garlands wound around the legs of the sign. Three wire-framed deer with white lights seemed to be prancing down the retreat road.

It was all so over the top, so unlike anything I would have done and yet wonderful, I was overcome with emotion. Knowing that I'd be out of the way, Lerlene must have had a team working feverishly to get this all done while I was gone. I loved it! I was so touched by the effort and fantastic outcome, I got choked up. Easing off the brakes, I followed the direction of the deer to see what else had happened while I was away. I'd have to send Lerlene a huge thank you gift basket.

The drive close to cabin nine was flanked with giant plastic candy canes. A young sand pine by the road was bedecked in oversized plastic ornaments and gaudy garlands. A twelve-foot step ladder that I didn't recognize was positioned next to it. There were still boxes of ornaments and whatnot scattered around the base of the tree.

I drove passed Arnie, the concrete Skunk Ape, who looked goofier than ever in a makeshift Santa suit and hat. My office porch had four-foot-tall blow-mold soldiers guarding the steps, garland, white lights woven through the railings. A massive wreath with oversized colored balls hung on the office door. I parked in front of the meditation hall, which was also lost in a sea of garland and lights.

Lorraine came stumping of the meditation hall, "Hey, welcome back! What d'ya think?"

"I'm overwhelmed! The new sign is fantastic, I mean, I really love it. And this—" I waved my hands, looking around. "I can't believe you got so much done so fast. It looks like a Christmas village! Like I should sell tickets or something. Surely you and the kids didn't do that pine tree out there. It looks great, but whose ladder-- "

"Urliss and Hollis did that. I think Max might've sent them. They showed up and Saint Eleanor put them to work. I think they left to get something. They're coming back."

Saint Eleanor stepped out, preening; she'd obviously heard me. This meant that she must have heard Lorraine call her "Saint" Eleanor too. So, she knew about her nickname then. Ha.

"We haven't gotten to the cabins yet, but when we began sorting by category, we got the idea to decorate each one with a theme." She referred to her clipboard. "We thought cabin one could be Santa Clauses, cabin two snowmen, cabin three, stockings and presents—we found several strands of lights with pretty packages AND some blinking wire gift boxes —"

Clover, Dee and Freddie Jay came running out, "Guess what we found?"

"Wait a minute, don't interrupt," Saint Eleanor admonished. "I'm telling Haint about the themes."

"Angels!' said Clover, bouncing.

"Toy trains!" yelled Freddie Jay.

Their enthusiasm was adorable, but the volume was a bit much. I gestured, pushing my flat hands palms down, "Okay, okay, I'm right here, no need to shout."

"Where was I?" Saint Eleanor continued, "Cabin four, angels —"

"Yay, angels!" Clover cheered.

"Cabin five, animals — you wouldn't *believe* the penguins, bears, moose — there are even outdoor light up flamingos wearing scarves," Saint Eleanor continued, apparently caught between being impressed and being appalled at all the animals represented.

The children began rattling off famous cartoon character animals. Some I knew, some I'd never heard of. I'm totally out of touch with recent trending cartoon characters.

"Owls, squirrels, giant reindeer, even a dancing llama —"

"Gingerbread house!" Dee exclaimed.

"No, wait," Saint Eleanor said frowning, studying her list. "Cabin six is classic toys, you know, toy trains, toy cars. Gosh, I think there was even an air-balloon. Cabin seven is candles and Victorian carolers. We found a family of almost life-sized carolers in a sled. They're going to look adorable on the porch.

Where was I? Cabin *eight* is the gingerbread house—" she nodded to Dee. "Would you believe there are giant marshmallow lights? And gumdrop lights? We'll put those on the porch with white garland to look like the piping on the gingerbread house."

"Yay!" Dee clapped.

"And cabin nine will be all candy canes and peppermints," she finished, looking triumphant. "Big Freddie's bringing some of his bowling buddies and more ladders tomorrow, so we'll have plenty of help."

"Come see what we found!" Dee urged, tugging on Saint Eleanor's sleeve. Clover and Freddie Jay added further encouragements, "Yeah!" and "Lookit!"

I glanced past them into the meditation hall and gasped. "Oh…oh…oh." There were pathways through mountains of stuff: candles, bedding, boxes of lights, gift wrap, stacks of ornaments, cookie jars, even Christmas themed pet toys. "Dear me, Donna Reed and Zuzu's petals…"

"Come see!" the children called from the end of the porch. Behind a forest of fake Christmas tree bundles was a shiny, red child-size, two-seat, fire engine complete with flashing lights and fake fire hoses.

"Urliss and Hollis said the battery was dead. They went to Skeeter's to get a replacement," Lorraine said. "Thought the kids would have fun with it, if we ever see a lick of sunshine again, that is. Between you and me, though, I think Urliss and Hollis want to play with it."

"That sounds right," I said, marveling at the detail of the truck. A mini ladder was folded on top behind the cab and the whole thing was covered in official looking stickers.

"There was some stuff that wasn't salvageable—it had gotten water damage or was just covered in roach droppings, so we filled up your dumpster. We found Christmas Bingo, jigsaw puzzles, and board games that'll come in handy for evenings or if the weather is bad."

Freddie's eyes lit up, "Yeah, there's a ball toss game with giant snowballs—"

"It's made out of felt for indoors," Saint Eleanor said.

"You have to throw the snowballs into Santa's hat!" Clover said.

"That sounds fun. This is great."

Saint Eleanor patted Freddie's head, "We can come back tomorrow and keep going. These kids need some supper and bath time! I've left a pile of things you should go through. We found some jewelry, some pretty holiday china. Let me know if you don't want it, I might like it."

"I will. Thanks again for everything," I said.

Lorraine said, "If I pack a bag, can I come over tomorrow with them to help out and then go home with you?"

"Sure!"

So far, so fantastic.

# PART TWO

## THE GUESTS

# Chapter 6

## DAY OF REST

In defiance of Aunt Moira's predictions, I had only two couples as guests that weekend. The first couple was bound for Orlando with a honeymoon package--all the attractions they could take in, theme parks during the day, shows and bars at night. The other pair was two female botanists heading home after an extended research study in the Everglades. Once they'd checked out, and they'd checked out right after breakfast, I closed down the dining hall, cleaned their cabins for the next guests and headed home.

Lerlene, Saint Eleanor et al. were planning to come decorate some time mid-afternoon after Saint Eleanor returned from church, and they'd had lunch. I had time to go home and get Naughty Britches. I'd bring her back and we could work on sorting Christmas stuff.

I wanted my office back.

I finished off some leftover soup with a couple crackers for a lunch and soon had a hankering for chocolate. The only chocolate I had on hand was a gift bag of chocolate covered espresso beans that one of my guests had given me earlier in the month. I tried a couple. The crunch was satisfying, like peanuts, the blended flavors of the dark chocolate and coffee was super. I stuck the bag in my pants pocket and took NB for a short walk, then we went over to the office. She was fearful of the piles of stuff at first, but after a few tentative sniffs, she settled into her favorite spot, yawned, and began her mid-day nap.

"Well kiddo, where should I start?" I asked, pulling out the little baggie of magic beans from my pocket. They sure were good. As with potato chips, a few wasn't enough. I had a few more. And a few more. Dang, those things were amazing. How had I not known about these before? I cranked up some music and began to focus on sorting. The first box seemed to be assorted candles in all sizes and flavors—caramel, toasted marshmallow, cookies, pine, cranberry. The smells competed for supremacy, giving me a bit of a headache. The next box was books about the holidays—crafts, cookbooks, trees from around the world. I could donate those to the library. I set them aside and chomped some more beans.

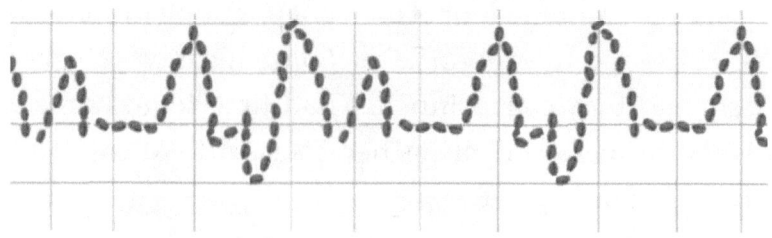

Iggy and his girlfriend, Louise, found me a bit later. I was up on a ladder with garland wrapped around me, trying to get it to swag in the blinds evenly.

"Hey, Haint, holy cow! Looks like Santa moved his workshop here!"

"Oh! Hi!" I said, dumping the garland.

Louise crouched to greet Naughty Britches who was being over-zealous with her vocal greeting.

Iggy said, "I tried to call you, you didn't answer, but we were out and about, thought we'd try you here."

"Oh? I must not have heard the phone. I'm in the zone. I got the tree up and all decorated, see? Isn't it pretty? Oh, Louise, for the love of all that is holy, please take some candles. You like candles, right? I've got so many. Did you see that cool wreath? I just love all the candies in it. Oh, do you like coffee table books? There was a whole box of them. I was going to donate to the library, but if you see anything you like please, help yourself. Do you like the garland on the window? Is it too much? I found some oversized snowflakes and was thinking maybe they'd look better —"

They both gaped at me.

"What? It's the garland, isn't it? Okay, you're right. I'll take it down. Snowflakes it is. Where'd I put them? Oh, they fell off the desk there. Here look, aren't they cute? Oh, I'm being a bad hostess. Are you thirsty? Can I get you something to drink?"

Iggy took me by the shoulders and made me look him in the eyes, "Haint, are you okay?"

"Yeah, why? Of course! I'm just on a roll here. Lorraine and Saint Eleanor are coming soon, and I wanted some time to just sort by myself. They did a super job yesterday, I'm really touched, but Lerlene said it's best if I keep away from Saint Eleanor and just let her go. So much to do! Did you see Lerlene's sign out there? Don't you love it? I'm so grateful. You know, honestly, in the beginning, I didn't like the old one, but I just love the new one, all the colors--"

"HAINT! Have you had anything to eat lately?"

"Yeah, why? I had soup a while back. Oh hey!" I said, fishing the bag of beans from my pocket. "Look. You've GOT to try these espresso beans. They're so good! I got them as a gift from a guest and I've been just chowing down on them. Please, take them away from me, or I'll eat the whole bag."

"Oh boy," Iggy said, picking up the almost empty bag and showing it to Louise.

"What? What's the matter?" I asked.

"Let's get you some protein and some carbs and a lot of water," Louise said. "You're jacked up worse than sugared up kids in a bouncy castle, honey."

"What? What do you mean? No, I'm not, I'm just in the zone."

"Riight," Iggy said, looking to Louise.

"Look at your hands!" Louise said.

I glanced down at my hands. I had to admit that they were shaking like bamboo leaves in a tropical storm.

"Right," Iggy said, releasing my shoulders and walking to my mini fridge. "You've got some water, here, dontcha? Ah, yup." He pulled a bottle out, unscrewed the top and handed it to me. "Drink this. What d'ya say we take you out to lunch? Want to go to Bev's?"

Had they said anywhere else, I could have said no, but Iggy knows I love Bev's burgers. "Oh, twist my arm then. Okay. Let me clean up super quick. Can we take NB and eat outside?"

"Sure," Iggy said, patting Naughty Britches. "Come on, cute stuff. Let's get your mom to come back down to earth, eh?"

NB adores Iggy. She happily followed him to the door.

I was about to set the water down when Iggy fussed at me, "Oh no you don't. Drink that all down."

"Okay."

Louise was about out the door when I yelped, "Wait! Stop! Take some candles! Here, I"ll get you a bag!"

Bev's wasn't crowded so we got seated and Kandi Jo took our orders.

"Drink this," Iggy said, pushing the huge ice water glass in front of me.

Louise's family was planning a big reunion over the holidays. I knew Iggy was nervous about meeting everyone, but I hadn't heard the details.

"So, when do you leave?" I asked, unwrapping the straw.

"We're going over to Louise's parents in Cedar Key on

Friday. We'll spend the weekend with them and then Monday, we drive with them in their van to Apalachicola—"

Louise interrupted, "My brother, Larry, runs a charter fishing company there and my sister, Larissa, runs a small bed and breakfast there. We're all going to stay at the bed and breakfast—"

Small red flags began waving in my head. If they were going with Louise's parents in the family van, they'd be stuck. I'd want my freedom to escape, even if just to get away for an hour. Iggy tends to me more gregarious than I am, but I could tell by his slightly hunched posture and wandering eyes that he was not entirely happy with the arrangement. As if reading my thoughts, he said, "It's right on the beach and within walking distance to town, so that'll be cool." He looked up at the moment. Our eyes met and I winked at him. *Gotcha, brat.* ♥

"So how many people are you expecting?" I asked.

Louise set down her burger and rolled her eyes. "Sounds like the usual mob—my parents, my brother, his family, my sister and hers, possibly an aunt and uncle from Georgia we don't see very often---they've got health issues... She's a drama queen, so I know it's mean, but I'm hoping they don't come."

"Gotcha," I said, hoping for their sake, she didn't show.

"What about you?" she asked me. "I thought you were going to Flagler?"

"I was but that got cancelled." I told her about Lorraine's septic situation and that I'd be hosting her family for Christmas.

---

♥ *Brat* in Polish and Russian, pronounced 'brott', like bratwurst, means brother.

"And Aunt Moira said something about a dream that I'd have a retreat full of guests. Hardly. It should be a pretty low-key week. Our biggest challenge will be dealing with Saint Eleanor. But you know, I've got to hand it to her. She did an amazing job yesterday. That woman was, perchance, a drill sergeant in a former life."

I had finished my burger and was picking at the last of the fries when Louise exclaimed, "Oh, I forgot something!" She excused herself from the table. She trotted back to the car and returned with an oversized gift bag. "Merry Christmas."

## GIFT EXCHANGE

Pulling out the heavy gift with a giant red bow on it, I began ripping away at the Santa-hatted, penguin-covered paper. A complicated bird feeder with squirrel baffles emerged.

"They say it's a fortress," Iggy said.

"We watched a video—this is the best bird feeder *ever*," Louise said.

Iggy knew my long traumatic history with squirrel invasions and bird-feeder fails. I'd given up completely at my house and had a cheap feeder at the retreat where guests could watch squirrels get fat. When they were too fat, the occasional songbird might slip in and get a seed. Racoons polished off the leftovers at night. Were it not for the occasional guest gushing about a cardinal at the feeder, I'd have given birdfeeding up.

"Golly, I can't wait to see if it really works," I said with enthusiasm.

"I really think this one might be the last one," Iggy said. "I know you love to see your birds. It broke my heart that you gave up."

"Aw, thank you!" I said, giving them both hugs. "I didn't know we were doing the gift thing. I've got goodies for you, too, but at home. Would you have time to run me home and back to the Lotus Lodge?"

"Sure!" they answered in unison.

We tossed our trash and got into their car. I felt a bit maudlin on the drive back to my house. The holiday wasn't going to be the same without Iggy, but I liked Louise and hoped that he fit in well with her family.

When we got there, Louise and Iggy waited in the living room as I strode to my guest room and picked their gifts off the bed.

"You know, I'm so used to spending Christmas together," I said, re-entering the living room, "I had it in my head we'd be together," I said wistfully. "Louise, can you take the one off the top? That's yours — and Iggy, this one's for you."

Over the past few years, I've really come to hate the requirement to shop for holiday gifts and it gets harder and harder to shop for people who already have everything they need, right? Well, I got lucky this year. Merinda Manor, one of my recent guests, runs a stained-glass studio in Gainesville. She encouraged me to visit her shop, so one day, I stopped in. I was amazed at the variety of themes there were: sports, wildlife, angels, and all sorts of hobbies.

I spotted a black and white piece with an infinity circle in black, surrounded by white, with a silhouette of a martial artist crouched in a dramatic tai-chi stance called Snake Creeps Down--an awkward and brutal move if you have knee problems. Iggy can do it flawlessly. Elegant and simple, the stained-glass panel was the perfect gift, especially since Iggy is the crouching partner in the martial arts studio, Crouching Blue, Hidden Chow. I know, it sounds like a peculiar restaurant, doesn't it? Iggy's friend, Joe Chow is the other partner. The quirkiness of the name has done well for them though on occasion they still turn away confused diners looking for Chinese food.

Louise was a bit trickier. I knew she worked at Quick Fit, a physical therapy gym and also acted in local theater productions. I thought she'd like a stained-glass panel with a gold Mardi-Gras-style mask surrounded by colorful flowers.

"Oh, Haint, this is gorgeous! I love the colors!" Louise cooed.

"Oh, wow, Snake Creeps Down? Did you have this done custom?" Iggy asked.

"Nope! But when I spotted it, I knew you had to have it."

"This is going to look great in the window at the dojo!"

"Well, I'm going to love the birdfeeder and the birdbath!" I said.

We chit-chatted a bit and then they dropped me at the office. Naughty Britches went nuts telling me all about how cruel we were to leave her, especially since she could smell Bev's burgers on me, and I'd neglected to bring her one. Iggy retrieved my new bird feeder and set it on the porch.

We hugged goodbyes and wished each other happy

holidays. My earlier expresso-bean mania was gone. Watching Iggy and Louse drive away, I felt deflated. The piles of decorations looked daunting.

"Well, kiddo, it's you and me," I said, hugging Naughty Britches. I got her leash. Soon we were performing a slow investigation around Arnie and the rest rooms. Her ears shot up. She began to bark. Soon I heard it too, the grumble of tires over gravel.

Saint Eleanor et al. were arriving.

## OH, SUGAR

Naughty Britches shifted her meandering pace to full tilt sprint to the parking lot to see who had arrived. The kids ran up to greet us. Saint Eleanor got out of the car, followed by Lorraine, who hefted a small suitcase with her. She had a brief conversation with Lerlene, waved and soon Lerlene was driving away.

"Good afternoon," Saint Eleanor said in a loud tone, to be heard over the boisterous trio of children.

"Wow, they're wired up today," I said, watching them pet NB who had rolled over to offer better belly access.

Saint Eleanor ignored that comment. "I think I left my checklist in the meditation hall."

"Oh, here, let me get that for you," I said, taking Lorraine's suitcase. I was going to set it in the office but didn't get that far. Feeding off the children's excitement, Naughty Britches jumped up and began lunging at and kissing the children. She promptly knocked Freddie Jay over and preceded to lick his face. The girls screamed, he yelled, Saint Eleanor scowled. I grabbed NB and held her, apologizing.

"Sorry, she gets excited."

Freddie Jay made noises of disgust while wiping at his face. The girls clung were afraid to move. Naughty Britches pulled and barked. I wrestled her back into the office and crated her. She protested mightily.

Before I knew it, Freddie Jay had seen the firetruck and ran over to jump in.

"Freddie! We're here to work, not to play!" Saint Eleanor barked.

The girls soon forgot their fear and took off to join Freddie.

Lorraine pulled me aside and said, "She gave them ice cream. They'll be flying high for a while, I'm afraid."

"Oh goodie."

"Freddie! Stop this instant! Let's go inside, we've got work to do!" Saint Eleanor demanded.

The children swirled around her and disappeared into the meditation hall.

"Can we put my bag in your truck?" Lorraine asked with the hope of a hitchhiker in the desert when a car stops.

"Sure," I said, realizing that I'd neglected it. "Why not get yourself something to drink and I'll be right back."

"Thank you," she whispered, like a prayer.

The afternoon was not as productive as I'd hoped. Dee cut herself on a broken ornament. Freddie Jay managed to splash through a puddle and get most of the dirty water on his clothes. Saint Eleanor and Lorraine got into a snit over what the centerpieces should be on the tables in the dining hall. And Saint Eleanor picked a fight with me.

I'd noticed that she'd been critical and edgy, quite different from the previous day. "Are you okay?" I asked. "I'm sure the kids have been a handful this afternoon. Want to call it quits for the day?"

Her nose twitched; her jaw tightened. "No, I'm fine."

"Can I get you something to drink? A snack?"

"No, I'm *fine*. I just don't agree with it all, that's all, but I'm not here to judge."

"Mom—" Lorraine began.

"No, it's fine. It's not my business, I just don't understand the hypocrisy, that's all."

"I'm sorry?" I asked. I had no idea what she was talking about.

"All this. Santas and candies and reindeer and snowflakes. It's got *nothing* to do with the Christian celebration of the birth of our savior. It's all commercialism. You're a *Buddhist*. What does any of *this* have to do with anything?"

*Take a moment, Sister,* the Inner Critic warned. *Breathe in and out.*

I felt attacked, but I tried to pull back from the urge to argue back with hostility. In truth, she had a valid question. It wasn't the question that got my goat, it was the arch way she'd posed it.

"Yes, I'm a Buddhist, but this isn't a retreat that espouses or eschews any religion. Buddhism is not exclusive, you can be a Jewish Buddhist, Catholic Buddhist, whatever you want. This is a retreat. I'm not asking or telling anyone to practice a faith. If people want to come here just to eat good meals and walk in the woods, that's perfectly fine. I offer yoga and meditation to help clear the mind. Maybe I shouldn't decorate at all, but I like it. It's winter and dreary. The cute snowmen and Santas make me smile. I love the red tablecloths and hanging mistletoe. The kids love it.

"But what is it teaching them?" she countered.

I was at a loss. I stink at arguing. I tried to summon a response, but nothing came out. Maybe she was having a weird sugar response or was dehydrated or something. She'd been in a good mood and excited about the decorations yesterday.

"Mom! You're being rude!" Lorraine said.

"I'm asking a valid question!" she said.

"I don't know, I really don't. Does a gingerbread man really offend you?"

She didn't answer.

"Well, what do *you* get the children for Christmas?"

Lorraine said, "She puts money in their stockings!"

My eyebrows went up. "Oh?"

"To teach them fiscal responsibility!" Saint Eleanor said huffily.

"By *giving* them money? I don't follow. Wouldn't it be better if they-- earned it?" I asked.

Saint Eleanor blustered. "I don't feel I have to defend what I give to my own grandchildren for Christmas! That's my business!"

"I assure you that I wasn't attacking, I was just asking —"

Fortunately, this awkward moment was broken by Dee shrieking, "Ew! Roaches!" She'd been pulling a small fake tree from a bag and several bugs scurried out. Freddie Jay began stamping at them.

"Hey, whoa!" I said, "Let's not kill them. Let's just escort them outside!"

"I hate roaches," Saint Eleanor said, stomping at one but missing. "*Disgusting.*"

"All God's creatures," I said.

Freddy Jay was having a grand time stomping about even though his kill rate was low. The roaches were too quick for me, running and hiding before I could find something to catch them with.

"I was going to show them how to catch them in a cup and take them outside," I said. "You know, thou shalt not kill?"

She stopped talking to me after that.

When Lerlene came to fetch them later, we waved goodbye to the kids while Saint Eleanor avoided eye contact. Lorraine turned to me and said, "I packed a bottle of red wine in my suitcase."

"Oh, yes. That sounds heavenly. Let's go home. I've had enough of the holiday spirit for one afternoon."

Saint Eleanor apologized the following day. She said she'd been tired and had forgotten to take her medication. Over the next few days, she was cheerful, helpful, and did a spectacular job of keeping us on task decorating the cabins in their assigned themes, the dining hall, meditation hall—even the bathrooms got some bling and color. Thanks to her organizational skills and diligence, we'd sorted, decorated, had dump runs to discard what could not be salvaged. She happily received items she'd requested—a set of holiday dishes, lotions, wall-hangings, etc.

Haint's Land of Christmas was ready for business.

At this point, I wasn't too worried. It all seemed like I had it under control.

Ho, ho, ho!

# Chapter 7

## THE GARCIA FAMILY

orraine is a low-maintenance, no-nonsense kind of woman. It hadn't taken long to get her situated in my guest bedroom. It was Sunday night, the 21st. I'd had a craving for eggplant rollatini, so we'd ordered takeaway from Tony and Al's, one of my favorite restaurants. I always get extra garlic. I had to pace myself or I'd snarf down the whole thing. I wanted to save some for lunch the next day.

"Mmm!" Lorraine purred, wiping sauce from her mouth. "This parmesan meatball sandwich is just the *bomb*! Thanks for picking this up."

"No problem. I had a hankering," I said.

After dinner, we migrated to the living room. I couldn't seem to stay warm, so I got a fire going in the fireplace for ambiance as much as heat. It was still early-ish, but I felt like getting into my jammies. Moments later, wrapped in my favorite old, oversized bathrobe, sitting by the fire, I announced, "I'm in my happy place. If I could purr like a cat on steroids, I would."

"I could go for another glass of wine," Lorraine said.

"A fine idea," I said, launching myself out of my seat. I fetched our glasses from the kitchen, refilling them and returned, settling back into the cushion.

We decided to watch a Dario Argento *giallo* movie. *Giallo* is an Italian style of mystery film, most popular in the 60s and 70s notable for weird dreamlike sequences, vivid colors, bloody but highly stylized death scenes, and stylishly dressed killers usually disguised by masks or hats. I'd really enjoyed the first two films I'd tried, though I'd wondered if the artsy death scenes weren't a twisted gateway towards more and more violence, a grooming, a conditioning. In *Blood and Black Lace* for example, there is a death scene where a woman is murdered in a bathtub. The last shot of her is, dare I say it, gorgeous. Her eyes are the color of the tub water, her face is beautiful, the balance of the picture is perfect. It is cinematic gold and yet, hello, why am I celebrating a woman getting strangled? Because it's not real. It's artistic. Her face framed by the porcelain tub, her dark hair, her peaceful expression — completely impossible. But *Opera* was really over my threshold for violence. I was on edge and eager for the crazy killer to be stopped.

It was cold outside, but all was toasty and snug inside. Naughty Britches was asleep beside me, Mischief was draped across the back of the sofa by my head. An exuberant fire burned in the fireplace. On the television, a terrified woman holding a knife crept around an opera house as loud heartbeats and opera music built to a crescendo and the inevitable confrontation with a killer. I was comfortable but on edge at the same time.

My phone rang.

I jumped, slopping a bit of wine.

Naughty Britches groaned with displeasure at having been so rudely awakened.

"Hello?"

"Haint? This is Yolanda."

In the background, I could hear animated conversation in Spanish punctuated by cusswords.

"Hi, Yolanda, what's up? Are you okay?"

"Yes, I am okay," she said, then in muffled, rapid Spanish, *"Puedes mantenerlo bajo? Estoy en el telefono!"*

In the background, I could hear Yolanda's husband, Paco saying, *"Te lo digo, probablemente Mingo pueda arreglarlo."* My Spanish is sketchy, but it was something about Mingo fixing it.

*"No las molestas!"* he argued.

"Sorry, Haint. Our stove at the restaurant stopped working. Something is wrong. It's gas. Sometimes it works and then suddenly *nada*. Sometimes I swear I smell gas. I'm not going to play with gas. I'm afraid of gas. The repair guy can't come out until Friday, the day after Christmas. He thinks Mingo can fix it, but I'm not trusting my whole restaurant to Mingo when it's a gas problem."

*"Yolanda, por favor!"*

"No, Paco, no," She yelled back. "What if Mingo doesn't do it right? *Quieres explotar a nuestras clientas?* You want to blow up the restaurant? Kaboom? Like that? No! We wait for a professional!"

I had a funny feeling I knew where this was leading. I took a big sip of wine. I glanced at the movie in time to see the woman with the knife put her eye to a keyhole. I flinched.

Note to self, never do this. What happened was really gross and shocking.

"…we were closing the restaurant to the public so we could have a big meal for the family. But now our parents and Yaya are coming. *Es demasiado!* Too much! Rocky and Osanna live here, so they could go home, but Yaya and all the kids… I could manage to cook for everyone, but —"

"Yolanda. Stop. Take a breath! How many people?" I asked.

"How many? Mingo, Rita, George, Mimi, Lulu, *eso es dieciséis*…Yaya, Mama, Papa…*diecinueve*, Pedro…*viente*, Clementina…*veinte uno*…uh, twenty-one."

I gulped the last of the red wine as a woman in the movie screamed her lungs out over the dead woman who'd previously been unwise enough to put her eye to the keyhole. I punched the pause button.

Lorraine was cringing, hands over her eyes, "Oh, that was so gross!"

Yolanda said, "I'm sorry, I shouldn't have asked. I should let you go."

"No, that wasn't *me* screaming, I'm watching a movie!" I said, "What I was going to suggest is, if you want everyone to stay together, I have two large cabins…How many children total?"

"Ah…let me see, ah…ten."

"They could stay in one cabin all together, like at camp, and the adults could stay in a separate cabin right next door. Everyone could be together. Comfortable. And you don't even have to worry about cooking."

I tried to make this last part sound effortless, but realized I wasn't prepared to cook for so many extra people with such short notice. Aunt Moira had tried to warn me, hadn't she?

"Oh, you do?" she said, sounding relieved. To Paco she said, *"Ella dice que podríamos tener dos cabañas grandes, una para los niños y otra para los adultos.*

"*Y Yaya?* You want to put *Yaya* in a cabin?"

"It's only for two nights. She would be with everyone. Do you want her to stay here with us instead? *La podemos hablar más tarde, sí?* We can talk about it later, yes?" To me she said, "Are you sure? I know it is so short notice."

I wasn't at all sure, but I could hardly back out now. Max's family, Lorraine's family, the Garcia clan. This would be the first time I'd have so many children at once. I have to confess that I'm not really comfortable around children. My mother was hardly a role model of loving comfort, and I never felt the calling to take on motherhood. The thought of screaming, snotty, sickly children made my ovaries shrink to raisins, but I did know some well-behaved, intelligent children who gave me a glimmer of hope about the future. They would be supervised. Their parents would be here. It wasn't like I'd be babysitting. With the retreat looking like wonderland, it just might be fun.

With a bit of apprehension I asked, "When will you be coming?"

"Is Tuesday okay? Tuesday to Thursday."

"But Thursday is Christmas. Don't you want to stay over?"

"We'll see how it goes."

That sounded a bit portentous.

*What could go wrong?* my Inner Critic jeered.

"Okay, until Thursday, but you can stay over if you want. I don't have anyone checking in."

"*Gracias*, thank you, Haint. You don't know what a relief this is."

"No problem," I said, staring at the freeze frame on the television—the distressed girl in hysterics over the dead woman. "Glad I can help."

"Oh, I feel silly asking this, but could we be in a cabin, oh, how do you say… *sin espíritus*—"

I heard Paco in the background yell, "No ghost!"

"Without ghosts--we'd appreciate it," Yolanda finished.

I drew in a breath and closed my eyes. How had she heard about the ghosts? I wished I could promise no ghosts, but the retreat was *slightly* haunted by a benevolent Native American Indian woman and her two sons who died from yellow fever. I had only seen glimpses of them. A few children had reported seeing two boys dressed in strange clothing playing in the woods. According to Shane, one of my guests, Spotted Fawn had tried to get in bed with him several times. The problem was, the sightings were not limited to a particular cabin or area of the retreat--my ghosts were free-ranging.

I had been silent for too long, thinking about how to respond. Yolanda said, "Pedro said he saw a woman in his cabin. By his bed."

"Pedro saw her?" I managed to say, masking a giggle. I had to hand it to her, Spotted Fawn had good taste in men. Both Shane and Pedro were quite handsome. If I were a lonely ghost with a libido, I'd have picked Pedro too. "Pedro didn't mention it to me."

At the mention of Pedro's name, Lorraine jerked upright and stared at me. "Pedro?"

I put a finger to my lips. "Shh."

Yolanda continued, "Don't tell him I told you. He was a bit afraid and embarrassed. But please. No ghosts."

"No, no," I said, reassuringly, crossing my fingers. What could I do about it? Note to self. Ask Aunt Moira to ask Spotted Fawn to stop getting overly friendly with my male guests.

She thanked me again and hung up.

Lorraine verbally pounced on me. "What's up with Pedro? Is he okay?"

"Yes, he's fine. That was Yolanda. The stove died at the restaurant. She wants to book the retreat for the whole family."

"Including Pedro?" she asked, wiggling like a puppy about to get a treat.

"I think so — o," I said in a teasing sing-song.

Back in September, Pedro Garcia had been a guest at my not-so-grand opening. Pedro was *smoking* hot — melty brown eyes, gorgeous brown skin, fabulous hair, perfect butt, not very tall, but that was fine, Lorraine was short. They'd be a super cute couple. His casual clothes seem tailor made. Lorraine had helped me out that weekend and had tripped over herself and stammered in his proximity.

"More wine?" I asked.

"Sure."

"Oh. My. God," Lorraine said as I walked to the kitchen. "I don't know whether to hoot or cry. Pedro will be there. He'll meet my whole crazy family. *Saint Eleanor!* Oh, she could drive Jesus away. I'm so screwed."

I refilled our wine glasses. "Maybe not. Hey, she was super all last week. Well, except for that one day of weirdness. Remember, you have that gimpy ankle. Automatic sympathy card."

"You think?"

I handed Lorraine her wine and shrugged. Glancing at the television screen, I wasn't sure I was up to the rest of *Opera* but needed to know that the heroine would survive, and the killer would die in some fabulously karmatic fashion. I know, bad Buddhist me, but he was nutzoid and needed to go.

I had just settled back down on the couch when Lorraine said, "Hey, forgot to tell you. The final head count--twelve."

I was glad I had gotten more wine. I took a big gulp. "Well, looks like I'll be grocery shopping big time tomorrow."

"How many Garcias?" Lorraine asked.

"Twen-ty-one Garcias," I said, feeling uneasy. So much for an easy holiday. "Hey, think of this: *his* whole crazy family will be there too. Maybe you could bond in commiseration. We'll put up extra mistletoe and spike the eggnog."

"Oh, Haint...don't tease. I don't know if he even knows I'm alive. I'll have to go clothes shopping. This changes everything!"

I laughed.

"What about Buster? Have you heard from him?"

"Sort of," I said, feeling squirmy, "I got this mangled postcard of a creepy fetish doll. Most of the message was obliterated by tire tracks or something. I think he might be in Africa."

"*Africa?*"

"The postage stamp was foreign and I'm pretty sure it said Congo."

"So, he's not going to be here for Christmas?"

"Let me get out the magic eight ball" I said, holding the imaginary oracle device up "Hmm, let's give it a good old shake," I said pretending, "Ah. It says "Signs Point to No." I picked up the remote and clicked the "play" button. "Let's see how this maniac gets it."

To be honest, I don't remember much of the movie after that. I was too preoccupied with planning for this onslaught of guests.

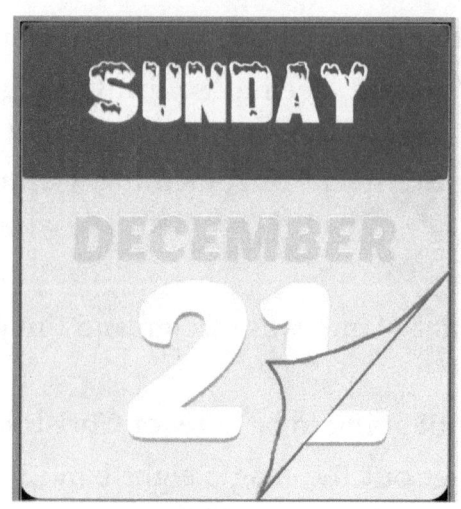

# Chapter 8

## Weather Outside is Frightful

Dizzied up about my first holiday season at the retreat, I'd neglected to pay attention to the weather forecast. Another cold front came through early Monday morning bringing close to freezing temperatures along with that wet cold that seeps right through layers of clothing. The frozen-lake-gray sky indicated that it must be snowing farther north. All in all, stay in bed with hot cocoa and a good book kind of weather.

But I had Max's clan, Lorraine's family and the Garcias coming the following day. Tuesday: the day before the night before Christmas.

Lorraine and I were in the kitchen enjoying coffee while I cooked eggs and made toast. Her phone buzzed.

"Oh! Got a text from Lerlene. Aunt Moira and her partner Gigi are coming...but they'll stay in their camper, they don't need a cabin."

"Wait. Aunt Moira's coming? I thought she was in

Kalamazoo."

Lorraine shrugged. "You never know with her. Keeping track of her is like trying to catch bubbles from one of those toy bubble wands—you know, like a giant squash racket riddled with holes? You can't. They move too fast. Oh… she says Moira and Gigi were going to Gigi's family, but they've all got the flu. Gigi's just as happy to beg off, she doesn't get along with her brother at all. Moira says he has *mucho* bad karma from a past life. "

"Don't we all," I murmured.

"Oh, come on, you sound like me. You are very blessed, and you know it."

"Yes, that's true. You're quite right. I think this weather's got me down."

"Yeah, no kidding! Couldn't we just hibernate like bears?" She pulled her bathrobe tighter.

I set her plate down in front of her. "Careful, it's hot."

"Speaking of hot, Pedro is really coming? Do you think I should get my haircut?" She flipped her curly hair around. "Maybe do my nails? God, I haven't put polish on my nails in years…"

I stared at her. "Who are you and what have you done with my no-nonsense friend, Lorraine?" I turned the burner off, got my plate, and joined her.

"Yeah, I know. I've got it bad, don't I? But honestly, isn't he just Mr. McLuscious?"

"Hmm. Since he's Mexican, not Irish, I think you mean Señor Soñador, Mr. Dreamy, and yes, he is, absolutely. Good thing he's closer to your age than mine or we'd be wrestling over him."

"Good thing. I love you, but it could get ugly."

"I've got some martial arts training," I reminded her.

"You have to sleep sometime," she replied with a wink. "So, what's on your plate today?"

"Stocking the freezer and the larder for home and the retreat, per Aunt Moira's warning."

"Good choice. I mean, I'm sorry you have to go out in this cold mess, but if she said to stock up, stock *up*. She's spooky that way."

"Have you asked her about your chances with Señor Soñador?"

"No way. I am holding onto the illusion that it's a possibility. Should I get my eyebrows done? Might as well, right?"

I considered this. "You know, Lorraine, in my almost-fifty years, I've never once heard a man have an opinion on a woman's eyebrows. You bake him one of your cakes. That's all you need to do."

"Ooh… good idea!"

"What's on *your* menu for today?"

Well, what with the weather being crap, and the fact that I'm going to be mobbed by relatives sooner than I'd like, I'm giving myself the day off. I think I overdid with decorating. My ankle hurts. Going to put it up, takes some meds and read a trashy romance. Naughty Britches and Mischief'll keep me company, won't you?"

Naughty Britches had her chin on Lorraine's leg, eyeing her eggs, and Mischief had jumped up on the table and was poised to bat at her toast.

"Get down!" I yelled, snapping my fingers. Mischief moved away, looking affronted.

"So don't worry about her," Lorraine said, patting NB. "I'll let her out and feed her for you. Shop all you want."

I looked out the window at the gray day. *Blech.* I'd love to play hooky, stay home, and read. How'd I get roped into all this again? Hadn't I wanted to escape to the beach? I could enjoy the beach, even in the cold and rain... I loved watching storms move over the ocean from the safety of a restaurant window.

## Mokèlé-mbèmbé

Patriotic Pete waved a handful of mail as he got out of his vehicle. "Hey, Haint! Happy Holidays! Since you're here I've give you the retreat mail and your mail at the same time. You got a package here. Say, I like this company. I order clothes from them too. Good quality, eh?" He held out the bundle. "Looks like you got a postcard from yer feller. Is he workin' at a museum someplace?"

I nodded, shrugged and yelled, "I DON'T KNOW."

"Heard you got a bunch of people stayin' with you. That's great! Happy to hear it. Place looks so cheerful with all the decorating. Warms my heart on this gloomy day. My sister and her family are comin' to visit for the holiday, so I got to keep movin' today. They're comin' later on. You have a good one, ya hear? Stay warm!"

He handed me the mail and scooted back to his vehicle. I almost felt cheated. Normally, interaction with Patriotic Pete is much like being hugged by an octopus. Takes a while to get disentangled as he always wants to talk but is deafer than my mailbox. A shouting match ensues. But not today. And soon he'd be outmoded by a boring lockbox. I waved and screamed, "Merry Christmas!"

I flipped through the junk and found the postcard from Buster.

On the front was a dinosaur (don't ask me what kind, I was never that keen on dinosaurs—one of the long neck and long tail variety, like a humongous lizard). Under the skeleton was a caption: Mokèlé-mbèmbé.

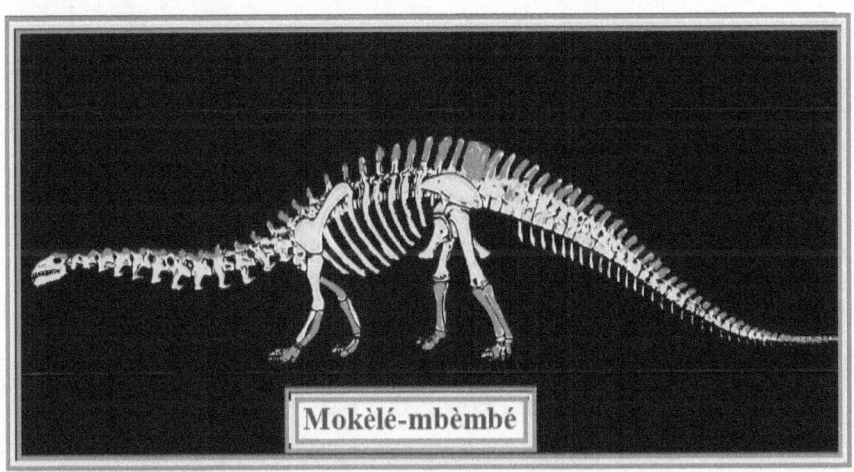

Mokèlé-mbèmbé

At least this time, I had something I could research. I flipped the card over, eager to read the message and dismayed to find that this time, while the card was intact, it had been splattered with oil. Most of the note was unreadable. "My

Darling Moon Eyes," it began. Aww. My heart went all pinky mushy like in my heart meditations. It said something about "to see you" but not when. Said he lost his phone and something about a viper! Wish he'd said more, but it was something to hold onto. Where was he?

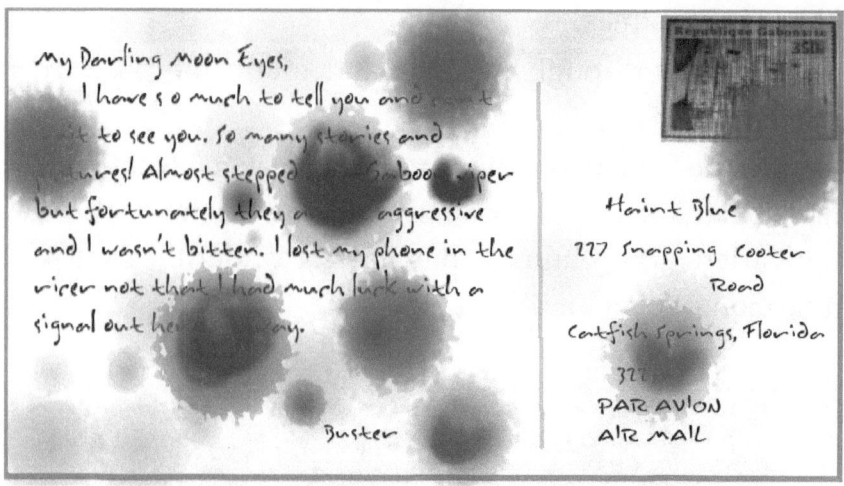

My Darling Moon Eyes,

I have s o much to tell you and ___
___ to see you. So many stories and
___res! Almost stepped ___ Gaboon ___per
but fortunately they ___ aggressive
and I wasn't bitten. I lost my phone in the
river not that I had much luck with a
signal out here ___ ny.

Buster

Haint Blue
227 Snapping Cooter
Road
Catfish Springs, Florida
327__
PAR AVION
AIR MAIL

When I got inside, I let my fingers hunt the internet for mokèlé-mbèmbé and bam! The mokèlé-mbèmbé is or was...hang on. Honestly, when you're talking about a mythological creature or a cryptid and there is scanty to no evidence that it ever existed, do you refer to it in the past or present tense? Well, according to the internet, it IS alive and well and living in the Congo River Basin in Gabon. It IS a **sauropod**, that meaning a lizard-like, water dwelling dinosaur known for a long neck and long tail. The name

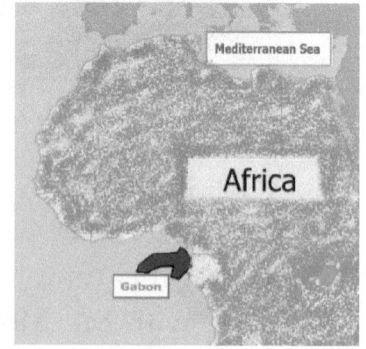

translates to "the one who stops the flow of rivers". Well, that makes sense. A sighting could stop one's heart, too.

Oh, and a history of sightings including a dire warning that a group of locals once caught one of the beasts, killed it, cooked it, ate it, and died. Either they didn't cook it properly, or it was toxic.

Note to self: Don't eat a sauropod no matter how hard the trendy restaurant pushes the exotic special. If offered up a plate of mokèlé-mbèmbé, just say no. I got the giggles picturing a silly T-shirt with a big X over a picture of the dinosaur. I could hunt up a print shop and make a stocking stuffer gift...

Ahh! The colors of the flag of the Republic of Gabon are green, yellow and sky blue, same as the colors on the dinosaur picture.

Buster was in Africa! Well, that sure explained why I hadn't heard from him in a while. Oh-ho! What? No way! There was an article about a recent discovery of footprints and dung attributed to the sauropod. There was even a photo of the dung pile and I have to say, that was a *lot* of poop. Dang!

Holy crap! (Sometimes the puns just insert themselves, sorry.) Buster was off chasing the mokèlé-mbèmbé!

I had a little Christmas tree decorated with dog ornaments on my kitchen counter. I propped the card against it and stared at it. *Oh, Buster.* I think until this moment I had hoped to hear from him. My mind kept spinning and banging about this like sneakers in the dryer. What was I doing getting involved with this man who was gone all the dang time?

"Why the glum face?" Lorraine asked.

I hadn't heard her coming up behind me from her bedroom. I showed her the postcard. She picked it up and read it.

"Well, at least you know why you haven't heard from him. He's somewhere in the jungle and dropped his phone in the river while hunting a dinosaur. Hey, he sent a postcard. That's so retro!" She propped it back up against the tree. "So, I just got off the phone with my dad." She laughed. "Oh, the drama!"

"What happened?"

"My cousin, Stuey, and my dad are pretty close, but you know, they have to talk on the sly, so Saint Eleanor doesn't hear about it. Stuey and his fiancée, Amy, were supposed to come to this family reunion thing, right? They *just* got engaged over Thanksgiving. And that almost didn't happen. Stuey had been working extra hours to buy her this big honking engagement ring, right? Well, she got suspicious that he was cheating on her. So, he proposed to her and explained why he'd been out so much. Then she felt guilty, so she thought she'd surprise him with a nice romantic dinner to make it up to him. She made it sound casual, he should come by for dinner. But she didn't say it was a big deal. Wouldn't you know, something happened at his job, and he had to stay late. So, she fussed and made the table pretty with candles, and cooked up a storm and then sat and waited. And waited. She got it in her mind that he was cheating, so she chucked it all in the garbage. Not half an hour later, he came over and said, "God, I'm starving, have you eaten dinner? Maybe we could go out?" She screamed and threw a box of cereal at him."

"Oh, no!"

Lorraine threw her hands up. "How was he supposed to know that she'd cooked this big dinner? Why did she throw it out?"

"Suspicion is not a good foundation for a relationship," I said, well-aware of my own nagging suspicions of Buster.

"No! So, Amy did the family thing for Thanksgiving, right? They spent time with both their families. *She* wanted to go skiing with her girlfriends in Vail over the holidays. Then Saint Eleanor came up with this family-together-for-Christmas plan, so Stuey wanted her to come. She's not a happy camper about it, as you might imagine. I mean, honestly, I can't say I blame her. Skiing in Vail versus a family do in Catfish in this crappy weather? Whoop-de-doo!"

"Yikes," I said, wincing.

"Personally, I'll be shocked if they both show up for this family reunion. Pop and I have a secret bet that they break up by Christmas Eve. Pop hopes they will, I bet they won't."

"Sounds awful."

"If he wins, I have to bake him a chocolate lava cake. If *I* win, I get a gift card for a spa day with the works."

"Ooh," I cooed, dreaming of a spa day.

"Stuey's dad is Mr. Agreeable, Mr. Let's-All-Play-Nice-Together. Stuey's mom hates Amy. The funny thing is, Dad and I think she's just like her. He calls Noni his 'blister-in-law'. I think Stuey sees his mom in Amy and will marry her and be miserable because it's familiar."

"Golly, can't wait to meet them," I said, fingering the edge of the postcard.

# Chapter 9

## The Nifty Thrifters

Heeding Aunt Moira's advice, I was grocery shopping in Gainesville stocking up. I'd already hit two local grocery stores and had circled up 13th Street for my final stop. I was pushing the laden cart down the meat aisle when my phone rang. I didn't recognize the caller ID.

"Hello? Lotus Lodge, how may I help you?"

A garbled mix of women's voices and road rumble came across with intermittent syllables ending with "again." The caller disconnected. The area code was foreign. In all likelihood, a phishing call. I passed an end cap with a Christmas display blaring tinny Christmas songs. A four-foot inflated llama with a red scarf was staring me down and a giant Santa seemed to be having caffeine jitters while looming over a puppy in a wire box covered in white lights. All this to sell massive tins of popcorn. None of it brought me closer to the spirit of the season, in fact, Santa was making me antsy to leave.

My phone rang again. The same number came up again with the ring tone.

"Lotus Lodge—"

"Is that better? Can you hear me now?"

"Yes, I—"

There was giggling. "We're just passing through Madison, Georgia and my friend was looking for a cool place to stay — do you have any vacancies?" More laughter.

"For how many people?" I asked. As long as it wasn't a group wanting the big cabins, it would be fine.

"Two."

"Yes, that's fine. Checking in tonight then?"

"Yes."

"And departing when?"

"We're not sure!" More laughter. Had they been hitting the eggnog early? "You aren't close to the beach, are you?"

This was a bit of an odd question. They obviously had no map skills. Cedar Key is an hour to the west and Flagler and St. Augustine are about an hour and a half to the east. "No, we're right in the middle. Like the spine of the state."

"Well, like, is there stuff to do around there? Well, hell, we don't care. Just as long as we don't have to shovel snow!" More laughter.

"That's highly unlikely here. Ordinarily, you'd be more likely to get a sunburn, but not today. It's drizzling and cold. But I promise, no shoveling snow."

"Perfect! Reservation for two please, Ceci Franks, that's me and Kate Keensey."

"The Nifty Thrifties!" Kate yelled then laughed.

"Would you like dinner tonight?"

"Nah… we'll come fed."

"Well, Madison is about four hours from here. That's perfect. I'm out shopping but I'll be back by then."

"Super!" Ceci said.

"Whoo-hoo! We're goin' to Florida! Ah-ha-ha!" Kate laughed.

"Drive safely," I said but I doubted they heard me over their laughing.

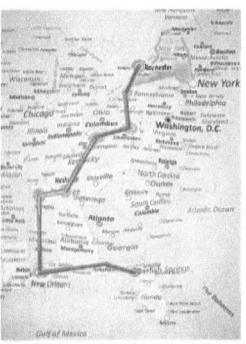

Ceci Franks and Kate Keensey arrived well after dark, looking simultaneously jacked on caffeine and exhausted from driving. They blew into my office in a boisterous burst of noise and exaggerated gestures, talking simultaneously.

"You can't believe how happy we are to have made it here," Kate said, flopping into my office sofa. She was thin with straight brown hair in a short pigtail that was coming undone.

"We came from Rochester, New York. What day is it? We left on Thursday…" Ceci said, setting her bulging purse down on my desk with a thud.

"No, we left on Tuesday," Kate corrected.

"Right! Oh my gosh, it was Tuesday!"

"We were just going to go for a long drive —"

"But we were having so much fun—"

"We drove along Lake Erie."

"We were just going to have lunch somewhere—"

But then we were passing Pittsburgh—"

"We got a bit Thelma and Louise!" Ceci giggled. "It was so great! Oh, where is my wallet? I've got so much shit in here."

"And who knew there were so many cool shops in West Virginia?" Kate added.

"Yeah, what was the name of that town where I got the lamp? It was just across the border."

"Morgantown, I think."

"Yeah, we'll have to go back that way." Ceci said, looking nostalgic.

"Then we got to Lexington...I'm not really a horsey person, but we went on this scenic tour of horse farms. It would have been amazing if we'd done it in the fall, but it was still pretty with a dusting of snow. Looked just like a Christmas card."

"That *was* fun," Ceci said, pulling out a notebook, a glasses case and an iPad and setting them on my desk.

"I called my neighbor, Mrs. Cabazier to watch my cats," Kate said in a knowing, reassuring way as if I knew she had cats.

"Oh, the waiter in the barbecue place in Lexington was so hot."

"He was also half your age."

"Doesn't hurt to look," Ceci added with a frown as she pulled more stuff from her bag—a packet of tissues, lip balm and a travel sized puzzle book. She'd have won for sure on the old game show *Let's Make a Deal* where you got paid for the random stuff in your handbag.

"We got last minute tickets for this old-timey radio show thing—with a special holiday theme. Really put you in the holiday spirit."

Ceci dropped both hands over the bag and looked wistfully at the ceiling. "Yeah, that was *real* nice. Kinda smarmy but a feel-good show. Made me nostalgic for my childhood. You know, the big family gathering with all the relatives. Most of them are dead now. We hardly do family stuff much anymore."

And Ceci kept going on about Graceland, so the next thing we knew, we were heading to Memphis," Kate said in a breezy tone.

"Wait, wait, wait," I said, putting my hands up in a stop gesture. "Stop the presses. You drove from Rochester, New York, to Winston Salem to *Memphis* to Florida?" I asked drawing an imaginary line on the map of the U.S. in the air with a big sideways lurch in the middle of the path.

"And New Orleans," Ceci added. "I mean, it wasn't *that* far out of the way, right? You *have* to go to New Orleans." She checked her pockets again. "Oh wait, I bet I put it in the side compartment when we were in Tallahassee."

"Yeah, why not? I mean, we were already heading south." Kate continued, stretching her arms over her head. "I'd always dreamed of seeing The Big Easy. We went on a ghost tour, heard some great music, ate too much—"

"Those donut things were sooo good!"

"And the coffee. And the seafood. Hell, everything in New Orleans was amazing," Kate said, eyes closed.

Ceci tugged on the snap of an outer purse pocket. "Oh, this damn thing always sticks. Come on. Ah!" She exclaimed as it released. "Oh yeah, New Orleans was *fantastic*!"

"It's none of my business," I began, "not to be nosy, but how did you just get in the car and go like that? Did you pack any clothes or anything? You said you were just going for lunch. I'm confused."

Head back and eyes still closed, Kate put a hand to her chest, "My husband's a merchant marine. He's not going to be around for the holidays, he's Lord knows where until March or April." She gestured to Ceci, "She's divorced, goodbye and good riddance, so for once, we're footloose and fancy free! We don't open the store until January, so what the hell, right? We can buy what we need—extra clothes—underwear--toothpaste."

"Ah! Found it. Thank goodness. Graceland was so over the top! And *so* pretty for Christmas." Ceci said, handing over her credit card.

"It really was. I was surprised. I didn't think I'd like it. And it was so out of the way. But once we got there, I fell under the spell. They had it decorated for Christmas with poinsettias on the white staircase and Christmas trees and garlands. They were playing Elvis's Christmas songs—I'm so glad we went."

"The dining room was so elegant with that giant Christmas tree—"

"We went a little crazy in the gift shop."

"Well, *you* didn't, *I* did," Ceci said.

"We couldn't face driving back—"

I ran Ceci's credit card and passed her the screen to sign.

"We found some cute shops in Mobile, Alabama," Ceci commented as she swept all her belongings off my desk and back into her carpetbag.

I printed out the receipt.

"Oh, you should see what we got!"

Ceci snorted, "I still think I should have bought that goddess statue."

"It had a broken arm. Bad luck. You didn't need it."

"I could've glued her together somehow. She was so elegant."

"Tacky."

"Well, maybe, but there was a 70's charm about her —"

I interrupted, "Here is your card and your receipt, and the room key code. You're all set. You must be exhausted. Let me show you to your cabin."

"Oh, yes, I could fall asleep right here," said Kate.

Ceci stored her card and receipt in her wallet then dropped it into the cavernous purse. "We were heading for St. Pete, but we're not in any hurry. I thought a retreat in the woods on a river would be dreamy. I found you on the internet."

"I'm so glad," I nodded, moving toward the door.

"I'd love to go to the Keys," Kate purred. "I've heard Key West is really weird and wild, but we're getting a little tired. That's like another day's drive to get there isn't it?"

"I think so," I said, "I'm not sure. I've never been. If you don't make it that far, you should consider St. Augustine. Lots of shops, history, ghost tours. I think you'd love it."

Ceci's eyes lit up.

Kate sighed, "Further south is out. Last time I talked to Mrs. Cabazier, she said Fritz had thrown up a few times and she wasn't sure he was eating right. Hard to tell, I have so many cats, but she thought maybe he was missing me. She said he seemed a bit lethargic. Fritz is fifteen."

Ceci rolled her eyes, "Jeez, Kate, Fritz is old. He's always lethargic. Looking at me she flicked a thumb towards Kate, "Kate is the Crazy Cat Lady you always hear about."

"Ceci, don't let me forget to call Mrs. Cabazier in the morning."

"You won't forget. You worry too much." Ceci said, adjusting the purse strap over her shoulder.

I held the door for them.

"Ope!" Ceci said, passing me, then turning to Kate, "You'll be on the phone before you even have coffee. I know you."

"Ope!" Kate said, passing me, then responding to Ceci, "I'm not that bad."

It seemed that "ope" meant excuse me. I guessed it was a regional thing.

"How many cats do you have?" I asked.

She stopped abruptly, giving me almost no room to close the door behind me. I had nowhere to go. I was mostly across the threshold hanging on the door handle for balance.

"Too many," Ceci grumbled. "Come on. I'm going to collapse right here in the road if you don't keep moving."

"Fourteen," Kate said.

For a horrible moment I thought sure she was going to tell me about each one as I hung there. I eased the door open to give myself more room. Then it occurred to me that these ladies were bone weary and I had to take charge just like parents had to guide over-tired children to bed.

"You're in cabin three, this way, right close to the bathroom pavilion," I said, pushing forward, bumping into Kate and closing the door firmly behind me.

# Part Three

## The Day Before the Night Before Christmas

# Chapter 10

## BREAKFAST

Naughty Britches had maneuvered herself crosswise across the bed nesting on most of the covers. I woke in the dark, butt hanging precariously off the bed, freezing. No hope of claiming any covers. Mischief was draped across the pillow above my head like a furry halo. Unable to read the clock, I had that uneasy sense that it was nigh unto alarm time. NB stretched and moaned, pushing her back feet into my belly.

"Sorry, am I in your way?" I whispered.

It would have been nice to stay and cuddle, but not without covers. I reached for my glasses on the night table and felt for my bathrobe that had fallen on the floor. NB shifted, immediately claiming the space that I'd vacated. Mischief lifted his head and opened half an eye before sliding into the space where my head had been.

"You two are killing me," I said to the sleeping cherubs while I pulled the sash tight.

FLORIDA

Plodding towards the coffee pot, a vague line from "Good Morning Vietnam" came to mind. Robin Williams was imitating Walter Cronkite: "the weather today is shitty with a continued crappy and a pissy little rain front coming down from the north". Quite. Only it was hot and muggy in Vietnam. Our weather would be gray with a side of grayer, drizzling cold, with and a high temp straining to reach 50 degrees.

*Think layers.*

At least there was no rush for breakfast; I only had the Nifty Thrifters as guests and they weren't likely to be up early. It was the rest of the day that could get crazy.

Lorraine surprised me; I hadn't expected her to be up early.

"Okay if I come for breakfast?" she asked over her shoulder, stumping with her boot to the bathroom. "I want to meet these guests you were telling me about and I'm craving a waffle."

"Sure. Short bus leaves in ten minutes."

"I'm on it."

As we were leaving and I was saying my goodbyes and please-behave-yourself requests to Naughty Britches, Lorraine passed my Word-of-the-Day calendar on the kitchen counter.

"Hey, check this out. The word for today is 'gelid'. Sure fits the weather forecast for today."

"Never heard of it."

"'Gelid', soft "g" adjective, comes from the Latin word *gelidus*, meaning icy cold or frosty."

"Ew. Sounds like one of those disgusting gelatin molds from the 60's with potted meat and canned peas. Hmm. Let me see…" I began to sing, "Ge-lid, the Snowman, was an aspic made from sause, dripping here and there all around the—"

"Oh, stop!" she said, covering her ears and disappearing into her bedroom.

"Let's go make you some waffles," I said, and we left for the Lotus Lodge.

The kitchen and dining hall were unwelcomingly cold. I bumped up the heat first thing. As anticipated, breakfast prep was easy. I made coffee, set out the juice, waffle batter, and a few pastries and waited until the ladies dragged in to find out if they wanted sausage or eggs.

Lorraine busied herself making a waffle. "Do you have dessert for tonight? I'm in the mood to get back to baking. I was looking at recipes yesterday. Does eggnog poundcake sound good? Or mincemeat cake with a drizzle of caramel?"

"They both sound like foods that the cherubim and seraphim pass around in the tenth realm of heaven, especially if you make them."

"Aww."

Prior to her ass-over-teakettle chihuahua tumble, I'd relied on Lorraine to bake cakes for my guests. She'd also provided cakes for local restaurants. Her sister, Lerlene, had tried to cover for her, but it wasn't the same. The Baking Muse loved Lorraine.

We sat down to eat.

"Well, you had me with the caramel drizzle, but anything that inspires you. You're not capable of making a bad cake," I said.

"Okay. We'll see what happens. Lerlene will be bringing Saint Eleanor over later, I'm sure she'd be happy for the excuse to run me to the store for ingredients. You won't mind if I take over your home kitchen, will you?"

"Not at all! Are you kidding?"

"What's on your plate today?" Lorraine asked.

"Same. Cooking. I watched a cooking show last night. Got me all excited about cabbage rolls. I thought I'd make up pans of cabbage rolls and freeze them. That way, I can pull them out as needed and reheat them. Green and red with grated cheese. That would suggest snow, right?"

She shrugged. "Sounds like comfort food."

"That's the idea. I'll do a meat version and a veggie version. Secret ingredients: green chili sauce and red chili and garlic sauce. And while I'm at it, I can make up some cranberry meatballs. They'd make a nice appetizer tonight before the lamb. I've got a beautiful leg of lamb for dinner tonight."

"Okay, I'm officially drooling. Holler if you need a taster. I'm in."

"Hey, have you got anything to write on? I need to make a list," Lorraine said.

"Me too."

I went to the kitchen and found a couple notepads and pens in a drawer and returned with them. "One for you, one for me."

We enjoyed our breakfasts in silence, happily scribbling.

As I expected, the Nifty Thrifters didn't show up until almost nine o'clock. That was fine. Lorraine was perusing recipes on her phone; I was mentally staging dinner for the mobs to come: Clan Max, Lorraine's tribe, and the Garcia family. *Can take the leg of lamb out an hour prior to cooking...I could do the cranberry meatballs once I got the leg of lamb and roast potatoes going--eight pounds times roughly twenty minutes a pound...should get the lamb in the oven by--*

"I thought it was sunny in Florida! Where's the sun? It's freezing out there!" Kate complained, shivering, making for the coffee machine like a hound tracking a bunny.

Personally, having lived in climates with snow, Christmas in Florida is always weird. If it's sunny and warm, it's not particularly special; the other option is overcast and dreary and that's just not cheery. There really is no perfect hot-chocolate-and-boots kind of winter weather like elsewhere.

As it was otherwise quiet in the dining hall with only the two guests, I couldn't help overhearing fragments of their conversation as Kate, in a louder than normal voice, checked in with her cat-sitter neighbor, Mrs. Cabazier.

"Choo-choo and Smirky got into it, she says, but that's nothing. Busker isn't eating and Smoochy puked up her pills," she reported, shaking her head.

"Busky misses you," Ceci said. She took advantage of Kate chewing a sausage patty to change the subject, "I know we were going to do Christmas in the Keys, but I've no interest in driving in this weather. I say we stay put. I like it here."

Kate nodded and covered her mouth, "Mmm-hmm. I wogee." She swallowed and tried again, "I agree."

Ceci wiped her mouth with a napkin and looked me in the eye. "It's awfully quiet at night. I had to go to the bathroom in the middle of the night. Kind of gave me the creeps, the dark woods, snapping twigs, an owl calling...don't you get scared out here?"

"Not really," I began, considering the question. "Guess I'm used to it."

My Inner Critic cleared his throat and muttered, *Sure you are, except for nights when you watch giallo films and jump at any little noise. Or when Waylon and Willie scare you have to death howling, or you find a massive poop with a dog collar in it...or find out that one of your guests is a psycho killer.*

"It's so remote," persisted Ceci. "I mean, this is the perfect setting for a horror movie, isn't it? Killer picks off people in cabins one at a time?"

*Almost happened, didn't it?* My Inner Critic said.

"Ce-ci!" Kate said. "I think you're upsetting her." Kate turned to me, "Sorry, she has no filters."

*You could tell them about the mysterious furry thing in the trail camera*, the Inner Critic sniggered.

*No. Not going there.* My thoughts bounded from Skunk Apes and trail cameras to Buster and his crypto friends, Shane and Rebel. Buster…wondered for the millionth time where he was and what he was doing.

Ceci sighed like a bored child, with a full-bodied slump. "Pity it's so bleak and we can't go kayaking or something…"

"Yeah," Kate said absently, more focused on sipping her coffee.

"Haint?" Ceci asked, "Is there anything fun in town like, a play or a show or something?"

"I think there might have been a parade, but with this weather, I bet it's been cancelled."

"Are we the only guests?" Kate asked.

"No. I've got three extended families coming this afternoon," I answered.

Ceci's eyes widened, "Oh my gosh! I've got an idea! Kate! We've got so much stuff, why don't we announce a Secret Santa event for tomorrow? If people wanted to do a gift exchange, wouldn't that be fun? Would you mind, Haint? Could we do that?"

Ceci and Kate reminded me of the old Judy Garland and Mickey Rooney old feel-good pictures where they needed to raise money for something or other and inevitably came up with, "Let's have a show!"

I felt like a sour puss but couldn't help myself, "But it's so late, I mean, people won't have time to shop. I hate to make people feel obligated—"

Ceci exhaled in disappointment, her lower lip forming the perfect, crushed-spirit-arc of a toddler. All that was missing was the lip quiver and the threat of tears. "Well, we ought to do *something*."

*Perfect opportunity to get rid of that junk,* my Inner Critic said.

Hmm. There's that. "Well, when they get here, I can ask, but I dunno..."

"Yes!" Ceci said thrusting up a fist.

"Don't get your hopes up," I warned.

*My, aren't we the buzz kill*, whispered my Inner Critic.

*Can't help it. I just can't get into the holiday spirit this year*, I thought.

## Nellavon and Mamma Sue

arlic, onions and chopped mushrooms simmered away in a skillet; cabbages were steaming in the biggest pot I owned. I was in the cooking groove in the retreat kitchen when my phone rang. Max. I wanted to defer a lengthy call but since he was in a retirement home, and you never know, I turned the heat off under the skillet and answered.

"Hey, Max, what's up?"

He dispensed with niceties and began with, "Nellavon just called me. She and Taylor have Mamma Sue; they're on their way to the Lotus Lodge. My son, Junior, and his wife, Olivia, are on their way too. The twins are comin' ta get me, so I'll be there as soon as I can."

"O-kay, is there something I should know? Why are you yelling? You sound like they're staging a strategic attack."

"That's about right. She always gets my blood up."

"I'm sure it'll be fine. Don't stress —"

"Nellavon can boss paint off the damn wall! You wait! She'll get you honked off soon too! And her husband Taylor is like a brainless prisoner stuck followin' her around. Don't look to him for support. He hasn't stood up to her since the day they got married. He'll disappear as soon as he can and then she'll set in on Junior. You got earplugs and a hard hat? You're gonna need 'em."

"That bad?"

"You ever known me to joke around?" Max growled. "I'll be there soon as I can. Oh, I think this is them now. See you, Sugar."

*Well golly and Edmund Gwenn, what kind of a Christmas were we in for?*

I was glad I'd thought to make several signs to hang on the office door with directions to either come find me or text me. I hoped to get to a good stopping point in this cabbage process before having to deal with guests.

About twenty-five minutes later, a couple entered the dining hall. A deep, smoker's voice called out, "Hello, anyone here?" Followed by, "Well, hell's bells, where is she?"

"Hello! Coming!" I called and turned off the burners. I washed my hands and trotted around the buffet counter.

No question, it had to be Nellavon, Max's sister. She was heavier than Max, but had the same sharp eyes, jawline, spindly legs and knobby knees. From head to waist, she was bundled for winter in an oversized jacket. She wore eggplant-colored yoga pants covered with a pattern of white snowflakes.

Her hair, the color of a black plum, was wound up on her head in a wide, red headband.

"Hello. You must be Max's sister."

"Hi. Nellavon," she said, shaking my hand. "This is some shit weather, huh? I don't guess he's here yet. Go figure, we drive all this way, and he can't make it across town. Just like him." As an afterthought, she turned to the man with her. "This is Taylor, my husband."

"Hi, Taylor," I said, shaking his gloved hand.

Taylor had a long face and high forehead, thinning hair, a weak chin, and dull gray eyes. "Haint is it? Hello."

I nodded.

Nellavon pointed to the door with her head and rasped, "I've got Mother in the car. She's in a wheelchair, you know. I hope the cabin is wheelchair accessible. So, where do we go? Where do I park?"

I'd been lucky that when Max owned the retreat, he'd added wheelchair ramps to the cabins. Not all, but most of the cabins had ramps, rails and extra wide doors to accommodate wheelchairs. It dawned on me that if Nellavon had ever been here before, she would know that. This told me that in all the years that Max and Charlene had been here, Nellavon had never visited.

"Yes, not a problem. Max should be here any minute. Let's go next door and I'll get you all checked in.

She huffed, indicating inconvenience, which I ignored.

Their vehicle was in front of the office, engine running. I could make out a bundled figure in the front passenger seat.

"Here, please come in," I said, holding the office door for them. I'd left the office radio on, so we were greeted by Paul McCartney telling us about our wonderful Christmas time. I tapped the wreath on the door. "Thank you so much for all the Christmas decorations. That was a Godsend!"

Taylor looked at the wreath in passing and made an undecipherable response. Nellavon brushed past me without giving it a glance. She made a noise somewhere between a hack and a laugh, I really wasn't sure which, "Are you kidding? I'm just glad to be rid of all that crap. My sister, Roberta, had shit everywhere. Her house was full, almost to the ceiling. What she could jam into the nooks and crannies went to storage units." She coughed a deep, lung-damaged cough. "Unbelievable. If you want more junk, just say. Weed only packed up the Christmas shit."

Wow. And I thought Lorraine was blunt. I had no idea how to respond, so I scooted behind the desk, pulled out a map and the key code card for cabin seven. "You'll be in number seven, just across the road. You can pull right up to the ramp if you like, then park in this lot here," I pointed out the window behind me. "Dinner will start at six, in the dining hall, where you found me."

"You got a bar? I could use a drink."

I blinked. "I'm sorry, this is a meditation retreat. But there is a liquor store in Catfish that's probably still open—"

"Meh!" she grunted. She swiped the map and key card off the table and left, walking with the same slightly unsteady but determined gait as Max. Taylor followed her like a shadow, looking back at me like a lost puppy.

As the door slammed, McCartney got more insistent.

I was simply beginning to have a headache.

# Rocky and Osanna, Benny and Cammie

Cabbage leaves were sticking together. I was carefully pulling them apart and separating them by size when I heard a noise close by. I looked up to see a stocky man dressed all in black from his hat to his boots. Dark eyes peered at me over a black scarf.

"Aah!" I exclaimed, dropping the cabbage leaves. I was about to step back and reach for a cast iron skillet to defend myself when he asked, "Are you Haint?"

"Yes?" I said, sounding unsure.

"I'm Rocky Garcia. We'd like to check in." An attractive woman with shimmery black hair cascading over a short, mauve, wool coat walked in followed by four children, two girls and a young pair of twin boys. The girls looked like copies of their mother; the boys had bright eyes and thick hair.

"Oh," I said, relieved.

"My wife, Osanna."

"Hi, pleased to meet you. "Let me just turn off the burner here—let's go next door and I can get you checked in. What beautiful children!" I pulled off my apron and stepped around the counter.

"This is Anna and Zelia," Osanna said touching the girls' heads lightly in turn. The girls whirled from her heading towards the artificial Christmas tree by the picture window.

"Girls! Don't be rude! Come say hello."

The girls flounced back to say quick hellos as Osanna introduced the twins. "…and the boys, Oro and Oscar."

"And how old are you?" I asked the twins.

"Four!" they answered simultaneously, then smiled the same smile and asked, "Can we go see the tree?"

"Yeah!" the girls exclaimed.

"Later," Rocky said. "You'll have plenty of time. Let's go find our cabin and your cousins, eh?"

With reluctance, they agreed, and we went next door.

I'd no sooner gotten them settled when a car pulled up and a couple in their sixties got out. He looked a bit like Walter Matthau, tallish, a bit heavy, with droopy jowls and a fleshy nose. He moved slowly with stiff limbs. The woman I presumed was his wife had short blonde hair with a shadow of darker roots. She was wearing a beige pantsuit with a large, clunky glass pendant.

"I think the office is over here," she said.

"May I help you? I asked, approaching them. "I'm Haint, the owner."

The man studied me head to toe like a Tiffany's jeweler examining a diamond through a loupe. "You are the whitest person I've ever seen! I guess I'd heard that you were an albino. How amazing! I'm sixty-three years old and I don't think I've ever seen a real, live one before. "

"Mmm, no doubt," I said, nodding. "So few of us escape from the zoo."

"Benny, don't be rude," the woman said in a voice that was

heavy with resignation and disgust.

A little cloud of confusion passed across his face. I could tell he was pondering my escape from the zoo. His blustery ego soon took hold once more as he puffed out his chest to say, "Benny Gagson, you know, like gag, joke, ha-ha. This is my wife, Cameron," he said raising a hand with effort to introduce her.

Cameron's composure wilted for a moment before coming to life again to greet me. I got the impression that she'd heard this awkward intro for painful decades. Then it clicked. Max had mentioned something about a relative he couldn't stand, hadn't he?

"Ah. Come up to the office," I said, following Cameron who was already heading that way. "We'll get you checked in. I think Pike and Betsy are already here…"

"Are you a natural blonde or a bottle blonde?" Benny asked as I held the door for them. Too stunned to respond, he barreled ahead, "No matter. Got a joke for ya."

"Benny, don't—" Cameron began.

"What do you call it when a blonde dyes her hair brunette?"

Cameron put a hand over her eyes.

Expecting the worst, I did my best Polish face (aka bitch face: neutral disinterested).

"Artificial intelligence. Get it? Artificial Intelligence!"

As blonde jokes go, it was pretty good, but he was as funny as a flat tire in August.

"You'll be in cabin seven, just across the road there. You

can park in the lot on this side," I said, pointing out the window with a pencil. "Here's the key code for the door." I passed them the key code card for cabin seven.

"What's with the gorilla out front here?" Benny asked. "That is the dumbest looking thing — what's that got to do with this place?"

"His name is Arnie. He was the mascot here when it was the Stinkin' Skunk Ape Fish Camp. Is this your first time here? Arnie belonged to Max before he sold me the property."

"My uncle, Max, had Arnie for *ages*," Cameron said. "He looks better than I remember and cute all dressed up for Christmas." She shot Benny a don't-say-a-word look.

"Well, you tarted the place up nice for the holidays, that's for sure. I'm sure the kids love it."

Cameron elbowed him in the ribs. "Benny!"

"Thanks. I wasn't going to *tart it up*, but Max and Nellavon kindly donated items from their sister's—" I searched for the appropriate word and landed on "estate."

"Estate? That's a laugh!" He said with a derisive snort that might have been a warthog mating call.

"Benny! That's enough!" Cameron said, driving the elbow deeper into his gut.

Benny didn't take the hint, in fact, it seemed to encourage him. "You know," he said, moving out of elbow reach, "my brother dated a hoarder once. He couldn't believe that she broke up with him. Like, he was the one thing she *could* part with! Get it?"

"Well, I'm glad you could put Aunt Roberta's decorations to use," Cameron said, glaring at Benny. She eyed my retreat brochure. "Meditation? I'd love that."

"I wasn't sure anyone would be interested—"

"Oh, I would be!"

"You are the first person to express an interest. We could have an evening meditation tonight after dinner."

"Sounds lovely," she said, clutching the brochure.

"It does." I could use some cushion time myself. I prayed that Benny wouldn't come. I had a sudden, wicked wish that he'd fall off my dock and float away down the river.

*No, no, no...no crime scenes, remember?* The Inner Critic warned.

Right. Cancel clear. Delete thought. May he fall asleep in the cabin early.

# Chapter 11

## Aunt Moira and Gigi

had just gotten the lamb in the oven when I looked up to see two women peering at me from the dining hall. Lorraine's Aunt Moira is a striking woman of about sixty who makes me nervous. For starters, her short and spiked gray hair suggests ferocity. Are porcupines susceptible to rabies? I don't know, seeing Aunt Moira in a peach-colored caftan adorned with a superabundance of gemstones and charms, sets my mind to pondering.

She was accompanied by a woman of about the same size and age, with a kinder more approachable demeanor. She wore bright red lipstick and had laugh lines that put me at ease-- unlike Aunt Moira who made me glad for the counter between us.

"I told you you'd be busy!" Aunt Moira said with a smirk. "We parked at the end of the first lot, out of the way. Gigi! Meet Haint Blue."

"Nice to meet you! Oh, aren't you a doll? Look at you! And this *place*!" Gigi said. "Pity the weather is so abysmal. I bet it's gorgeous when it's not so dreary. Oh! You've got hot water and tea—" she continued, moving towards the tea station. "Oh! And hot cocoa mix! I love you! Do you mind? I'd kill for a hot cocoa right now."

"No not at all," I said.

"Is Saint Eleanor here yet?" Aunt Moira asked with trepidation.

"Not that I know of," I said.

"Stu and Noni got a late start, as usual," Aunt Moira said, shaking her head. "I hate to say it, but my brother would be late to his own funeral."

"I thought you said Stuey Junior couldn't get off work on time?"

"Yeah, that's what Stu *says*, but he'd be late anyway. Saint Eleanor drives him nuts." She looked at the oven. "Oh, that lamb is going to be lovely."

How did she know? I just put it in the oven. Could she smell it? Best not to ask. Besides, another question came to mind. "Did you know when you called me about the dream that you'd be coming for Christmas too?"

She made a dismissive *pppth* sound with her lips. "Oh, hell no, Hon. We thought we were going to be in Minneapolis over Christmas. Plans change."

"We brought some goodies for the gift exchange," Gigi said with an excited twinkle in her eyes."

"How did you—" I began.

"Oh, it's nothing crazy," Aunt Moira said, "We hit a shop that was having a blowout candle sale—oh, that's funny!

Blowout! Ah-ha-ha!"

Not knowing what else to say, I offered, "Your family'll be in cabin six — Lorraine has the pass code.

"Okay to go to the meditation circle?" Aunt Moira asked.

"Huh? In *this* weather?" I glanced to the window to be sure that by some miracle the drizzle had stopped, the sun had come out, and guests were walking around in short sleeves.

"I don't mind cold. Hell, this is downright balmy when you've been in Kalamazoo."

"Sure then. Have at it."

"Great. Come on, Gigi. Let's go commune with spirit. We'll be back for dinner. I'll be first in line for that lamb. Hope you've got mint jelly."

"I sure do!" I said waving to them and turning back to my checklist. What next? Oh yes, make cranberry meatballs. I turned to the refrigerator and was startled by something white fluttering to the floor. An old favorite phrase of an Italian boyfriend came back to me: *Cosa sta succedendo?* ♥ What is going on?

I stared at it in disbelief.

I had not been plucking white chickens in the kitchen. Ever.

---

♥ pronounced co-sa sta su-chay DEN-do? Means: What's going on? It's just fun to say, isn't it?

# SAINT ELEANOR AND ENTOURAGE

The first batch of zucchini-and-green-chili-sauce cabbage rolls had gone in the oven, and I was working on the second when Lerlene's husband, Freddie, found me in the kitchen. How shall I describe Freddie? Agreeable, breezy, and attractive, with an odd sense of humor. He has a habit of babbling nonsense; often it's hard to tell if he's spinning a fairy tale or telling the truth. He's the fun dad, the best drinking buddy, the life of the party kind of guy.

Freddie drew himself up and began to pontificate like an ancient minister, "The altar of Saint Eleanor has been anointed with oil and strewn with flowers. Our Lady of the Immaculate Cleanliness and Virtue will receive penitents for blessings and guidance in cabin six by appointment only. Visitors are advised that photography and smoking is strictly forbidden." He finalized the announcement with a salute and click of heels.

"Ah. Good to know," I said. "Will her Ladyship be dining with us this evening, or shall I send round the carriage and courtiers with a hamper?" I asked, dropping a quick curtsy.

He broke his rigid character, "Nah, she's coming. How are you?"

"Stressed. You?"

"I've got three kids, an A-type personality wife, a saintly mother-in-law, an eye tic, and an ulcer. Got any antacid?"

"Maybe in my purse…"

He waved me off. "Just kidding. I'm fine." He looked at the leftover, innermost cabbage leaves. "Say, you ladies always say that size doesn't matter. What're you hiding in those cabbage leaves?"

"Moo-wah-ha-ha" I laughed maniacally. "Shh. Don't tell. I put the poison in the smallest ones. KIDDING. I'm trying to make equal portions of sausage rolls and zucchini rolls. It helps to secure the meat in a smaller leaf and wrap it with a bigger leaf."

"So, no need to feel like Hansel in the Witch's kitchen?" he asked, eyebrow raised.

I smiled. "You never know. I wouldn't get too close."

He feigned fear and stepped back. "Saint Eleanor is playing cards with our little cherubs. I thought I'd take a stroll. I was here a couple times when Max had it as a dingy fish camp. You've really transformed it."

I smiled, "Thanks! It was a lot of work." I made a face. "It's gross outside but help yourself. Feel free to walk the trail. It loops. There's a meditation circle out in the woods. Oh, you might run into Aunt Moira and Gigi."

"Oh boy. Wonder what they're conjuring up. Speaking of witches! Maybe I'll just go sit on the dock then. I just need a bit of silence. Might  make the kids walk the trail later--away from the damn gadgets. Get the stink of nature on them, a bit."

"Yeah, um, I think most intelligent animals are denned up," I said, spooning the sausage mixture into the first cabbage leaf.

"Well not me. I'm off. See ya later, unless a Skunk Ape gets me."

"Right. Arnie will save you."

"Yeah, right!" he laughed.

# PART FOUR

## THE ACCIDENT

# Chapter 12

## The Accident

I would find out later that around 3:30 PM on Tuesday the 23rd, a horrific accident took place on Interstate 75 just south of the High Springs exit. In a fit of road rage, the driver of a delivery truck overloaded with roadside, pop-up shop goods (you know the kind: cheap fringed rugs draped over the body of the vehicle, red-lacquered, knock-off "Oriental" furniture occupied by oversized, dead-eyed stuffed animals, gaudy standing lamps, etc.) had been speeding and weaving between vehicles like a cocaine fiend in a roller derby championship. He switched lanes ahead of a tractor trailer loaded with Christmas overstock. Unfortunately, he didn't see that there was an express overnight delivery truck *also* changing lanes in front of the tractor trailer. The left-front fender of the tractor trailer clipped the back bumper of the delivery truck and sent it careening into the express truck. All three vehicles spun out of control across the road causing a multiple car pileup.

All but one northbound lane was closed as the highway was strewn with vehicles, overnight parcels of all sizes, car parts, broken glass, Teddy bears, small appliances, gift sets of tea and cocoa, shaving sets, makeup, snuggly blankets, fluffy slippers with reindeer antlers, "nibbler" boxes of cheese and mini sausages, cases of broken jars of mincemeat, and demon-eyed, oversized, stuffed panda bears.

By some miracle, there were no fatalities, thank goodness, though many were hospitalized for injuries. The road-rager was in critical condition. It was rumored that the express delivery driver was high as a kite on marijuana. Several accident victims reported that prior to the accident, they had avoided his truck noting that he seemed to have difficulty keeping it in one lane, while a suspicious fog emanating from it with that telltale, cloying smell. The driver of the express truck was treated for injuries and arrested for possession of copious amounts of weed. It was rumored that paramedics, injured parties, and witnesses closest to the crash experienced a mild contact high. The local evening news reporter came close to giggling inappropriately while describing the scene.

It was shortly after four o'clock when the flurry of calls began--anxiety-ridden people asking if there was any chance I had vacancies.

"Hello? I know so close to the holidays, you're most likely all booked up, but is there any chance you'd have room for two? My wife would prefer not to stay in a chain motel. We were hoping –we'd pay extra--"

"Hello? We've been stuck in traffic for over two hours. My client needs to rest. She'd like someplace quiet. Do you have *anything*?"

"Hello? Is there any way that you might have a cabin for a

small family — two adults and two children... and...do you have any open space? We are travelling with three alpacas and need a place to walk them."

## Lame Brains

The first call of the rerouted travelers sounded like a group effort in a noisy vehicle--multiple people talking at once over music.

The male caller asked, "Do you have any rooms?"

Before I could answer, a volley of background voices chimed in and it became a conference call — well, really, more like an old-fashioned party line:

Whiny female voice, "We could just stay in *that* motel — it looks cheap."

Other male voice: "But it's like, in the woods."

Caller's voice: "Please can we try this first?"

Different female voice, "Or that one... oh, crap, look at the line."

Caller's voice: "Shh! I'm trying to talk."

Other male voice: "We'll never get a room."

Me: "For how many people?"

Caller: "We're seven total, but, ah, we're on a bit of a budget, so if you have anything where we could be all together, that would be so extra."

Me: "My biggest cabins are already booked up, I'm afraid. I've got the mid-size cabin for four to six —"

Other male voice: "You got a ghost, right? Could we get a

haunted cabin?"

Whiny female voice: "If there's a cabin, just take it!"

Caller: "She said a cabin for four to six."

Male voice: "Shh! It's worth asking—"

Giggling.

Different male voice: "I got a bag; I can sleep on the floor or something."

New female voice: "Just take whatever we can get! Geez!"

"How did you hear it's haunted?" I asked. It wasn't common knowledge that the retreat was mildly haunted.

Caller: "Oh, my mom's best friend, Gwen Luster stayed at your place. She said she saw a ghost. We love all things spooky, and that would be slaying, but we'll take whatever you have."

"There is a little sofa—" I started to say.

Male voice: "But it's like, out in the ass end of space!"

Other male voice: "Wanker Town."

Giggles.

Female voice: "It is not!"

Whiny female voice: "Shut up!"

Caller, louder, speaking over other voices: "Yes, we'll take it!"

Me: "Great. Will you be paying all together or--?"

Whiny female voice: "Can't the club pay for it?"

Male voice: "Can we use the club money?"

Multiple voices: "Yeah!"

Caller: (aside) "I'll cover it, we can figure it out later."

To me, louder, "One charge. Lame Brains will pick up the

tab."

Me: "Sorry?"

Laughter.

Caller: "We're the Lame-Brain Zombie Apocalypse Bell-Ringers."

"Okay, gotcha. See you in a bit." I shook my head and typed Lame Brain in the slot for cabin five on the computer.

Caller: "Thanks!"

Laughter.

## MR. AND MRS. SILLYCLOWN

The next call came from a woman with a voice like an old lady on helium, frail but cartoonishly high pitched.

"Hell-o? Is this a recording or a real person, can you hear me?"

"Yes, I can hear you."

"Hello?"

"YES, I CAN HEAR YOU," I said, practically shouting.

"Oh, thank goodness, listen we were hoping you had a room available? We're just two people, me and my husband."

"YES MA'AM, I DO, I CAN PUT YOU IN A SMALL CABIN."

"Oh, thank goodness! If we can figure out how to get there, we'll be there soon."

I prayed I wouldn't have to shout directions.

"Oh, Henry, pull over there. I've got to go the bathroom," she said.

I waited as if I hadn't heard that.

"We'll get directions if we can at this service station. Pull in there, Henry."

"WHERE ARE YOU NOW?"

"Henry? Where are we? Oh, here, you talk to her, I've got to *go.*"

"There was a pause, a door slam, some shuffling sounds, then a man's voice. "Hello? We just got off the interstate. We're in High Springs...I'm lookin' at a boot outlet store and a donut shop."

I gave him directions step by step, to which he responded, "uh-heh...uh-heh" and asked me to repeat several steps. I was sure he was scribbling it all down. "Okay, left just after Night Swamp Glen. Look for the sign. Blue's Lotus Lodge. Got it."

"And what's the name?" I asked.

He sighed as if it pained him to tell me, then said something that sounded like "Loopy Clown".

"Sorry?"

He sighed again. "It's a Czech name. Spelled H-l-o-u-p-y-k-l-a-u-n."

"Oh, how fabulous! You're a Silly Clown!" I said excitedly, then immediately regretting it. I'd heard of this funny name phenomenon in the Czech Republic. Back before there was any kind of unification, i.e., taxation going to a central government, people did not have surnames, only first names: John, or, John, son of John, etc. In order to get them on the tax register, they had to have a last name. The first census takers were given a tough task. Ask for something that doesn't exist. It was like a

Monty Python skit or an Abbot and Costello routine.

"What is your last name?"

"John."

"That's your first name, what's your family name."

Shrug.

"Come on, out with it, I haven't got all day. What's your last name?"

"I don't know."

Census taker writes: J-o-h-n I-d-o-n-t-k-n-o-w. "NEXT!"

"I don't know" and "I don't care" became common surnames. I'm not making this up! Whatever the responder said was written down. The questioners were apparently oblivious that they were being called names Either that or they took glee in forever marking a man's family with a ridiculous name. Wild things like "Potato head" and yes, "Silly clown" became family names. This man's family was from way back. He was a Sillyclown. "I'm sorry," I backpedaled, "My mother was Russian and Polish," I said. "I've heard of the unusual names in the Czech Republic."

"Oh, you have? Then you know. Good. Well, we'll be there in a while, assuming we don't get lost."

"Call me if you have any questions. See you in a bit."

I called Lorraine. "If I come get you, could you come check in people in? I've got more guests coming and I can't be cooking and doing check in at the same time."

"Sure."

"You won't believe this. I just got a reservation from a

group called The Lame Brains — "

"Let me guess. A group of attorneys? Oh, no, they're catfish, right? Bottom feeders."

"LARPers."

"Uh-huh. Right. Whatever."

" — and another one from Mr. and Mrs. Sillyclown."

She was silent for a beat, then said. "What *have* you spike your eggnog with? I didn't think you drank in the daytime."

"I'm serious! Be there in a jiffy."

"You aren't putting me on?"

"Nope."

"You're seriously okay to drive?"

"Yup."

"O-kay--I'll be ready quick as I can."

"Bye!" I hung up and took a deep breath. I'd run over to pick her and Naughty Britches up. She would love being a greeter. All good. Then I could get back to the kitchen.

*Don't get nervous, you got this, just keep going*, the Inner Critic said.

# Chapter 13

## PRINCE ALBERT OF
## UPPER BALDERDASH ET AL.

ust as I was heading home, a faded, four-door truck pulling an animal trailer came into view.

"Crap, crap, crap! I gotta pick up Lorraine," I muttered, turning the truck off and getting out. The truck pulled up in front of me and the driver, a tanned man with dark hair and a cowboy hat, rolled down his window.

"Howdy! Boy, am I glad to find you. Thought we'd never get out of that traffic. I've never seen so much debris all over the road. It was like a tornado hit a shopping mall. Hope nobody was killed. Total standstill. Took the first available exit. I called a bit ago—name's Warcloud, Chaz Warcloud, we're the ones with the alpacas—" he said, gesturing to the trailer.

"Hi, I'm Haint Blue, welcome to the Lotus Lodge.

The woman next to him in the passenger seat smiled and waved. A teenage boy's head popped up over the console, he waved also.

"Yes, Mr. Warcloud. You'll be in cabin one, it's just that way," I said pointing, "If you'd like to come inside just a moment, I can get you checked in."

He got out and followed me to the office. I checked him in, gave him the key code for the cabin and showed him the map. "There's a parking lot just beyond this set of buildings, or, if you want, you can park just beyond the cabin here," I circle the area by the beginning of the hiking trail. You'll be across from the dining hall. The bathrooms and showers are here—"

"Where might we exercise or graze the alpacas?"

"Oh, right. Well, you are welcome to walk them on the trails," I said, letting my finger trace the trails, "and there's a field in the middle of the woods here where the meditation circle is—will they run away?"

"I wouldn't leave them unattended. Mehitabel is pregnant, I don't think she wants to go far and the other two will stay by her. Is there a feed store near here?"

"Yes, Everymans –" I glanced at the clock, "I'm not sure how late they'll stay open today. You can call and ask. It's in Catfish. There's another feed store in Alachua, too."

"Good to know. We're okay for now, but I'm not sure how long we'll be here. It'll depend on Mehitabel. We hoped to get her home, but we'll just have to see how it goes."

"I don't remember ever seeing an alpaca before, except in pictures," I said as we walked back outside. "I met a few llamas before, in fact, one tried to eat my dress when I was a child visiting the zoo, and one spat at me at a carnival.

"They're similar to llamas but cuter in my opinion. They're

shyer and less likely to spit in your face--that's a big plus," Chaz said, getting back in the driver's seat. "I just go down there?"

"Follow the dirt road off the parking lot, around the bathroom pavilion. You can park just beyond your cabin. I'll follow you down there."

He nodded and closed the door.

Well aware that I needed to go pick up Lorraine, I followed the trailer over to cabin one. I was curious to see the alpacas, especially the pregnant one.

When I caught up with them, they were just getting out of the truck.

"This is my wife, Robin and my son, Rain," Chaz said.

Rain said, "Mom says you're an albino. I never heard of that before. You're pretty."

"Rain!" Robin said, looking embarrassed. "I'm so sorry."

"He's fine," I said.

She pulled her jacket tighter. "Golly, are we in Florida or what? Dang that *wind*!"

Chaz unhitched the trailer gate and led the first animal down the ramp. "Meet Prince Albert of Upper Balderdash."

All my predisposed wariness disappeared as this silly, cute, fluffball-headed, gangly-legged creature gave me the once over.

"You are *ridiculously* adorable, Prince Albert!" I said.

"You can pet him if you like, but please wait until I get 'em all out. He'll inspect you in the meantime to decide if he trusts you," Chaz said as he passed Price Albert's lead to Robin and reached in for the next animal.

Price Albert looked like a lost Jim Henson character making curious grunts and snorfles as he inspected me head to foot. He shifted his weight and moved his mouth as if he had a popcorn hull stuck in his teeth. He was a creamy beige with streaks of pale brown on his head.

"Do you sheer them and make wool?" I asked.

"Yes," Robin said. "I sell sweaters in a little shop near me and online."

"And this is Archy, Prince Albert's son," Chaz said, leading a smaller and dark chocolate version of Prince Albert down the ramp.

"Hello, Archy," I said. "Don't you have some rambling title as well? Are you also from Upper Balderdash?"

Archy snorted and stomped in reply.

"He feels he has to show off in front of his dad," Robin said with a tiny laugh. "He's going to be two next month."

A raucous *screee-haww*! erupted from the trailer, making me jump.

"And that would be Mehitabel," Rain said, rolling his eyes. "She doesn't like to be separated. Yes, yes, I'm coming," he said, entering the trailer.

"She just adores Rain," said Robin. "Stand back. She's kind of unpredictable lately and doesn't like people behind her."

"Holy Rosemary's Baby!" I exclaimed, as a painfully round back end of an alpaca backed up out of the trailer.

*Screee-screee – scree -haww!* Mehitabel roared.

"Yes, yes, good girl. We're going to stretch those legs," Rain said as he emerged with the front end of the ridiculously pregnant Mehitabel. She looked around and tap-danced a bit.

"Whoa, I gotcha," Rain said in a gentle voice.

"Hello, Momma," I said, patting her neck. Turning to Chaz I asked, "Are there two babies in there? She's huge!"

"No, just one—"

"A baby alpaca is called a cria," Rain said, patting Mehitabel's neck.

"Oh," I said dumbly. I knew so little about alpacas, I mean four legs and llama-like pretty much covered it. Now I knew a baby was called a cria. I was going to ask if they knew if it was a boy or a girl and stopped myself. Probably not.

*Did you think they'd throw a gender reveal party?* The Inner Critic sniggered.

"That way?" Rain asked, tossing his head in the direction of the trail.

"Yes," I said, taking the lead. "I wish I had a barn you could use, to keep them out of this nasty weather."

"We'll make do," Chaz said.

"You know," I said, thinking out loud, "my neighbor Hollis has a bunch of outbuildings…he lives just over there…they're used to having animals. Used to have goats and chickens. I wonder if he's got something big enough for them… hard to say, he and his twin Urliss have a lot of equipment, tractors, mowers, trailers—"

"We wouldn't want to trouble him."

"Well, hey, let me call him. Worst thing that happens is he says, no, right?" I pulled my phone out and punched his number.

"Haint! We were going to call you. What time do you want us over tomorrow?"

"Dinner'll start at six. Hey, listen, the reason I called is, well, I've got guests with a trailer full of alpacas and one of them, Mehitabel, is profoundly pregnant—"

As I said this, Mehitabel stopped, let loose a *scree-haw*! and flicked her tail. She turned her head around to look at her rear end.

"Seriously pregnant, as in, count the minutes to birthing..." I added.

"Are you serious?" Urliss asked.

"She's looking at her rear end now as if it might pop out," I said nervously.

"Not yet," Robin said, encouraging Prince Albert. He had stopped abruptly to watch Mehitabel.

"So, I was wondering, would you have space to shelter them? It's so nasty out here," I said, shivering. "I know you've got outbuildings—"

"Hollis!" Urliss hollered.

I pulled my head from the phone.

"Mebbee. We could move the tractor and make some space. Hang on—Hollis! Where're you at?"

Soon there were muffled sounds as the twins conversed for a moment. Meanwhile, Mehitabel began strutting forward, so Archy and Prince Albert followed. We were moving down the trail into the woods towards the circle.

"Don't put them to any trouble," Chaz said.

"They're retired. Trust me, if they didn't want to help,

they'd say no, no problem."

Mehitabel stopped and swished her tail. Her head swung around again, eyeing her back end.

Rain looked back at me earnestly, "Did you know that alpacas come in twenty-two colors?"

"No, I didn't!" I said. "I'm not sure I could even think of twenty-two colors."

"It's a fact." Rain said this so earnestly, that I began to wonder if he was on the autism spectrum. I'd noticed that he didn't look me in the eye, he looked off to the side and unlike Aunt Moira with her aura checking, this was avoidant.

"Wow," I said, wishing that Mehitabel would start walking again. I was directly behind her. Bad idea. I stepped back and to the side, putting Rain between us.

Mehitabel had huge brown eyes and long lashes. She had hanks of wool hanging down over her eyes like a teenager in desperate need of a shower and a haircut. Her expression was goofy, but what did she want? Was I bothering her? Was she fixing to spit at me?"

"Why is she staring at me?" I asked.

"I think she likes you," Rain and Robin said simultaneously.

"Oh good. I like her too."

"Haint? You there?" Urliss asked. "Yeah, we can put them in the tractor barn and move the tractor to the pole barn. I've even got some hay if they want. Do alpacas eat hay or sleep in it?"

"I've no idea," I said while nodding that the plan was a go

to the expectant faces, human and animal, looking at me. Chaz and Robin looked relieved. Chaz gestured that he wanted to talk to Urliss. "Let me let you talk to Mr. Warcloud a second," I said, handing the phone over.

Prince Albert expressed his relief by bending his back legs as if straddling an invisible toilet and taking a huge whiz. He regarded us with a dopey bliss. I felt a bit embarrassed for him, it seemed rude for us to all be standing around while he did his business. Silly thought, isn't it? Why would an animal feel embarrassed? It's we humans who make everything so complicated. He widened his stance and kept peeing. And peeing.

"Are they related to camels?" I asked, half-kidding.

"They are," Chaz said. "Same family, camelid."

"They can hold a *lot* of liquid," Rain said, solemnly. "He usually takes a minute or more."

Chaz was talking on the phone, "We really appreciate this. Are you sure we aren't putting you out? Okay. Good. About a half hour? That's perfect. We appreciate this so much." He wiped a hand across his forehead. Poor man looked exhausted. He handed the phone back to me.

"They could use the exercise, so we'll keep walking around a bit then load them up and take them over. It's just that way?" Chaz gestured behind us.

"Go out, turn left, turn into the next drive on the left. You can't miss it. The mailbox looks like a largemouth bass."

I was putting the phone in my hip pocket when it rang. It was Lorraine. "Hey, are you coming?"

"I'll be right there," I said. "I got waylaid by a family of alpacas. Urliss and Hollis are going to bed them down. Got it all sorted."

"Wait, *what*? A little while ago, it was lame brains. Now it's alpacas? Girl, what are you *smoking* over there?"

"I'll tell you more when I get there," I hung up and turned to Chaz. "Sorry. I've got to run out for a couple minutes. The path is a loop; the circle is in the middle. There are signs to direct you." I gestured down the path. "Call me if you need anything."

"We'll be fine, thanks for your help," Robin said.

I half-ran to my truck and sped over my house to get Lorraine. She and Naughty Britches were ready to go. I got out to lift the dog up into the cab. She wiggled and wooed, happy to see me.

"Were you good for Aunt Lorraine?"

She gave me an indignant look.

"Yes, she was. Were you serious about alpacas?" Lorraine asked, getting in.

"Yes. Did you know that they come in twenty-two different colors?"

She looked at me as if guessing if I were kidding or not. "No."

My phone rang as I put the truck in reverse.

"Hello? Blue's Lotus Lodge."

"We're here at the office waiting to check in," a baritone voice said. I could hear multiple voices in the background.

"This place is cool."

"I'm freezing."

"Is she not here?"

I shifted to drive and apologized, "I'm so sorry, I'll be right there. Three minutes." I hung up and turned to Lorraine. "The Lame Brains are waiting to check in."

.

# Chapter 14

## Zombies

A van pulsing with hip-hop music was parked in front of the office when I got back. Four people were huddled on the porch by the door. They looked like college students.

"Hi!" I called, "Sorry to keep you waiting."

Lorraine got out while I helped Naughty Britches out.

The driver, a dark-haired woman with a round face and dark round glasses got out and slammed the door. "Hi, I'm Cindy. We called a few minutes ago—we're the Lame Brains. You're the owner, right? She told me your name, I'm sorry, I can't remember it. Spooky or something, isn't it?"

"Close. It's Haint. And this is Lorraine, she'll help you check in."

"Aw! What a cute dog!" Cindy said.

"Thanks, this is Naughty Britches."

Cindy followed us up the steps to meet the others. NB was eager to greet everyone.

"Right! Sorry. I'm so *lit*! I love this place! You have yoga classes, right? I do yoga. I heard the food was great too."

"I'm sorry the weather is so bad. It's pretty here in nice weather."

She ignored me, waving to get the attention of a man coming back from the dock. "Hey, Linwood! You're paying with the club card, right?"

A young man and woman emerged from the van and waved. Judging by their close proximity, I assumed they were a couple.

"We'll be back!" the woman called, adding, "I need a cigarette!"

The man I assumed was her boyfriend was tall and stoop-shouldered. His hair was shaved almost to skin at the back of his head but longer in front with a tuft of bangs over his forehead. His hairstyle was strikingly like Mehitabel's. His jeans and shirt were toffee brown. A long gray scarf with fringe swayed from his neck. The woman was also thin and dressed in browns and blacks.

I opened the office door. Lorraine went in first, the others followed, greeting NB as they passed us.

"Come on in," Lorraine encouraged, taking a seat behind the desk. She studied the reservation screen. Haint? What cabin?"

"Five."

I'll get you the passcode and give you maps."

NB merrily followed them in. "Anyone allergic to dogs or not like dogs? I can put her in her crate—"

"Aw, no, we're cool! Come here, baby girl!" said one of the men.

I unclipped her leash and let her mingle.

"We're so grateful you have a cabin," Cindy said. "We sat in traffic for *hours* and the first motels we tried were already booked up. This is *so* much better than some smokey room with highway sounds all night. Kind of tricky finding you though. Glad you warned us about the detour."

"I rolled my eyes. "That culvert collapsed over the summer. It's taking forever for them to fix it. Drives me nuts."

Lorraine passed out a couple maps and the key code card. "You'll want to park in the second lot over that way," she gestured. "You're in cabin five, just across the way."

"Okay," Cindy nodded, passing out the maps.

Oh, um, this is Ray," she said, tugging on Ray's arm in a possessive way, "and Linwood—"

"Hi—"

"...and Kirby—"

"...and Wendy—"

"Hi, welcome," I said.

"...and Kandi and Lloyd disappeared for a smoke," Cindy finished.

I had my hand on the doorknob to leave but couldn't get the chance to excuse myself.

Lorraine asked, "Where were you headed?"

"To a LARP event in Kissimmee tomorrow afternoon."

"Sorry. What's a larp?" I asked.

"Live action role play," said Kirby.

"Oh. How does that work?"

"A LARP is like a convention. There's a lot to it, but the main thing is, we take over a few floors of a hotel. The zombies hunt the people. It's epic," said Ray.

"There are other things too…vendors, talks, videos--" said Linwood.

"We've worked up a special show for Christmas," said Cindy almost bouncing with eagerness. "We're like a zombie bell choir."

"O-kay. That's different." Lorraine said.

My phone rang. "Excuse me just a moment," I said, stepping outside.

"Hello? Blue's Lotus Lodge. This is Haint."

A weary voice with a French accent asked, "Is it possible, by any chance that you have a non-smoking room for two adults and a child?"

I stepped back inside and had a gander at the reservation screen chart. I had one vacant cabin left. *Oh, Aunt Moira, how did you know this would happen?*

"You are in luck. I do."

"Oh, *magnifique!*"

I gave the caller the warning about the culvert being out and the detour. "Stay on Route 27 and turn right onto Night Swamp Glen. You'll see the sign for the lodge on the left."

"We're just getting through Catfish Springs now." I was amused that with the accent, the town sounded like Cot-feesh Spu-rrings with a rolled 'r'. "We'll be there soon. Name is Joliecoeur. Violette and Duran Joliecoeur."

I heard a child's voice in the background yell, "And Angejolie!"

"And Angejolie," Violette added.

"I'm sorry to do this, but I'm going to pass you to my assistant. She will be happy to help you."

I pointed to cabin four, held up three fingers and dashed to the door. "Sorry folks, I hate to be rude, but I have to get back to the kitchen if we're going to eat tonight!

## Señor Soñador

Some time later, Lorraine buzzed me on the phone. "He's here. Oh. My. God. He just checked in. They all stayed in the car, except for him and his sister, Clementine — that's a pretty name, isn't it? She's pretty. Young. Gorgeous, lush, long hair. I'm so jealous. He remembered my name and, oh, Haint--"

I had the phone cradled in my neck and was sprinkling minced spring onions over a pan of sausage cabbage rolls. "What? Who are you talking about?"

"*Señor Soñador*! Oh, Haint, he's wearing this gray, full-length coat...I swear it was cashmere. Are you sure he's in banking and doesn't do modeling on the side?"

"Pull it together, girlfriend!" I said laughing. I gotta go. Need to get cabbage rolls in the oven."

"Oh, hey, your Sillyclowns arrived I thought you were kidding. It's not spelled that way exactly though. . Super cute old couple. They look about a moon cycle shy of a hundred."

"Great. Gotta go."

"Wait! I've got questions. I'm getting calls from people with campers and trailers and stuff. They don't need cabins, just a place to park. The motels around here are full. What do I say?"

"We can take a few, I guess. The parking lots are pretty full already. Depends on the size. Use your judgement, err on the cautious side."

"Got it. Oh. People coming. I hear footsteps. Bye."

## THE JOLIECOEURS

With dinner mostly under control, I took off my apron and thought I'd see how Lorraine was doing. I was putting on my jacket, but before I could get to the door, there was a crazy, high-pitched sound as if King Kong was playing with a monster-truck sized squeaky toy. *Wee-kee-wee-keeee---wee-keeee!*

"*Co na świecie?* ♥" I muttered as a shudder of fear shot down my spine. I stepped outside to see a child running pell-mell towards Chaz, Rain, Robin, and the alpacas. They were just coming back from the woods heading towards the truck and trailer in the second parking lot.

"*Maman! Regarde!*" she called with glee.

Her parents were running behind her. "*No! Angejolie! Attend!*"

*Weeeee-keeee! Weee-kee, weee-keee!*

"Angejolie, wait!" her parents called, running after her.

---

♥ Polish: pronounced tso na sehvee-chay = What in the world?

"We don't run in the road!"

Lorraine had heard the commotion too. She came trotting from the office. I could hear NB barking her most hysterical bark, incensed that she was excluded from the goings-on in the parking lot.

The alpacas shied. Prince Albert of Upper Balderdash craned his neck as high as it would go and let out another raucous squeal. Archy hid behind Mehitabel who pranced in place, nostrils flaring.

Robin held up a hand, "Hi, sweetie. You can visit with them, but slow down, don't scare them."

"Okay!" the little girl said stopping abruptly, letting out another high-pitched squeal. Her parents also slowed, and the two parties converged.

Rain asked, "What's your name?"

"Angejolie."

Lorraine nudged me. "That little girl is adorable, isn't she?"

"Sure is. Who are they?"

"The French family who were on the phone before."

"Oh. Gotcha."

Her voice changed to awe as we got closer, "I don't think I've ever seen an alpaca…you weren't kidding. Wow."

*Weeeee-keeee! Weee-kee, weee-keee!*

"Angejolie, that's a pretty name. Say hello to Mehitabel and Prince Albert and Archy," Rain said, patting Mehitabel's neck with one hand and pointing to the other two with his free hand.

The little girl shivered with excitement. "Hello, Ma-belle. Prince! He's a prince? That's a funny name! And Archy!"

Chaz looked to me. "We had a good walk. I'm afraid that they chose a spot in the middle of your meditation circle as their toilet."

"That's okay. With all this rain, it'll wash away. I *highly* doubt anyone is going to be out there meditating today."

"It's a beautiful spot," Robin said, shivering, "that is, I can imagine it would be peaceful and relaxing if it weren't so cold and nasty."

Chaz looked at his wife. "Why don't you go get a shower? Rain and I can run them over. We don't need to all go."

"You sure you don't mind?" Robin asked, rubbing her hands together. "I'm about half-frozen."

"Where are you going?" Angejolie asked Mehitabel.

"We're going to a place just next door where they have a barn for them to sleep in tonight." Rain said.

Robin excused herself and walked around the trailer on her way to cabin one.

"Why is Ma-belle so fat?" Angejolie asked.

"She is going to have a baby," Rain explained.

"There's a baby in there?" she asked, cocking her head. She contemplated Mehitabel's belly for a few moments before asking, "Can I touch it?"

"They're kind of wet and a bit dirty," Chaz said.

"Come on, sweetie, let's let them alone." Violette said, trying to take her by the hand. "We have to go find our cabin. Maybe you can visit with them again."

"Hi, I'm Haint Blue, the owner," I said, offering a hand. "We talked on the phone."

"Oh yes. We are so hop-py to find you. We were telling Miss Lorraine, the traffic was *terri-ble*," Violette said. "We were on our way to Orlando for Christ-moose, we have teek-its for all the attractions, but then we got stopped for hours and the weather is so bad, there is no point." She waved a hand in a gesture of futility. Angejolie is tired. Perhaps tomorrow we can go."

Angejolie, still as curious about the alpacas as they were about her, resisting her mother's hand. "Ohhh. Okay. G'bye Ma-belle. Funny Prince and...what's his name again?"

"Archy." Rain said, leading Mehitabel into the trailer.

"G'bye Archy."

The remaining two alpacas regarded her with comical curiosity. Archy waggled his head side to side as if trying to balance in a fun house. Prince Albert turned his head to the side and studied her with one matted wool-covered eye.

"They smell like the zoo!" Angejolie observed, looking up at her mother.

"Come on, it's cold. Let's go find our cabin," Violette said, picking her up. The little girl wrapped her arms around her mother, resting her head on her mom's shoulder. "Papa, do you have the key card so we can get in?"

Duran felt in his pockets. "No, I must have left it in the office when she ran out of the car."

Lorraine and I headed back to the office with them. Their car was parked out front. As they got closer, the little girl turned her head, and a smile overtook her sleepy face. The twinkling lights from the porch decorations danced in her eyes. She pointed to the artificial, poinsettia-dominated wreath on the office door. Scattered amongst the huge flowers and gold garlands were mini twinkle lights. The dreary gray surroundings enhanced the magic of the twinkle lights reflecting in the glass panes of the door. She beamed with delight as if her whole being was pure happiness. Even with the nippy air, I felt my heart and core warm. Seeing it through her eyes, the wreath was no longer a somewhat tacky, second-hand item, it *was* beautiful.

In that moment, as her smile transformed my world, I realized she had the eye folds, small nose, and mouth characteristics of a person with Down's Syndrome.

Angejolie looked like she was falling asleep with visions of sugarplums dancing in her head. Actually, I'm not sure what that would look like to be honest, true sugarplums are an expensive combination of dried fruits and nuts rolled into balls and covered with confectioner's sugar. I've only made them a few times myself. Let me rephrase that. She looked like a contented cherub saturated in the holiday spirit.

"Dinner will begin at six in the dining hall," I said, rather automatically, as I glanced through the office door window at the wall clock. *What? How was it four-thirty-five already? Kurwa!*♦♦

*You better get back over there,"* my Inner Critic said.

The office phone rang. Lorraine ducked in to get it. We followed. Naughty Britches was elated to greet the new guests, trilling out a half-howl, half-yodel. This woke Angejolie from

---

♦♦ All-purpose Polish cuss word equivalent for "shit" or the f bomb, depending on context.

her dreamland. I spotted the key card and handed it to Violette.

"*Maman! Le chien!*" she cried stretching out her hand towards Naughty Britches.

"What size is your RV?" Lorraine asked, giving me a what-do-I-do look.

Violette let Angejolie down. NB wagged furiously and licked the child's face. She giggled and squealed putting up her hands defensively.

"Thirty feet?" Lorraine repeated, giving me the hairy eyebrows.

I nodded, grabbing NB away from Angejolie. "That's enough, you'll overwhelm her."

Violette pocketed the card and picked Angejolie up again. "Let's go, *petite.*"

"Bye doggie," Angejolie said, waving.

"Do we have hookups?" Lorraine asked, wrinkling her nose.

"No, but if they want to run a generator, they can."

Lorraine nodded and repeated it back to the caller.

Naughty Britches stared at the door, looking sad that Angejolie had left.

"This is getting nuts," Lorraine said hanging up the phone.

"Tell me about it," I said.

# Chapter 15

## Timing

Much as I had heeded Moira's advice about being prepared and stocking the freezer, I was beginning to have a full-on panic attack about feeding everyone. Did I have enough food? I was supposed to be serving dinner in less than half an hour. I sure hoped they'd go for the cabbage rolls. The retreat was now at full capacity, possibly beyond, *if* you counted the toddlers, which I was sure a fire marshal would. Urliss and Hollis were coming, and they could eat a whole turkey each. The added guests resulting from the accident tipped the scales of my preparedness. The parking lots were full. My head was swimming with how many adults, teens, and kids were present, zombie LARPers, not to mention a pregnant alpaca—"I think I need a paper bag…" I muttered, "aren't you supposed to breath in a bag?"

Lorraine hung up only to have the phone ring again.

"We're full. No more," I said, holding my head and pacing.

"Okay," she said, picking up the phone.

Naughty Britches mewled and looked at me more pitifully than an orphaned child on a save-the-children poster.

"Yes, yes, I'll feed you, sweety," I said, fumbling for NB's bowl. It had kibble dregs and dog hair in it. I picked it up and wiped it out.

The weather was dreary. The usual retreat activities — walks, the river, kayaking etcetera were kiboshed. In the midst of a growing sense of panic, a hot flash blazed up all over my body. My lip broke out in a sweat, my core felt like molten lava. I looked down to see if steam was truly coming off my clothing. Was this it? Would I self-combust and disappear? Would tomorrow's local news report that my shoes and feet were found here facing the desk as I held on to meditate my way through the heatwave? "This is too much!" I wailed. Even my ponytail was sinking.

"Hello, Lotus Lodge," Lorraine answered yet another call.

As the engulfing heat subsided, I began pacing in my office liked a caged tiger. "I should have hired help! How can I cook and serve for all these people? Stupid, stupid, stupid! I'll never find help now." I let loose my melt-down fears in a roaring fit, "Shit, shit, shit, AHHHRRGGGH!"

Lorraine glared at me and apologized to a caller, "No, that wasn't me, *sorry*, my co-worker just found out that she doesn't qualify for the extended car warranty — no, I'm sorry, we don't have any vacancies at this time. We're full. Best wishes for a safe holiday."

I was in full on crazy when the door opened, and Buster walked in and stopped mid-stride. "Uh-oh, Mebbee I should'n'ta come without callin' first."

My mouth fell open. My ponytail that had been slipping lower and lower, fell out. "No, this isn't happening!" I wailed.

Lorraine looked up. Her mouth fell open.

Of course, what I meant was that the timing couldn't have been worse. But Buster pivoted and was almost out the door before I grabbed him. "No! Wait. It's not you!" I hugged him hard and began blubbering about meal planning, the horrible weather, and alpacas.

"Your parkin' lot sure is full. You got so many RVs in the front lot, it kinda looks like a trailer park."

"I know. It's crazy. There was an accident on I-75—the motels are full--" I said, my voice warbling with emotion.

"Glad I missed it. I came from Jacksonville. Real sorry I didn't call. I'd no idea you'd be so busy."

"Me neither!"

He looked exhausted, like standing up and keeping his eyes open was about all the effort he could muster. I caressed his jaw with the palm of my hand. "Hey, you look, um, --" I didn't want to say what I was thinking. I tried again, "Are you sick—?"

"I'll be fine. I'm beyond exhausted. Mind if I sit?"

"Of course!" I said, gesturing to my little office couch. "Buster, this is Lorraine, Lorraine, Buster."

"Hi!" Lorraine said. "Want something to drink? There's water and soda in the mini-fridge."

"Water'd be great," he said, collapsing into the couch.

"Could you feed NB?" I asked Lorraine, while getting a drink for Buster.

She nodded and retrieved the bowl from the desk where I'd abandoned it mid-meltdown.

I brought him a bottled water and sat next to him. "I got your postcards. Well, sort of. They were hard to read. One was ripped up and the other had tire treads on it."

"I'm shocked they even found their way to ya," he said, then drank about half the bottle at once, letting out a satisfied, "Haahr, I sore needed that. And didn't even have to bribe you for it." He patted my knee. "I'm so glad to be back. That was somethin' else." He tipped the bottle back and finished the water.

"You *were* in Africa, then?" I asked.

"I was."

"What were you doing?"

He shook his head. "Long story. Tell ya later." He looked at me with eyes that spoke of horrors that couldn't be put into words because they shouldn't exist in the first place. He tried to smile and when that failed, he changed the subject. "All them guests are here on account o' the accident?"

I filled him in on the highlights from the restaurant stove going on the frizzle to boarding alpacas at Urliss's house.

"A pregnant alpaca? Max's mother? Aunt Moira? Saint Eleanor? Sure glad I got here in time," Buster said, patting my hair. He lifted my chin and kissed me gently. "So, ya ain't mad with me? I lost my phone in the river an' then I kinda wanted to surprise ya for the holiday, but never thought you'd be so busy."

"I know. Me either. I was going to close the retreat and go

to the beach."

He kissed me again. And again. His scent of woodsy, musky, manly clean — the comfort of his tight embrace--I was so glad to see him. "Please tell me I'm not dreaming this. You're really here."

"I was thinkin' the same thing. Tell *me* I'm really here," he said, cradling my head.

I leaned into his chest savoring the moment. I had so many things to ask. What was he doing in Africa? When did he get back? Then I pulled back, "Shit! I've gotta serve dinner!" I trotted around to the desk drawer where I lock my purse. I fumbled to find my keys. "Here. You can get settled at my place. Could you take Naughty Britches with you? On a leash, please. Always. She can't be trusted on her own."

I pressed my keys into his palm, kissed his cheek, and was half out the door, heading for the dining hall. I stopped abruptly like a cartoon character, my body swaying over my feet. "Oh! Almost forgot! Lorraine is staying with me. Her house is a biohazard. I'm sure she'd be thrilled to see you strutting around *au naturelle*, it sure thrills *me*, but I thought y'ought to know."

Lorraine let her eyes give Buster the once over and said readily, "Fine with me."

Behind me I heard him say, "Biohazard? Uh, yeah, o-kay...Hey--I might not make it to dinner...don't be mad."

"I won't!" I yelled back. I would want him there of course, but I wouldn't have time to sit and talk. I was going to be a food service tornado.

# PART FIVE

# DINNER

# Chapter 16

## "I Just Need an Outlet"

With all the unexpected guests, I was in a stew, (pun intended) over dinner. My mind was in overdrive. *Would there be enough food? Should I add a spinach salad with mandarin oranges and gorgonzola? The leg of lamb was looking good. The roasted carrots should be ready on time. Did I have enough dinner rolls? Don't forget them…*

I was so distracted by the mental bubble gum that I hadn't noticed that Aletea, Yolanda, Rita and Osanna were trooping into the kitchen carrying huge slow cookers and serving utensils.

Yolanda began, "We had so much food at the restaurant that we couldn't cook—"

Osanna interrupted, "Do you have an outlet? If you don't mind, we need someplace to plug in the posole and black beans mole to keep it warm." She nodded her head to Aletea, "Mama says it's not the holidays without her mole, and *my* little angels begged me for posole…"

"Uh, okay —" I began, looking around for an outlet.

You know, thinking about it now, I should have known what was coming. I swear I didn't. I was stressed and distracted. And naïve...

Good thing it all turned out okay!

Aletea gave me the kind of matronly smile that indicated it would be a dire mistake to deny her mole concoction in my kitchen.

Avoiding Aletea's commanding gaze, Rita said timidly, "Mama's mole is too spicy for Mingo and my children. This is my mole without the hot chilies."

Yolanda said apologetically, "Sorry to take over your kitchen, but we are happy to share — we've taken over your retreat —"

"Oh, wow, no —" I mumbled looking for a place to plug them in close to the buffet. "Here, I'll move the waffle maker." I rushed over to make room. Yolanda whipped out an extension cord strip and plugged it in. In a moment, every vacant outlet was taken.

Aletea nodded her approval. The ladies set serving utensils next to the hot pots.

"This is amazing. Are you sure you don't mind sharing? We've got a lot of people tonight." I'll make up some sign cards to explain what the dishes are."

And then it seemed that while I kept doing my thing, more and more people were in my way every time I turned around. "I'm just going to warm up this sauce" and "I'm just making my guacamole" and "I'll make Yaya's salsa." Mingo appeared and plugged in a boom box.

"Bachata!" Osanna cried out, moving her arms to the beat.

The kitchen and dining hall soon felt more like a dance hall as a peppy beat of guitars, keyboards, maracas and various other shakers and clackers accompanied a mellow voice crooning out thoughts of love for the holidays.

"I need a pot-holder," Osanna said. I pointed to a drawer.

"Did Mingo remember to bring ice?"

"Where is Clementina?"

"Guys—" I began, feeling outnumbered and powerless. Over the music, multiple conversations flew back and forth as the women chopped, stirred, and simmered various dishes. They did the samba. They clapped wooden spoons together to the beat.

"I'll sit with Yaya to make sure she takes her pills. You have to watch her, or she'll throw them on the floor when you aren't looking."

"I know! I told her it's dangerous if the dog or cat eats them."

"Dog or cat? I found *Zelia* about to put one in her mouth!"

"Oh, that's terrible!"

"Why didn't Pedro bring his girlfriend?"

"I don't know. Do you think they split up?"

"I think so. He won't tell me though. Fine with me. I thought she was a stuck-up bitch."

"She was crazy high maintenance."

"Taste this. More onion you think?"

"I thought they were still together."

"Maybe she wanted to be with her family."

"What does she do again?"

"Did you take my tortillas? They were right here."

"More chiles."

And that's just a sample. There was a whole lot of Spanglish that was so fast I didn't understand any of it.

I was pressing my fingers to my temples when Yolanda appeared in front of me, holding a red cocktail in a plastic party cup.

"Here, you look like you need this," Yolanda said, taking a sip of her own.

A sprig of mint stuck out of it and there were red balls, possibly cranberries swirling in the ice.

"What is it?" I asked.

"Cranberry punch. Try it," she said with a nod of encouragement.

I did. "Wowee! Oh, you are a goddess," I said, taking another sip. "This is fantastic." It was the perfect blend of tart and sweet with an attention-getting kick.

"Cranberry juice, vodka, mint, jalapeño —"

"I don't have a liquor license," I said, anxiously looking around the kitchen.

"Relax. Mingo set up his mini bar in the back of his van. You aren't serving alcohol. It's BYOB. You aren't even offering ice cubes. We got it covered," she added with a wink. "Enjoy."

# Chapter 17

## Dinner with a Punch

inner was a crazy blur, thanks in part to the cranberry tequila punch. Here are highlights that I remember:

Clan Max arrived early in a mob like snowbirds descending on an all-you-can-eat-buffet. Nellavon was pushing Max's mother, Mama Sue, to the head of a table. Again, I was struck by how much Nellavon looked like Max. Mama Sue sat slumped in her wheelchair in a formless blue housecoat, her legs mostly covered in white circulation support stockings and nondescript slip-on shoes. She looked darned good for 101 years old.

"Haint, this is my mother, Mama Sue," Max said, touching her on the shoulder.

I nodded.

Mama Sue sized me up and made an incoherent grunt that I assumed was a hello.

"Welcome to the Lotus Lodge," I said.

Mama Sue looked at me, looked around the dining hall, twisted up her face in something between confusion and irritation, looked back at Nellavon and asked, "Where's the television? Shouldn't *Animal Planet* be on now?"

"Later, Mama. Let's enjoy that your family is all together. We're going to eat now."

She grunted again and flickered her eyes. Was she winking at me, or did she have a nervous tic? I wasn't sure. I *think* she winked. I got the feeling there was a lot of activity hiding behind the watery eyes. If Max was The Trickster, this was the Great Mother Grand Master Trickster.

Taylor shadowed Nellavon, his face devoid of animation. Something about his demeanor made me think of a paper doll. Flat. No substance. Empty. Once Nellavon had gotten Mama Sue situated, he helped push in her chair and sat next to her. It was all gentlemanly but performed like an automaton.

Max gestured to the couple coming up behind Mama Sue. "My niece Cameron and her husband, Benny," Max said, emphasizing the "B" with distaste, the way a vegetable-hating child would say "*broccoli*". Benny patted Mama Sue's shoulder as he passed her, making his way to a chair opposite Taylor.

Cameron stopped to give Mama Sue a hug. "I'm so glad you're here, Mama Sue."

"You too, dear. You're a good girl," Mama Sue replied, adding a "mwah" as they air-kissed cheeks.

Benny looked at Mama Sue and said in an attention-demanding voice, "You know, Mama Sue, I've heard stories about you —" He looked around to see if he had an audience.

Mama Sue put a hand to her forehead.

"Benny, don't—" Cameron said, pushing him to find a seat as other relatives came in and took seats at the adjacent table.

Benny persisted, "They say that it's dangerous huggin' on you, you know that?"

Max interrupted, "This here's my other beautiful niece, Betsy and her husband, Pike."

"Nice to meet you," I said nodding. "I'm Haint."

Pike shook my hand. "This is our son, Austin—"

Benny repeated "They say that it's dangerous huggin' on you, 'cause you'd hug a good kid and a bad kid the same, but if the kid had done bad, you'd hug on 'em extra and tell 'em you were sizin' 'em up to know how big of a hole to dig in the yard! I heard you even told the kids they had an older sibling you'd already sized up and buried!"

An awkward silence covered both tables. It was hard to know if Mama Sue had heard Bennie. She didn't react.

Nellavon muttered, "It wasn't funny."

Austin scowled at Benny and rolled his eyes. He looked to a petite woman standing close to him holding a toddler. "This is my wife, May, and our boy, Vonnie."

"Hi," we said.

Someone muttered, "I can't believe he said that."

Someone else muttered, "What a jackass."

Mama Sue asked, "Where is the television? I'm missing *Animal Planet*."

Max, who hadn't committed to sitting at either table and had remained behind Mama Sue, fixed Benny with a searing look. Good thing he wasn't pyrokinetic or Benny would have burst into flames. "It's not funny, Benny. That's true." Max said in a gritty voice. "I got myself in trouble at school once. After dinner, she hugged me real tight an' told me that she was sizin' me up. I dreamed about being buried alive for weeks. After I kept wettin' the bed, she got tired of changing the sheets and finally told me it warn't true."

Oh, Mercy and Myrna Loy! And here I thought *my* mother had been harsh. At least she hadn't scared me into wetting the bed.

Mama Sue's head jiggled a bit. Was she laughing or denying it? Hard to say. Her face was still covered by her hand.

Max took a few steps and claimed the head of the second table with a proprietary hand on the back of the chair. He looked straight at Mama Sue. "Roberta watched some revolting horror movie or other that had ghoulish phantoms and shadows. Silly girl got obsessed and terrified. Mama Sue told her, if she was scared of ghosts, she could suck 'em up in the vacuum cleaner. Heh-heh, kinda clever actually, but Roberta drove us all nuts! She vacuumed at least three times a day! Woke me up in the middle of the night! She was vacuuming her closet and under the bed! The house was never so clean as then."

Mama Sue looked up suddenly and hissed, "Don't you dare talk about Roberta. You let that woman rest in peace."

Oh, dear. What a family reunion. I could see why Max had been dreading this.

An uncanny thing happened then. It was one of those things that you might assume was caused by someone bumping the table. Austin and May were still getting seated at the second table, and May was making her way between the two tables, squeezing past people, carrying a squirming baby. There was a fair amount of activity, with chairs moving and people bumping.

Making a sharp smack, a glass saltshaker fell over, the lid flew off, and a spray of salt flowed across the table in Benny's direction, almost as if pointing to him. The distance from where the saltshaker had been and where it now lay was a few inches. It had not just fallen over sideways--it was as if it had jumped or been picked up by an invisible hand and knocked over. The pepper never faltered. I looked to see if anyone else had seen what I'd seen. Nellavon was staring at the saltshaker. Perhaps she had.

"Oh, gosh," I began, dismissing what I thought I'd seen. "I'll get something to clean that up," I said, adding, "The buffet line will be open momentarily. Please help yourselves and don't forget to save room for dessert."

Behind me, Benny began in his brash voice, "That reminds me of the one about the blonde who bought a new vacuum cleaner..."

I was halfway to the kitchen congratulating myself on escaping another awkward Benny moment when I heard a scratchy old woman's voice call out, "Hey Benny! Come give Mama Sue a big ol' hug," followed by laughter.

I had returned and wiped up the mysterious salt spill with a damp cloth. Something about the way it had just pitched kept bugging me. It wasn't natural. Was it my imagination or had it been aimed at Benny? I wondered if the saltshaker had had supernatural guidance, and if so, by my ghost, Spotted Fawn, or their recently-deceased Roberta? If she was lingering on this earthly plane, she could have come with them or with all her Christmas decorations. *They were everywhere*, I thought looking around. Centerpieces on each table. I was on my way back to the kitchen when Kate intercepted me.

"Remember we talked about the Secret Santa thing? Have you asked? Is it a go?"

Nellavon, coming back from the buffet line, tilted her head, obviously overhearing the question. "What's this about a Secret Santa?"

"The ladies were suggesting that we do a Secret Santa exchange tomorrow — something fun since it's so bleak outside and all —" I began.

"You know, something silly and fun —" Kate interrupted, bubbling with enthusiasm, "--nothing expensive. We've got a trunk full of stuff I'm sure we could part with —"

At first Nellavon looked about to say something catty or dismissive. In fact, "stupid waste of time" practically ran across her face like an alert streaming across an electronic message board. You know, like a traffic delay sign on the freeway. But then it changed. She lit up like a tree topper, "Ooh! Yes! Hold that thought, I'll be right back."

"But the Garcia family — they've already had to do Christmas for the kids —" I began, and then thought about all the leftover holiday decorations I had stashed away.

Ceci busted out laughing, "Oh, have we got some gag gift options!"

Meanwhile, Nellavon hovered over Max talking rapidly. He nodded and bellowed, "Hell yes, great idea! Cripes there's even a closet of wrapping paper--enough to wallpaper Catfish Springs!"

Nellavon tromped back to us, looking triumphant. "You know, Roberta was a hoarder, and we have to clear out her house... Max agreed that we could go over there later. I'm sure we could find lots of crap—you can have all you want."

"And I'll ask the Garcia family if they are interested," said Kate. "I promise, if they aren't comfortable with it, we won't do it."

As is often the case, I felt like this event was getting away from me. I wanted to be sure that the Garcia family wanted to participate, and I was pretty sure they would not need the added responsibility of gift hunting. Yolanda was in the kitchen making a new batch of jalapeño punch. I waited until she turned off the blender.

"Wow, that smells fantastic," I said.

"It's the cloves, cinnamon, and coconut. Good, ya?" she said, pouring the contents into a pitcher.

"I have a question," I began, a bit intimidated by how brisk and efficient her movements were.

"Ya?" she asked, not looking at me as she scraped the last bits of liquid from the blender with a spatula.

"Uh, I was wondering, since the weather is so bad and we're all cooped up, some of the guests were talking about maybe doing a Secret Santa gift exchange—"

"Secret Santa? For the kids?" Her face was stern. I couldn't tell what her mood was.

"Well, see, Kate and Ceci have lots of small stuff because they run a thrift shop and I have some extra Christmas ornaments and things and Max's sister—" I stopped myself. Was I really going to say that we'd be giving away a dead hoarder's collection of junk? "Has some small things to give away—so it would be anything small, inexpensive, you know, like a white elephant gift exchange—"

"White elephant?" she asked with a scowl as she washed the blender vigorously with a brush.

"Well, I've also heard it called Chinese present exchange, but that's probably not politically correct—"

She looked more confused than before.

"Everyone brings a gift to give away and we do a big gift swap. If you don't like the gift you got, you get an option to trade it for someone else's gift. None of the gifts have any great value, it's just for fun."

Yolanda shot me a doubtful glance as she grabbed the pitcher and headed toward the dining hall. "No value?"

"Well, it can be silly or cute, but not expensive. I think the thrift ladies are going to offer up stuff from thrift shops…"

She set the horchata down near the iced tea pitchers and turned to me, "Oh! For everyone? Kids and adults? You know, my brother, Mingo, does the flea market over in Waldo—I'll ask him. He usually has all kinds of small stuff. Are food items okay? He has all kinds of stuff like socks, cheap toys, overstock pancake mix, canned goods, kitchen gadgets…"

I shrugged, "Why not? I'd be happy with a tin of

pineapples or new socks."

"When would we do it?"

I hadn't thought about that. Christmas Eve? Christmas day?

"We go to midnight mass on Christmas Eve and mass Christmas morning."

"What about mid-day Christmas Eve, before dinner, like, four o'clock?"

"Okay, that should work," she shrugged. "I'll ask him."

And just like that, the Secret Santa plan was set in motion.

I was refilling the iced tea pitchers when Rocky came up next to me for a coffee. When I'd first met Rocky, he'd been bundled up in a coat with gloves and a scarf. Now he was wearing a collared shirt with the sleeves rolled up. I'd not realized he was covered in tattoos, even down his fingers and creeping around his neck.

I'll confess that I'm not a fan of the full-body tattoo look when the ink is black, and the images are of skulls and other dark subject matter. It kind of creeps me out. Rocky is a stocky guy, too, so I'll confess he made me a little uncomfortable. As he poured his coffee, I noticed that in script over his knuckles on the left fist was the word *resiliencia* and over the right knuckles, a dark red hear and *corazón.* Heart and resilience. He caught my eye and I smiled reflexively. He smiled back. Warm. Friendly. "Thank you so much for having us. The kids are having a great time. They think having a cabin to themselves is like having a secret hideout. They love it."

"Oh, I'm so glad," I said, smiling again.

Just then his daughter, Anna, wandered over and hugged his leg. "Hey, *flor pequeña, what are you doing?*" He said patting her on the head. "You need something to drink?"

She shook her head.

"Okay, come with me. We'll go back to the table."

She nodded and trotted after him, obviously a Daddy's girl.

The Hloupyklauns sat with the Warclouds. Rain broke the ice by telling them about the alpacas and Mehitabel's pending delivery. It turned out that until his retirement in the mid-nineties, Mr. Hloupyklaun had been a zoologist and manager of the Brno Zoo in the Czech Republic. He was eager to see the alpacas, as camelids were one of his favorite animal families. Chaz would take them over to Hollis's barn for a short visit after dinner.

Meanwhile my happy meter ticked over to high as both Mr. and Mrs. Hloupyklaun raved about my stuffed cabbages.

"This is one of our *favorite* dishes," she said in her helium voice. "I like what you did with the chili. Puts a little kick in it. And I *love* your sausage. So flavorful. I'm going to have a second one and I *never* do that. What the heck. It's almost Christmas, right?" She winked at me.

Her compliments sure put some air in my insoles.

Urliss and Hollis had arrived with massive, disposable tin pans of cheesy, tater tot and veggies casserole. Oro and Oscar were fascinated by the adult twins. They were both keen on tater tots too, so the younger twins hovered near the Oakey twins like yellow jackets over soda cans.

"Are you a pirate?" one asked Urliss. "You got a scar like a pirate."

I snorted. I never envisioned pirates wearing overalls and sporting beer bellies, but, on second thought, Oro or Oscar, (whichever one had asked) was not far off the mark. They *could* be modern day pirates, I supposed.

"Arrr mateys, I could be!" he answered.

The other twin cuffed the first one on the head, "He isn't a pirate, he doesn't have a *peg leg*."

Hollis said, "That's not true. His pirate name is Blue Skink because he lost his leg in a gun fight but it *grew back*."

"Whoa!"

"Did you have a HOOK too?" the first boy asked, raising his hand in the shape of a C.

"I did! It was awful! Couldn't drink my beer! I had to grow my hand back, too!" Urliss said, waving his fingers.

"WHOA!" the boys cried in unison.

I wouldn't have guessed that the Oakeys were fond of children, but they seemed happy to entertain the youngsters, who in turn adopted them as long-lost uncles. The conversation meandered towards porch pirates and boobytraps. The boys were transfixed.

I caught Max bemusedly watching them discussing porch pirates. "Those boys are on Urliss and Hollis like two roaches on a bacon scrap."

It seemed that Rocky knew the Oakeys, so he and Osanna

glanced over from time to time but seemed relieved for the break in monitoring their high-test boys.

There was tension and loud silence hovering around the table where Stuey and Amy sat with Noni and Stuart Sr., Gigi, and Aunt Moira. I gathered that Aunt Moira had dropped some unfavorable predictions on someone.

"That's all a load of bullshit," Stuey snarled.

"I just thought you should know," Aunt Moira said defensively.

"Hey! Keep it civil!" Stuey's father barked.

"Scorpio, am I right?" Gigi asked Stuey.

"I think I'm getting a migraine," Amy said, closing her eyes.

Gigi said, "Look on the bright side, forewarned is forearmed, right?"

Stuey stared at the floral centerpiece.

Amy pushed her chair back and announced, "I'm going to lie down." Stuey patted her back, but she pulled away from him and scooted toward the door like a sandpiper running from a wave.

I glanced over to the next table, where Saint Eleanor, Leander and Lorraine were sitting. Leander winked at Lorraine and passed his hand over his belly in the universal yummy sign. She grinned. She loved her dad so much, dollars to confectionary creations, she'd bake him that chocolate lava cake even if she lost the bet.

I was carrying Lorraine's amazing caramel drizzle cake out to the dessert table when a loud outburst at one of the Garcia tables got my attention. Rita had pushed back her chair and rushed to the other end of the table, shouting in Spanish in the kind of tone of alarm that makes you want to drop and cover. I couldn't see what the issue was. I set the cake down and quick-stepped over. Gorge was folded chest over legs in his chair, puking on the floor with all his might.

"Oh!" was all I managed to say, staring at the disgusting mess on the floor. Was he ill with food poisoning or ill with flu? Lord, *please* let it not be food poisoning from my food.

Rita was still streaming her concern and what appeared to be anger. Nothing like hurling your life force out while your mom screams at you. Dang.

Pedro caught my eye. "Don't worry. He'll be fine."

"What is it?"

"Gorge has a lot of food allergies. Unfortunately, he doesn't pay any attention to what he eats, so this happens a lot."

Oro and Oscar had crept out of their chairs, thrown themselves on the floor nearby and began imitating Gorge hurling.

"Do they know what he ate?" I asked, bracing myself.

Mimi, Gorge's sister, who was sitting close to us answered, "He ate the lamb off my plate. He can't eat lamb."

I felt awful for Gorge, but relieved that it wasn't because of tainted food.

Rocky stood up from his table and began to unhitch his belt

buckle. "You twins better pray that your *traseros* find your seats before my belt finds your *traseros*!"

Osanna began yelling at Oro and Oscar.

Rita stopped yelling at Gorge and wiped at his face. "Come on, we'll go to the bathroom."

Gorge allowed her to pull him off his chair avoiding the mess. They were halfway to the bathroom when he stopped, bent over, and hurled again. Oro and Oscar levitated off the floor in a hurry and yowled back to their chairs.

"Oh, for the love of Lucy," I said.

"This brings back bad memories," Pedro murmured and covered his eyes.

I trotted to the kitchen for cleaning supplies.

Max came out of the men's room and found me on the floor, mopping up after Gorge. "Say, Honeybun, I thought that man o'yours was back. Expected to see him here. Did he miss a flight? Have you heard from him?"

I looked up at him. If Buster didn't have a phone to call *me*, how did Max know when he was coming? "How'd you know he was coming today?"

"Did he come? Where is he?"

I noted his evasion and gave up. "He's at my place. He was exhausted. Said he might skip dinner. I'll take a plate home if there is anything left. The buffet line looks decimated."

"Is he okay?"

I stopped wiping and looked up again. "Well, yeah, why?"

He nodded. "Well, I'm sure you'll pamper him good."

"What are you not telling me here, Max?"

"Oh, nothin'. I just know that he went places that foreigners ought not to go over there in the Congo. That was a stupid thang to do, and I won't mind tellin' him when I lay eyes on him, not that it matters." He set his jaw.

That was all I was going to get. I finished the mopping, putting all the soiled towels in a bucket.

I thought back to how tired and haunted Buster had looked. What had happened to him? Should I have left him alone at the house?

I caught up with Lorraine as she was leaving dinner.

"Hey, dinner was superb, Haint. You outdid yourself. You need help cleaning up?"

"No, I think Yolanda and them are staying to help. You go on home. Relax. Get that foot up. Do me a favor though, would you?"

"Sure."

"Check on Buster. Max said something that made me wonder if he's really okay."

"Oh, sure. My goodness, Haint," she said, fanning herself with her hand. "You told me he was good looking, but you didn't say he was smokin' hot! Dang, girl! He's a hunk sandwich with hot sauce!"

At that moment, Pedro and Clementina were pulling on their coats and passing us. Pedro and Lorraine exchanged a glance — that kind of deep glance that warps time; eternity in a nano-second. He smiled. She blushed.

"Good night, ladies," he said. "Dinner was out of this

world. And you are the one who made that caramel cake, right? That was the *best* cake I've had in a long time." Then he winked at her and left with Clementine.

"Oh my God! Do you think he heard me?" Lorraine gushed. "How embarrassing. I bet he thought I meant him-- which would have been totally right, only I wasn't."

"He winked at you. He liked your cake. Now he thinks you think he's smokin', which we both know he is. I'm not seeing a problem."

"OoooH! I'm dying here!" Lorraine said, knees going weak.

I laughed. "I'm not used to this jelly-legs Lorraine. Who are you, and what have you done with my staunch and stoic friend? Are you a doppelganger?"

"I know. One look at him and I just lose my brains."

"Well, put your brains back in your head. I gotta get back to cleaning. Epic mess in the kitchen. See you later maybe," I said, giving her a hug. "Tomorrow we have to find you some mistletoe to ambush him under."

"In your dreams!" she said laughing.

# Chapter 18

## HOME AT LAST

"He's fine," Lorraine said, meeting me in the hallway when I got home. "He was foraging in the kitchen for sandwich fixings when I got here. He looked kind of stiff, but said it was nothing. Actually, I think he said something like 'it don't do me no never mind'. Oh, that voice is something else, Haint! I can hardly understand him sometimes, but who cares, he sounds Sam-Elliot sexy. Dang. He could read the owner's manual to my lawn mower, and I'd probably orgasm!"

I laughed. "You didn't have to stay up," I said.

Naughty Britches came wiggling her way down the hall to greet me with pitiful whines. "Shh, sweet girl. Keep it down."

"Eh," Lorraine said. "I was too wound up to sleep. My foot was buggin' me, so I was just getting some water and a pill. You must be dead on your feet."

"I am."

"Miss Thing here has been fed and let out. She had water

and cookies. She was sleeping on the bed next to Buster 'til just now."

"Perfect. Well, I'm going to dive into that bed. Goodnight."

We hugged and I made my way to the bedroom with Naughty Britches tagging along as if every step was a hardship. Buster was lying naked in a freefall position, halfway between being on his side and being on his belly, arms and legs bent, resembling a sauwastika, (reversed swastika, often still used on maps in Asia to denote Buddhist temples.) Even in the dim light, I noticed splotchy, green-purple bruises on his neck, lower back, forearms. *Dear Lord, Buster, what happened to you?* His pillow was on the floor. The covers were twisted around one leg like a still-life tornado. He was *out*.

I undressed and took a short hot shower. When I came back, Buster had moved to the edge of the bed and was in more of a fetal position, head down, fists clenched like a defensive boxer. I placed my hands over his and whispered, "You're home now. You're safe." I imagined a blanket of soft light covering his body in protection, safety, and blissful relaxation. I stroked his hands, willing them to relax, repeating, "You're safe now."

It was hard not to look at the bruises around his wrists. There was a patch on his back that looked like either a boot kick or a rifle butt. What had happened to him? I worked at freeing the bedding from around his leg. Once freed, I tucked them in around him and walked around the bed, getting in on the other side. Naughty Britches waddled in and stomped up the doggy steps to find a spot at the foot of the bed. I removed my glasses, turned out the light, and spooned against Buster's back.

"Heh-LO?" Mischief called from the doorway.

"Come on, Mischief," I whispered.

Soon Mischief was tiptoeing over Buster to claim a spot on my pillow. *Merr*, he said, whiskers tickling my face.

"Shh."

It had been a crazy long day. I heard one contented moan from Buster and one from Naughty Britches before I slipped into the dream world.

## ᏨHE ᗪREAᎷ

Five a.m., Christmas Eve morning, I woke up with a gasp. I'd been dreaming I was on one of those crazy, gladiator shows where contestants have to run through a giant obstacle course, climb massive rope nets, run over moving logs before a huge, swinging mallet coshes them, lobbing them into a moat, or throw as many balls into a hoop as possible while a moving barricade shimmies in front of the hoop deflecting potentially successful throws.

I was at my retreat, only everything was on a massive scale; it was more like a monstrous fortress with walls half a mile high. There were people rushing through the gates like in an epic battle film. They were all yelling at once and waving their arms.

"I can only eat vegan meals!"

"I hope the bed is comfortable."

"Where's my room?"

"Do you have hot cocoa?"

"I need a toothbrush!"

"There's no television in my room!"

I was acting as a goalie, wearing protective gear like a roller derby queen holding glowing directional indicators like the ground crew do at airports. As the mobs rushed me, I would point them towards a cabin, yelling out cabin numbers. "You — cabin three!" "You — ten!" They would follow my directions, darting around me, but only after bashing into me first.

"What's the Wi-fi password?"

"You're really an albino? I've never seen one before. Why don't you use a tanning bed?"

"Where's my room?"

"Is that alligator real? Here's my phone. Take a photo of me with it. How do you get it to show its teeth?"

With each question came a hit to my shoulder, a push to my chest, manic, angry eyes in my face. I kept moving my arms, gesturing right, gesturing left while trying to sidestep like a bull fighter. I was feeling bruised and overwhelmed.

"Hey, Moon Eyes," Buster said, nuzzling into my neck. "What's up?"

"Ugh. Stress dream. Guests were coming at me like angry townsfolk with torches in a monster film, stuff like, 'Where's my room!' 'I said medium rare!' 'Why is your place so far from the highway?' There were so many of them. They just kept coming."

"Shh-shhh. Ever-thing's gonna be jus' fine. Here. Settle on down an' go back ta sleep. I got yer back. If they start atcha ag'in, you jus' tell 'em ta grow up an' solve their own problems or go ta hell and show 'em the door."

"I've got to feed all those people. And I offered a meditation session in the morning. I don't have time for that! I'll barely get breakfast all finished before they come back again for lunch. I don't have time to lead a meditation!" I covered my eyes with my arms.

"Hey, hey," he said, pulling my arms away. "You need a meditation class? No sweat. I gotcha covered. What time?"

"What? *You'd* lead it?"

"Sure, Moon Eyes, I'd be happy to. I could use me some meditation myself."

"Really? After breakfast. Nine-thirty."

"Right, then. See? Problem solved." He kissed my neck and hugged me to him. His firm body cradled mine. He was really here. His breathing slowed and a moment later his foot twitched. Then his hand on my belly twitched. A faint snore started up, tentative at first, but it soon found a steady pattern, nothing jarring, just a steady, comforting sound. Buster was in my bed. It was Christmas Eve morning. Did anything else matter? I nestled against him and fell asleep feeling gratitude and love.

I awoke again a bit later with panicky thoughts of making breakfast for everyone. Naughty Britches had wedged herself between me and Buster; I had about four inches of space, my butt was hanging off the bed and the only thing keeping me from falling out was the counterweight of Buster's head on my arm. This was sweet and all, but my hand was completely sleep. It took a few moments, but I slid my arm out from under his head and oozed off the bed without disturbing either of them.

Naughty Britches groaned and wiggled, expanding herself to claim the space I'd just vacated.

Flapping my hand to regain circulation, I found my glasses on the nightstand and slipped them on, then felt around with my feet for my slippers. I always leave my bathrobe on the bed for easy access in the morning. Naughty Britches was lying on the bathrobe sash. I felt like a snake charmer coaxing the sash out from under her. She groaned again and Buster rolled over, throwing an arm over her. She wiggled her butt closer to his belly.

Rain pattered on the roof. How festive.

Next stop, the coffee pot. As I went through the ritual, the alarming images of the dream came back to my mind.

It was going to be a long day. Coffee in hand, I flipped the Word-of-the-Day calendar. December 24. **Shivoo : noun— Australian for raucous party, shindig, or blowout.**

That sure fit. At least the retreat was decorated for a 'shivoo'."

The weather was supposed to be "gelid" again, so the usual perks of the retreat like kayaking or walking in the woods were scrapped. I was grateful to Aunt Moira for encouraging me to decorate the place—it sure helped to offset the gloomy, wintery conditions.

Part of me was antsy to get to the retreat and start with breakfast, but as the coffee pot wheezed to life, I saw the image of a glass of water in my mind, accompanied by phrases from meditation lessons  like "seek clarity" and "can't see properly in murky, choppy water."

*"You've got time to sit your ass on the cushion for a few*

*minutes,"* my Inner Critic suggested. *"I think you need it."*

I started to argue but realized it was absolutely true and poured a small glass of water instead. I went back to the bedroom with my coffee and the water and sat down on the cushion in front of my altar. I lit several candles and a stick of the new rose scented incense I'd recently purchased. I sipped the coffee and stared at the glass of water.

*Calm surface, clear water, clear mind. I welcome peace and clarity,* I thought.

Unfortunately, the only place in the bedroom where my meditation altar would fit was by a door that goes to the back yard. The door has a long window that I'd rigged up with a curtain so I could have privacy or watch NB in the yard. Having this door is splendid for letting NB outside in the middle of the night but not so splendid for meditating. The window is drafty. The space is cramped. Rain was pattering gently on the roof; splats of rain hit the concrete slab outside. Funny to think that *just* on the other side of the door, inches away, was cold and miserable, while I was wrapped in my thick, ancient bathrobe, enjoying the calming smell of roses and delicious coffee excited my tastebuds and warmed my core.

*Clear water, not cloudy like coffee. Focus. Clarity. Calm. You can be like this water. Still. Pure. Clear. You can greet this day with clarity. Remember this moment. The water is so many molecules bound together. Fluid, not rigid. Fluid. Go with the flow. Seek stillness and calm. The color in the glass is the same where there is air and where there is water. Remember this moment.*

My tranquil abiding was interrupted by Mischief head-butting me in the spine. *Merr — ow? Merr? Merr-ow?*

"Shh. Come sit with me," I whispered. Every once in a while, this works. Mischief will sit with me and purr while I meditate. Truth be told, he spends far more time on the cushion than I do, though he's usually sleeping on it. This morning, he wasn't having it. He squirmed away from me with more protests as he headed toward the kitchen. His yowling complaints woke up Naughty Britches. Telltale tail thumping sounding just like someone beating on bongos.

Buster rolled over, throwing his arms around. *"Fara na na sa! Fara na na sa!"*

This alarmed Naughty Britches who must have thought he was in distress. She responded by throwing herself on his chest and licking his face—her version of mouth-to-mouth resuscitation. He thrashed and sat up, *"Fara na sa*! Bleh! Okay, what? Yeah. Oh, hey, little girl, whatcha doin'?"

I blew out the candles. Meditation was over. The room was illuminated only by the glow of nightlights in the bedroom and bathroom.

"Sorry. I was hoping not to wake you. You can go back to sleep. Once I feed her, she'll settle down again."

"It's okay, I wasn't sleepin' too good anyhow," he said, propping himself on his elbows.

"What does *fara na sa* mean?" I asked, standing up with my coffee.

"Huh? Did I say that?"

"That's what it sounded like to me."

He wiped his face and blinked. NB nuzzled his arm. "Hey, sweet girl. I'm fine." Then to me he said, "It means, "go away" in Mande, a Congo language. It's one o' the few phrases I picked up to keep trinket vendors from swarming me."

The rain on the roof was shifting from a gentle patter to a more persistent and frenzied pounding.

"Izzat rain? Damn." He squinted, focusing on my coffee cup. "Izzat coffee? I could do with some o' that. Brrr."

"You don't have to get up."

He swung his legs out of bed and sat on the edge of the bed. "Brrr!" He shuddered. "Right little girl?" he added, patting NB.

"Want a bathrobe?" I asked, then felt stupid. My spare men's bathrobe was the only garment I'd kept that had belonged to Dillon, my husband, who'd died from cancer a few years previously. I'll confess that I have a bathrobe fetish. Well, maybe fetish isn't quite right, but *thing*. A bathrobe represents leisure time to me. Being able to lounge about in a bathrobe is a luxury. A good-looking man in the right bathrobe can look sexy as hell, as Dillon had, before he got sick. In my childhood in Japan, a man in a black silk kimono assumed a manly air of authority and masculinity. But Buster wouldn't welcome another man's, a dead man's bathrobe. What was I thinking?

As often happened, Buster surprised me. "If it ain't pank and frilly, and ya think it'd fit me, sure." The way he drawled out "pink" sounded more like it'd rhyme with "spank".

I pressed my lips together and walked into the closet, flipping on the light. The robe was in the way back. I pulled it off its hook and hugged it. *"You wouldn't mind, would you, Dillon?"* I asked mentally.

*He'd want you to be happy,* answered my Inner Critic.

I emerged from the closet and presented it to Buster. "It was Dillon's. I couldn't bring myself to… I think he'd like you to, um, if this is weird —"

Buster took it from me with solemnity. "Oh wow. Ya sure this ain't weird for *you*?" He opened it out and began to put it on. "This is perfect. Soft an' warm. I sure hope he won't mind. I'll wear it with honor. Thanks." He was now sitting on the edge of the bed. He pulled me into him, wrapped his ankles around the backs of my legs and kissed me. "Mmm. Yum. Good coffee. Sorry if I got mornin' breath.'

Naughty Britches bumped her head under his arm, wedging between us. *Raaaooauuuurrr!*

"Oh really?" Buster asked.

NB licked his face.

I wished we had more time to enjoy a leisurely morning. I wanted to enjoy my coffee. I wanted to cuddle. I wanted to find out about his bruises and what happened in the Congo.

"Reckon I need ta get myself into a sha-arr," Buster said, releasing me. He kissed my forehead and headed to the bathroom.

"I'll see you over there," I said. "Turn off the coffee pot before you leave."

"Y'okay."

NB bounded down the doggie steps by the bed and clawed at the door to go outside. The day had begun indeed.

With NB leashed up and me bundled up, I opened the door to go out. Mid-stride, two things happened. Naughty Britches balked about going out and chose to back up. My right foot was heading for the doormat, but I spotted a single camellia flower in the center of the mat, shifted the direction of my foot and lost my balance. I fell against the door, dropped the leash, and caught myself before hitting the floor.

Naughty Britches, startled by my noisy fall, retreated further down the hall, leaving me to reset myself.

*Not the best way to start the day, eh?* The Inner Critic murmured.

"*Matka Boska,*\*" I grumbled, then regretted it. This was my mother's go-to Polish cuss phrase that she peppered into her daily vocabulary. When Iggy and I were in our teens, we thought cussing in foreign languages was cool. I'd really love to quit cussing, especially in English, but sometimes it just flows out. As the owner of a retreat, I really wanted to scrub up my language. It's not professional to cuss, especially when advocating tranquility. It wasn't easy.

I straightened and stared at the perfect, candy-cane flower. I had several camellia bushes around the house, but none even close to the door. Camellias are a bit peculiar in that when the flower fades, it doesn't wilt and drop petals, the whole flower falls off the stem at once. I was told that Japanese samurai did not like camellia — bad luck-- implies head chop.

But this flower was perfect. New, perky, beautiful. Not faded. How did it get to the doormat like that?

NB crept timidly toward me then stretched herself out and keeled over. "You can pet me mom, but I'm not going out."

"Come on. Up! I don't have all day to wait on your

---

\* Polish curse, "Mother of God"

Highness. We're going out."

She resisted.

I persisted.

Wrangling, coercing, and prodding her out the door for the walk, I forgot about the camellia. When we got back, it wasn't there. Had it been blown into the bushes by wind? Yes, but there wasn't much wind and how far could it have gotten? I didn't see it. Weird! I had other things to think about.

# PART SIX

## CHRISTMAS EVE

# Chapter 19

## BREAKFAST

ancake batter, check; fruit salad, check; yogurt, check; juice, check; sliced cucumbers, check; and pastries from the Art of Tarts, check. I was in the retreat kitchen crazy-early getting breakfast ready. Go, go, go. I was getting my groove on when Yolanda came in and asked if she could make horchata.

"Uh, sure, I guess. What is it?" It sounded familiar, but I didn't really know.

She looked at me with incredulity, her neck retracting, as if I'd just asked, "What is milk?"

"Horchata is a rice drink with cinnamon. I add *agave nectar*," she said with pride. She shrugged up her shoulders, face beaming with delight. It is de-li-cious." She kissed her fingers and set them free.

"Oh, sure, fine," I said.

She nodded and sashayed away with a satisfied air.

I was in my own little reverie, working on sausage and eggs

when I realized that Osanna had appeared beside Yolanda and was cutting up Florida avocados while Yolanda was opening a bag of soft tortillas. I swung my head to the counter to see what had become of the horchata. It was there in a pitcher next to the coffee and juices. A glass of white liquid had appeared next to me. I glanced at Yolanda. She smiled, "Try it. You'll be hooked."

I gave it a go. "Mmm. That's friendly." I took another sip. Oooh, I saw what she meant. It *was* good.

Osanna looked up with a bright smile, "Good morning!"

Yolanda said, "I hope it's okay, her twins will only eat burritos for breakfast. My Eliazar is the same way, and I have so much food from the restaurant—" She turned her head as Paco walked in carrying a huge cardboard box.

"Here," she pointed to a space in the corner of the kitchen.

"Good morning," he said, coming around the buffet counter into the kitchen. He looked into the box as he spoke, "I'm so glad this won't go to waste. Look at these tomatoes."

He set the box down on the island in the middle of the kitchen. The box was full of peppers, tomatoes, fresh cilantro, and cucumbers.

"Where is the cheese?" Osanna asked.

Paco nodded. "It's coming. The eggs and cheese are in the next box."

Buster and Lorraine arrived together while I was setting a pan of hash browns in the buffet.

"Hey guys," I said.

"Good morning," Lorraine said.

Buster gave me a hug and brushed my forehead with a kiss. "How's it goin'?"

"Great," I said, tucking a stray strand of hair behind my ear.

He looked to the kitchen, taking in the mob and the mariachi music. "Are all them people workin' for you?"

"Yeah-uh, not exactly."

His eyebrow rose.

I leaned closer and whispered, "They sort of pitched in and took over."

"Oh?"

"Yeah. It kind of just happened. I know, I know. Should I have allowed them in my kitchen? Technically not. But they ran a restaurant; they were savvy about kitchen cleanliness—"

I shrugged. "It's the holidays."

"Rr-iight," he said, giving me the hope-you-know-what-you-re doing eye.

"Oh. I almost forgot to put the yogurts out," I said, retreating to the kitchen.

I was glad he didn't challenge me further. I knew I was skating on the bumpy edge of the pond. Before breakfast was over, all of the Garcia family women had been in the kitchen except for Grandma Yaya.

So many people, so much food! Osanna and Yolanda were amazing helpers, helping to keep tabs on the food levels—did we need more eggs? Were we low on juice? Time to refill the pancake batter pitcher for the electric pancake maker.

And the conversations! I only caught snippets, but what snippets! There was Kate's steady litany of cat illnesses and treatment methods both successful and unsuccessful as she and Ceci ate breakfast. We all overheard her conversation with poor Mrs. Cabazier, the cat-sitter.

"Oh, I'm so sorry Boo-boo scratched you. Did you wrap him in a towel? If you pull it real tight, he can't move. You can jam the pill in his mouth—"

Whoever was in earshot got to practice eyeball yoga having to suffer Benny's jokes: "What do you call a smart blonde? A golden retriever!"

"Why'd the blonde nurse carry around a red pen? In case she needed to draw blood!"

I recited a mantra in my head, "Gone in one more day, one more day, just one more day."

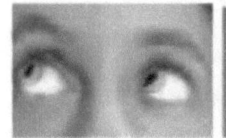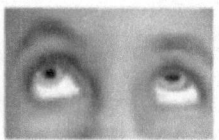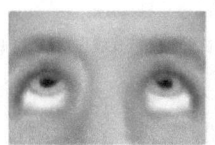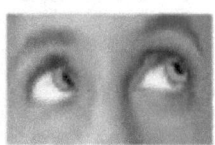

**Dear Lord, Please grant me strength and patience...**

Max snarled, "Benny why don't ya ever tell a *good* joke? Say, I got a great blonde joke for Christmas." He looked to me and said, "Honey, you won't take no offense, I hope."

"Can't be any worse than Benny's jokes," I muttered. "Go on."

Max leaned forward; his eyes gleamed. "Okay. It's holiday time, and, as usual, the mailman is doing his usual rounds. He gets to the door of the Miller house and he's just about to put the mail in the box when the door opens. Mrs. Miller, this attractive blonde is standing there in a negligee, face all made up pretty, hair all perfect—she invites him in, takes his hand and guides him to the bedroom. She undresses him and they proceed to have sex. Now she's amazing, he's, ah, quite satisfied, but she seems to be on a schedule. She hurries him along to get dressed. Next, she takes him by the hand and leads him to the kitchen, where she sits him down, gives him coffee, juice, and cooks him up a plate of eggs and sausage. He is kinda hungry, so he's more than happy to have breakfast. As soon as he sets down his fork, she says, "Okay then" and leads him to the door. 'Here you go,' she says, and hands him a dollar bill. She pushes him outside and closes the door behind him. Well, as you might imagine, the mailman is real puzzled. He starts to walk down the driveway but then he turns around and knocks on the door.

"Yes?" the blonde asks, surprised.

"Uh, I just have to ask. What just happened? Not that I'm complaining or anything, not at all, it was great, but you know, I've been doing this mail route for months. What was all that about?" He twirled his finger indicating the interior of the house.

"Oh!" she says. "Well, last night, my husband and I were talking about Christmas giving. We like to do nice things for people around the holidays, you know, charities and stuff and people who do nice things for us. I asked him, 'what about the mailman?' My husband said, 'Screw him! Give him a dollar'...breakfast was my idea!"

This got some genuine chuckles around the table.

"Now *that's* a funny joke," Max said with pride.

"That's cute!" I said.

Instead of taking the hint that his jokes were terrible, Benny took Max's joke as a challenge to tell more. He began, "You know why the blonde was putting lipstick on her forehead?"

"Benny —" Cam said, touching his arm.

"She was trying to make up her mind! Ah-ha-ha! Now that's funny!"

Max shook his head, looking dangerously close to telling Benny exactly what he thought of him. Buster interrupted the pending outburst. "Hey Max, I been puzzlin' over this muddle for some time. I hate to pull you away but, I'd sure like to pick your noggin. Got a moment for a chinwag?"

Max about leapt of his seat as ever-blustering Benny bellowed, "What d'ya call a bunch of blondes in the freezer? Frosted flakes! Get it? Frosted FLAKES!"

A small part of me couldn't help wishing he'd choke to death on his breakfast, but the image of EMTs arriving and Sheriff Dave serving me with lawsuit papers  helped me dismiss the wicked wish.

*You don't really want another death here, do you?* my Inner Critic asked.

Images from the double homicide back in September came to mind. No, I absolutely did not want a death. I took a deep breath and tried to muster positive thoughts about Benny but the only one that came to mind was that he'd be leaving the following day. I could muster compassion for Cameron. She must see something in him that I couldn't.

May approached me, bouncing Vonnie. "Haint, I just wanted to comment on the amazing job you've done with this place. I remember when I was little, and Grandma brought us out here to see Great Uncle Max and Great Aunt Charlene. I remember everything was painted gray...the cabins smelled funky, and the ice machine leaked and made all kinds of horrible noises. I was afraid of it! It's all so happy now, especially with the decorations. Baby Vonnie loves the candles and lights in our cabin. Those papier-mâché carolers on the porch look so lifelike! Twice I've almost said, 'Oh, excuse me!' thinking I was in their way. They're amazing. I've never seen anything quite like them."

"I haven't either, to tell you the truth. Your Great Aunt Roberta had quite the Christmas collection. You know, Nellavon and Max gave me all that stuff, but if you want it—"

"Oh, no!" she said, looking a bit horrified. "Actually, they look *too* lifelike. They're almost creepy." She looked down at her boy. "Right Baby Vonnie? They scared you, didn't they?"

*You're not the only one*, my Inner Critic mumbled.

I happened to pass by the Garcia table and caught a little scene where Pedro looked mighty uncomfortable, face flushed, waving a fork defensively as Clementina, Osanna, and Rita grilled him.

"Did your ghost girlfriend visit last night?"

"No."

"What cabin did you have last time?"

"I don't know. Six, I think. The one by the picnic pavilion."

"Was she pretty?"

"Look, I don't want to talk about it."

"Why didn't she come find you last night?"

"Are you kidding? After that cranberry punch, nothing could have woken me up."

"Were you going to say you slept...like the dead?" Clementina laughed, pawing his shoulder. The other two ladies cackled.

Osanna cooed, "Oh, she wants you alone, Pedro. She didn't want to find you with your family."

"That's just fine with me."

"Oh, poor Pedro, maybe she's got a new boyfriend."

"Look, could I just have breakfast? I'm hardly awake. Go away."

The Joliecoeurs, Warclouds and Hloupyklauns were sitting at the same table sharing an in-depth discussion about alpacas and llamas.

"Did you know that alpacas don't have front teeth?"

"Ever?"

"Nope."

Angejolie said, "I lost my front teeth. They were *baby* teeth. Now I've got big teeth." She showed them off. "When is Mehbelle going to have the baby?"

"Real soon. We checked on her a little while ago. Dad says

she is lying down, getting ready. He's going to go back over again after breakfast."

"Can we see it?"

"Dad? How long after do we have to wait to show everybody the baby?"

Chaz patted Rain's shoulder. "Let's see how it goes. Hopefully, it'll be an easy delivery. We can go check on her after breakfast."

Mr. Hloupyklaun asked, "May we tag along? If it's not far, I'd love to see them before we hit the road."

Then there was the Nifty Thrifter conversation about weird things that happened in their shop.

"We found dentures in a man's jacket—" Kate said.

"You remember that time we got a lamp with someone's ashes in it?" Ceci said, looking horrified. "It was this gaudy old 70s monstrosity. Some kid bumped into it, it went crashing to the floor and whoosh—shards of ceramic and Great Aunt Susie or whoever went flying. We never did find out who it was. What could we do? We said a prayer and vacuumed."

Ceci said, "Then there was the time we got a model airplane made of popsicle sticks that had a weed stash stuffed inside!"

"Someone donated a kitty litter box with the dirty kitty litter in it."

There was a sudden disruption at one of the Garcia tables. Chairs scraped the floor, moving in haste, and a collective "oooh", the kind of "oooh" that one hears in a second-grade classroom when a child says a cussword. This was followed by a hush, then a murmur in Spanish.

"It wasn't me; it was him," the seated twin said, pointing to the twin who was sneaking around behind people's chairs.

Osanna hissed at him in Spanish, something about sit yourself down or suffer the consequences.

"Oro! Listen to your mother!" Rocky snarled.

"Oro, come here to Aletea," purred Aletea.

There was a collective intake of breath as Oro hesitated. Aletea's voice was gentle and sweet as a pure mountain stream, but there was something predatory in her eyes.

"Can't help you now, Bro," Pedro said, getting up from the table and retreating to the buffet line.

"Oro, my angel, precious grandchild, come here, I want to tell you something," Aletea purred.

Oscar leaned over in his chair and hid his face in his father's arms.

Aletea shot out a hand snatching Oro by the ear, forcing him to come close so she could whisper to him. The rest of the family murmured sympathetic phrases like, "Uh-oh" and "Ohhh" "Oh, Oro."

Oro yelled and grimaced as Aletea talked rapidly in his ear. Huge tears formed in his large eyes. His lower lip quivered.

Osanna covered her mouth and looked away.

Aletea released Oro's ear and kissed his cheek before turning him around and pushing him back to his chair. He covered his eyes with his hands and moved blind as family members patted his back, propelling him towards his seat.

I happened to pass Pedro as I was heading toward the kitchen. He looked pale and shaken.

"Are you okay?"

"Yeah, sure," he said, touching his ears. "Flashbacks to my childhood."

"I'll bet. She's pretty intimidating."

"You've no idea."

I had hoped to get a little down time, just fifteen minutes to have breakfast with Buster. But I'd just sat down across from him when he got a phone call.

"Oh, hey, Boris, Mur-ray Christmas. You got what? Oh, say, that's great." He mouthed "sorry" to me as he stood up. "Well, I reckon ya could, but if I was you, I'd tie a neutral squirmy on top, an' a mop fly on bottom...yep, yep, sure, a spider could work just as well, or, hey-hey, a Buster Popper on top, an' a Glam Mop on bottom—yep! That's a popper hopper mop dropper—now that's just fun ta say, ain't it?"

He mouthed "be right back," patted my back and headed for the door, saying, "Idaho? Ooh, not sure when I'll get out thattaway..."

Well, there went breakfast together. Buster had been sitting with Max, Max Jr., and Olivia. I learned that Olivia had a homemade olive-oil soap business.

"We finally get a weekend to ourselves for once! I've been gone every weekend for months—farmer's markets, craft festivals, street fairs. Then during the week, I'm busy making more soap."

"She's really got a gift," Max Junior said proudly. "Her business has really taken off this year."

"We're taking January off," she said, patting his thigh.

Junior grinned, "And soon I'll be off every month. I'm selling the RV business and retiring. We close on January the fourteenth. We're thinking of taking a little tour of America."

"Ain't that somethin' else?" Max said. "Me and Charlene did that once. Had a ball. Do it while ya can, I say."

My heart hurt for Max. I know he missed Charlene.

The LARPers dragged in towards the end of breakfast and became more animated once they downed some caffeine and ate some protein. The snippet of conversation I overheard was regarding a big dinner party event with a Latin name, something like *monstrum convivium*.

"It's going to be *so* dope!"

"I can't wait."

"Remember last year?"

"It's going to be way better than last year."

Wendy came back through the buffet line while I was putting out more juice.

"Big party tonight?" I asked.

"Well, we check in tonight and there's a small party, but then tomorrow, it's just *cra-zy*, stuff all day. We have a couple performances during the day, and then later it's The Lusus Naturae! The Festival of Freaks!"

"But it's *Christmas*. Don't most folks have family obligations and stuff?"

"Not for the hardcore! There's a church service in the morning — we perform for that-- and the daytime stuff is family friendly! The kids dress up too! Then there's the Lusus Naturae where the Zombie hunters chase the zombies through the hotel. It's so fun!"

This made me feel old. There was a time back in my youth when running around a hotel in costumes would have been appealing. Were my costume party days over? Where had my sense of frivolity gone?

## Chocolate Kisses

Cleanup after breakfast would have been a nightmare, but Yolanda, Rita and Osanna, my kitchen angels, helped wipe tables down and dry serving dishes. I was tremendously grateful.

The Hloupyklauns checked out after breakfast, thanking me for a lovely time. They promised to come back if the opportunity presented itself. They drove out following the Warclouds and Joliecoeurs field tripping to Hollis's house to see the alpacas.

I would have loved to sit in on Buster's meditation class, but it was already underway when I was finally free. I didn't want to interrupt. I figured I'd change out cabin two while I had time. Taking a quick trip to the laundry room for clean towels, fresh sundries, and the laundry bag, I headed towards the river. The retreat was quiet as everyone was indoors, the sky and water were desolation gray, the ground was wet enough from recent rain that my footsteps made little noise. A hint of woodsmoke in the air suggested one of my neighbors had a cozy fire going in their fireplace. And it was while sniffing the air that my gaze happened to catch movement across the river. A brown fluffy blur jumped over cypress knees and disappeared deeper into the woods. Fat bunny? No. Pointy ears. Fat paws. Bobcat.

It had been ages since I'd seen a bobcat. How exciting. What a glorious animal. I replayed the moment in my head as I punched the key code and let myself in.

Holy Charlie and the Chocolate Factory! I walked closer to the bed. The beautiful quilt was mostly on the floor, which was a good thing. It seemed to have missed out on the main event that had happened in the sheets. I stared at the mess and tried to imagine the sequence of events that had led to this result: one side of the bed looked like toddlers had gone to town on it playing fingerpaints with chocolate. And at least it *was* chocolate and not something far worse.

I usually left out a bowl of chocolate for guests. In the holiday spirit, I'd left a bowl of chocolate mini-bites wrapped in shiny red, green, and silver foil. The bowl, now empty, was where I'd left it on a set of drawers. Bits of tightly rolled foil were scattered about the bed, the nightstand, and the windowsill nearby like snow in a tornadic snow globe. There was a clean patch at the center, presumably where the perpetrator had sat or lain. Maybe one of them had fallen asleep and the other had stayed up reading and gorging on chocolates, with a nervous habit of twisting the wrappers? Or — maybe the

Sillyclowns had been Friskyclowns? Had that cute old couple kanoodled in chocolate? I looked at the scene again and couldn't unsee the image in my mind.

This was the cabin decorated with a snowman theme. I swear some of the snowmen and snowwomen had stunned expressions and open mouths as if they too were recovering from what they'd witnessed.

Well, *that* was a new one. Hey, power to them, I just wished they hadn't done a number on my sheets and blankets. I forcibly removed images of them in coitus while trying to remember tricks for getting chocolate out of fabric. I pulled the bedding off the bed, swept the wrappers, changed out the towels, set the sundries up on the bathroom counter and went about the turnover process. I hesitated about refilling the candy dish.

Leaving the cabin with the laundry, I was almost to the parking lot when Ceci and Kate appeared heading in the opposite direction.

"That was *amazing!* I don't think I've ever been able to shut my brain off like that."

I hid behind the bathroom pavilion, eavesdropping.

"I know! Who'd have thought with that country-boy accent that he'd be a meditation guru. He sounds like a rodeo announcer!"

"Oh, and he's so easy on the eyes! I sure wouldn't mind some private meditations from him, if you get what I mean."

As they giggled their way towards cabin three, I swallowed a big lump of proprietary possessiveness and forced my legs to move. *He'd done a good job with the session then. Good.* It would take some time to get the chocolate stains out. I'd deal with it later. I dropped the bundle off in the laundry room and went around to the meditation hall. I wasn't checking up on Buster exactly, but I was curious to know how many people had been in the session and how he thought it had gone. I wanted to thank him.

Okay, yes, after Ceci and Kate, I had images in my head of women flocked around him like groupies on a rock star. I was pleasantly surprised to round the corner of the office and run into Gigi and Aunt Moira.

"Oh, Haint!" Aunt Moira said, jangling her bracelets. "Sorry you missed it! Your man led the most amazing meditation. He is *good*! That was *wonderful*! It's too early in the day, but I could go for a long nap after that. I went *deep*."

"He *was* good," Gigi agreed, nodded.

"Oh? Oh, good," I said, squelching a pang of jealousy. The way they were oohing and ahhing, you'd think they'd come from an orgy.

"That man is something *else*," Aunt Moira added.

Yes, he was. It would be something else if I got to spend any time with him.

They toddled off to their trailer as I passed Arnie. Amy and Stuey were strolling back to cabin seven, holding hands.

"That was interesting," Stuey said. "I feel better."

"Me too," she said.

I was just about to the door when Buster, Lorraine and Pedro came out together.

"Thanks, man, that was great." Pedro said. "I needed that."

"Glad to hear it," Buster said nodding.

Pedro shot a pained look at Lorraine and rolled his eyes. "I gotta—" he gestured to the Garcia cabins.

"Yeah," she said with a sigh as Freddie Jay and Clover came running from the dock. "Aunt Lorraine! Aunt Lorraine!"

"See you later," Pedro said.

"Bye," Lorraine said.

Lorraine watched Pedro walk away as the children slowed in front of us huffing and puffing. "Grandma was looking for you. Come on!"

"Bye," Lorraine said to us as she was pulled away.

"Hey," I said, hugging Buster. "The camp is abuzz at how amazing you are. Sorry I missed it. How'd it go?"

"That's a right nice space ya got there. I used yer CD player –the water music—an' we did some centerin' an' clearin' –then we did some chakra balancin', some relaxation an' ended with a focus on generatin' love."

"Seems like you got a good crowd."

"Nice group. How're you?"

"Jangled." I told him about the chocolate mess.

He raised an eyebrow.

I shivered and sighed, "I've got to get back and take NB for a walk. She hates when I'm gone."

"Me too," he said kissing me. "I'll meetcha over there. We can walk together. It'll be nice."

"The weather's terrible!"

"Aw, Moon Eyes, that's why hot cocoa was invented."

# Chapter 20

## Mystery Gift

Buster got to my house before me as I'd gotten held up by a text asking for a vacancy. Approaching the front door, I noticed something dangling from the door handle. What in the world? It was a necklace beaded with tiny whitish shells and flat, metal medallions. No note. The medallions were not quite round, nor completely smooth. There were edge marks suggesting they had been hammered flat by a hammer, not a machine. It looked old and fragile. Had Buster left it here for me to find? Why here on the door handle? Perhaps it was Lorraine's...but if so, I'd never seen it before, and why the heck would it be on a door handle like that? Why not leave it inside, say, on the coffee table? Buster would have seen it and taken it in, wouldn't he?

I was going to go on the assumption that it was a playful gift from Buster. Wanting him to know that I'd found it, I tied it around my neck. The metal rounds were cool on my breastbone. I felt a wave of rightness and wellbeing--the same sort of feeling when you put on clean jeans that fit just right, but even better--a spiritual sort of rightness.

On the other side of the door, Naughty Britches was beside herself at being left for so long.

"I'm here! I'm coming!" I said, opening the door.

She barked and circled, wiggled, and bucked out her protests. I got down on my knees to hug her.

"I'm sorry I was gone so long. Did Buster let you out? Where is he? We'll go for a walk, hmm?"

She bounced and barked.

I stood up and called out, "Buster?"

"Back here," his voice called from the bedroom.

With NB at my heels, I walked to the bedroom. Buster was pacing the floor, talking on his phone.

"The slogan's 'It's a *Drift* Queen 'cause ya cain't catch a fish with Drag'. Didja git them pitchers I sentcha?" He nodded to me and kept pacing.

"We're going for a walk," I said.

He winked at me.

I hooked the necklace with my thumb and held it out. "I love it! Thanks!"

A wave of confusion passed across his eyes, "Yeah, it's got silver flashin' and danglies to mimic mosquito killer legs. Drives the fish crazy."

"Let's go kiddo," I said, leashing NB. Once at the door, her momentum dragged as she looked out the window to see the rain. "I know. Let's do it." She looked up at me with the most pitiful eyes, as if I was asking her to walk through acid rain puddles.

"I'll take you back with me, I promise. You can meet the guests after dinner, Hmm? Would you like that? But you have to go potty first."

It was a short endeavor. The rain was enthusiastic. Buster met us in the living room when we got back. "Seems like if it rains much more, the animals are gonna team up in twos."

"Yeah. I'm soaked," I said, peeling off my raincoat.

"Sorry 'bout that," he said, thumbing toward the phone. "I got a new fly comin' out called the Drift Queen. A friend was askin' about it. Wants to sell it in his shop. So, where'd the necklace you got there come from?"

I froze. "It wasn't from you?"

"No," he said, looking at me like I was overdue for a psychological evaluation.

"I found it on the front door handle when I came in. I thought maybe you put it there for me to find."

"The *door handle*? Weren't nothin' there when I came in."

I studied his face to see if he was teasing me. Couldn't tell. "You aren't messing with me, are you?"

Moon Eyes, if I was goin' to give you somethin', I sure wouldn't just leave it on no door handle. It weren't in a gift bag or nothin'? Just like that? Lemme see."

I unhooked NB's leash and moved closer to show him. He fingered the beads. "Looks old. Shells of some kind. You know 'at reminds me of somethin' – cain't think what—oh, I know. Reminds me of the purty costumes the women wear at a Powwow. They got these billowy lookin' tops with them coin-lookin' things. In fact, seems like I was told they was old coins hammered flat. You got a secret admirer or somethin' I should know about, mebbee?" he asked with a sideways smile.

"No," I said frowning. "That's weird." If it wasn't from Buster, I had no idea. "I'll ask Lorraine, but I don't think it's hers."

"She didn't come back after breakfast. I think her family was off doin' somethin'. Aw, what's the matter? You look disappointed. I do got somethin' for ya. It's just a little ol' stockin' stuffer. You want it now?"

Tempting, but no. I didn't need a consolation prize. "No—I can wait until Christmas."

He winked at me. "You sure, Moon Eyes?"

"I'm sure. You here is gift enough for me."

He cradled my face with both hands and kissed me, tenderly at first, soon building in intensity. With remorse and reluctance, I pulled back. "Please don't be mad, I'd love to stay and savor this moment, but I've got a camp full of guests to feed here shortly. I gotta feed this little girl and get back over there."

"Later maybe, eh?"

I kissed him back. "Definitely."

"It sure is good to hold you again, Haint," he said touching his nose to mine.

"Oh, Buster," I said, voice cracking with emotion, "I almost can't believe you came. If it weren't for those postcards that I couldn't read, I'd have thought you were ghosting me."

"What? Never, honey. I ain't like that. I might get too riled up to talk. I might walk away to go git me a think on, but I'd never ghost you, you kiddin'? You're about the best thing 'at's ever happened to me. " He kissed my forehead.

I felt it in my toes.

He sure made it hard to get back to the retreat.

## Got Rain and Showers, Too

I'd been texting back and forth with two ladies I'd assigned to cabin two. I had warned the navigator about the annoying detour due to a culvert collapse. Based on the questions and the frequency, I got the impression that the navigator was from the city. Directions like "Turn left after the Bubba's Backhoe sign" got a response of: "What street?" It was unfortunate that the detour routed my guests past a sign for Jethro's Meat Processing and Taxidermy that was written in blood red and looked like a Halloween prop. It wasn't a prop. I did NOT give directions based on this particular landmark. After texting her the key code for cabin two and saying I'd be in the dining hall kitchen, there was a reply of "K" and nothing after that.

Focused as I was on cutting up potatoes into bite size chunks, I hadn't heard the door.

"Are you the owner?" a voice behind me said.

I spun around to find a woman in her twenties with an ornate hairstyle, braided extensions pretzeled around her head. Expensive looking gold earrings with tiny diamonds in them sparkled, contrasting with her gorgeous, dark skin. She wore a deep red shade of lipstick that made her perfect white teeth look luminous.

"Yes, can I help you?"

"I texted you. We're in cabin two."

I looked around for the other person in her party.

"Ms. Showers is already in the room," the woman said. "She's resting. I just came to check in. I'm Essie Jane, Ms. Shower's personal assistant."

"Haint Blue," I said. "Let me just wash up a sec." I began washing my hands. "Did you get into the room okay?". It seemed like a stupid question once I'd said it. She would have texted if there was a problem, but the locks were fairly new; I wanted to be sure.

"Oh yeah, no problem. She loves the cabin. She's a very private person. She didn't want to be in a motel. "

"I don't mean to pry," I said, drying my hands, "but what does Ms. Showers do?

"You don't know? I guess I've been in the art bubble too long. Ms. Taquira Showers is an opera singer — a contralto. She was Erda in Wagner's Ring cycle at the Metropolitan Opera last year. She's performing in Sarasota tomorrow night –good thing she wanted to visit a relative and get there a day early, I guess."

"Oh! What's the opera?" I asked, expecting her to answer, *La Boheme*.

"Hindemuth's *The Long Christmas Dinner*."

"Oh? I don't know that one." I pulled off my apron. "If you want to follow me, we can pop over to the office, and I can get you the retreat map and a map of the area."

"Sure," she said, following me to the door. "It's sort of

modern. Do you like opera?"

"Some. I like Puccini." I said, scrunching my shoulders. "This weather---brrr!" We walked quickly. "I've seen some wild modern ones that left me cold." I held the door for her. "I'm old-fashioned. I like scenery and a melody line, not abstract stuff. I saw *Of Mice and Men* sung in English. Not my cup of tea, I'm afraid. Too discordant. "

She raised her eyebrows and pursed her lips suggesting that I wouldn't appreciate this one.

I got around my desk and collected the maps and retreat brochure. "Dinner will be from six to seven-thirty."

Essie Jane took pamphlets. "She might want to eat separately. She wasn't feeling well earlier. Would it be possible for me to bring her a tray at dinner?"

"Sure, not a problem."

"I'll let you know. I can never tell. She changes her mind a lot."

"Please let me know if you need anything."

"Oh, not to worry," Essie Jane said with a hint of a smile, rolling her eyes toward the door. "You'll hear from me." She was wrestling with the door handle when she paused and turned back. "Oh, and please don't tell anyone who she is. She's very private."

"Gotcha," I said.

She nodded again and left.

For a moment I was a bit offended that she'd thought I would run around and tell my guests, "Guess who's here? The famous opera singer, Taquira Showers!" But the offense faded with the next thought that bubbled up: the thought to call up Iggy and tell him exactly that.

## Fun and Games

Naughty Britches was delighted to get loaded into my truck and beside herself when we arrived at the retreat to find Saint Eleanor herding a passel of Watts and Garcia children towards the meditation hall. They were all wearing colorful, puffy, winter jackets and jumping over and around puddles, reminding me of Easter marshmallow chicks.

When one of them spotted me helping NB down, she exclaimed, "Oh, a puppy dog!" This disrupted the procession. Not all, but most broke away to come pet Naughty Britches.

"Let's get out of the rain," I said, urging everyone to the porch. Naughty Britches didn't care, she was going to get her fair share of attention there on the spot. She wagged and rolled over, throwing her feet in the air. Her lips fell back, showing her canines.

"Look, it's smiling!" Dee exclaimed.

"What's his name?" Clover asked.

"It's a girl dog," Gorge said, pointing.

"What kind of dog is it?" Mimi asked.

"A basset hound," I said.

"It's a wiener dog!" Freddie Jay cried out.

"No, those are Dachshunds," I said. "Her name is Naughty Britches."

Gorge covered his mouth and giggled. He whispered to

Eliazar.

Eliazar popped him on the head. "No, stupid, "*britches*", not bitches!"

"Oh, mercy!" Saint Eleanor exclaimed.

Gorge looked confused. The other children laughed.

"What's britches mean?" Gorge asked, looking hurt.

"It's an old-fashioned word for pants," I explained.

"Oh! He said a bad word!" Clover said, looking shocked.

"Yes, but he didn't know," I said. "Her name is Naughty Britches," I repeated, emphasizing the 'r'.

"Is she bad?" Gorge asked. "Does she bite?"

"Let's go, children," Saint Eleanor advised. "I don't want you catching colds out here in the wet."

Lorraine and Lerlene came out of the meditation hall. "Oh, there you are," said Lerlene, looking relieved. "We wondered what was keeping you."

Lorraine said, "Hope it's okay, since the kids are restless and the weather is so dreary, Eleanor thought they could play some games in the meditation hall. She's got some ball-toss thing set up. We invited the Garcia kids too."

"That's a great idea, so long as they don't get too rambunctious. Shoes off. No tearing up my floor."

"Shoes off, absolutely."

"Come on, kids!" Lerlene called.

Lerlene and Saint Eleanor directed the children inside. Without the audience, Naughty Britches rolled to her feet and shook herself.

A utility truck pulled in and drove towards the dining hall.

The driver waved as he passed.

"Who's that?" Lorraine asked.

"That's Paco and Yolanda," I said shaking my head. "I wonder what they are making for lunch?"

"You don't know?"

Where to begin? "No."

"Aren't they catering?"

"Not exactly. It's complicated."

"What's going on over there?" Lorraine asked, looking towards the second parking lot. Kandi and Lloyd were pacing in a heated argument. Kandi gesticulated with a cigarette. They were joined by Wendy who threw up her hands in the universal "I give up" signal.

"Let's go see," I said, tugging Naughty Britches.

We rounded the corner at the end of the meditation hall, to find the LARPers milling around their van. The hood was up, and Linwood, Kirby, and Ray, were peering around the engine.

"Well, this is just fan-freakytastic!" Kandi said, taking a deep drag on her cigarette.

"It might be the starter."

"No, it didn't sound like it. I think it's the alternator."

"Crap! No one's going to be open today! We'll be stuck here!" Cindy whined.

Chaz Warcloud wandered out of the men's room not far away. Seeing the vehicle in distress, he wandered over. "Can I help?"

Linwood, Kirby and Ray gave him a rundown of what they'd diagnosed so far.

Yolanda came out of the dining hall heading to Paco's truck. She saw the crowd and came over, "Dead battery? I've got jumpers."

"No, it's not the battery," Linwood said.

"We think it's the alternator," Kirby said.

"Alternator, eh?" Yolanda said, holding out a finger for us to wait while she pulled out her cell phone.

I was torn. I wanted to see that they weren't left in the lurch with their vehicle, but there wasn't much I could do. I wanted to get back to the kitchen. I had to get Naughty Britches back to the office. I put a hand to my throat, deciding what to do, when I thought of the necklace. I didn't feel it. Bare skin. "What? Where is it?"

"What—did you lose something?" Lorraine asked.

"Well yeah," I said, feeling around my neck and inside my shirt around my waist. "I wanted to ask you about this necklace I found, only it's gone. How is that possible? It was kind of bulky and made noise. How could I have not noticed—no, it's gone."

"Necklace?" Lorraine parroted.

"I found it this morning after breakfast—it was draped over the doorknob at the house. I thought it was from Buster, but he'd never seen it before, so I thought maybe it was yours."

"I don't wear jewelry much, you know that. What did it look like?"

"It was made of beads and tiny shells, and had these round, metal pendants at the bottom." I felt around my waistline once more in vain, just in case the clasp had let go and it had slid down. Nope. Nothing. "It looked antiquey."

"Not mine," Lorraine said, looking at me skeptically. "Sorry, can't help you."

"Maybe it slid off when I was getting NB out of the truck," I said. I've got to get her to the office anyway. I'll go look.

"I'll check in on the kids," Lorraine said.

We headed back. She went into the meditation hall. I went back to my truck. Seat, floorboards, down in the crevasse by the console. No necklace.

"Well, that's a mystery," I said to NB. "Let's get you squared away, eh, little girl?"

Some twenty minutes later, I checked on the van situation. Dante and Paco were crawling back out from under the van, Chaz, Kirby, Linwood, and Ray were shaking their heads, leaning against the hood. The women were milling around trying to stay warm.

"But even if we call roadside assistance, they'll just tow it. We won't get it fixed today or tomorrow," Cindy said, huddling in her jacket.

It'll be a couple days before you could get a new alternator," Chaz said.

"I've got an idea," I said. "I think Skeeter is a roadside assistance guy. He has a repair shop in Catfish. It's a long shot, but I can try…" I pulled out my phone and called Urliss.

"Hey Haint. We ain't late, are we?" Urliss asked, sounding

worried.

"No, no, " I assured him. "Listen. There's a group of folks here with a van that blew an alternator. You think we could get Skeeter to open his shop?"

Dante held up his hands, "I can fix, maybe. Need my tools."

"Oh, wait, Dante thinks he can fix it."

Dante and Paco were talking rapidly in Spanish.

No surprise that the Lame Brains stayed for lunch.

Long afternoon short, the next update that I got on the van repair was that Dante and Paco had removed and disassembled the alternator. Rain had gotten a bit overwhelmed by the games in the meditation hall. He was listening to his father explain the fundamentals of auto mechanics. Urliss had called Skeeter; they both came over to see if they could help. Urliss brought beer. A portable radio was blaring. The second parking lot became a mechanic's club meeting as the alternator was repaired by group effort as the fix-it guys were drawn together like tool hoarders to a swap meet.

Kate and Ceci had gotten chatty with the cranky female Lame Brains during lunch and lured them over to their cabin to hang out afterwards. Ceci advised them that the weather report was for heavy rain and plummeting temperatures. The Thrifters and Lame Brains got on like a, God forbid, cabin on fire, and soon Wendy, Cindy and Kandi were less anxious to get on the road in the inclement weather and more inclined to join in on the gift swap and impromptu talent show they were also cooking up.

It was close to four o'clock when Cindy found me and

asked, "They're still working on the van. I should have asked sooner, but could we stay another night? Paco seems sure he'll get it fixed but I dunno, it's getting dark already and it's supposed to pour."

I had turned the cabin after lunch but hadn't had any guests clamoring for a group cabin. "No problem. You are in luck."

# Chapter 21

## A Feel-good Party Game

Have you ever had to attend an event with an awkward "ice-breaker" party game that failed? A baby shower where you thought to wear a pastel-colored dress, then had to play a guess-the-taste-of-the-baby-food game and ended up dropping the flimsy paper plate in your lap? Ended up wearing baby food for the rest of the party? Or how about a gender reveal where the mom-to-be wanted to be genuinely surprised though she knew it would be a little girl because she always wanted a little girl, she was sure it was a girl. Then a *blue* smoke bomb released from a barn loft causing the air to get thick with cringy discomfort as the mom-to-be's face fell in stages like Bette Davis cracking up in *What Ever Happened to Baby Jane?*

Generally, I'm not a big fan of these forced, contrived events, so I was not enthusiastic about this white elephant gift exchange. I attended a bridal shower with a gift swap game where stealing presents was allowed. The point of the game was for the bridesmaids to get to know one another. It had gotten ugly quickly, ending in a giant cat fight as two ladies screamed profanity, and pulled each other's freshly-styled hair while wrestling over a package of hair products. A few cans of hairspray repaired their coiffures, but they eyed each other with contempt throughout the wedding ceremony. When the bride threw the bouquet and the two collided while trying to catch it, another fight broke out. The bouquet was thrashed to tatters. One of the women got a black eye; her assailant broke her pinky finger. The wedding photos were something else! Ah, precious memories…all over forty-dollars' worth of cream rinse and conditioner.

I prayed that this proposed gift exchange would be an entertaining event that did not require emergency services.

Whether it was the crappy weather or the holiday spirit, I'll never know, but to my amazement, the wrapped presents just kept coming. Now, mind, some weren't wrapped in pretty paper with bows, some were in paper bags and looked like retro school lunches or were in plastic shopping bags. But we had so many we needed to set up another table.

We had sixty-six participants and a whopping one-hundred and forty-three gifts, so each person would receive two and we'd figure out what to do with the leftovers later. When this game is played on a smaller scale, each person gets a numbered piece of paper and upon his/her turn, picks a gift. We needed to speed up the process or we'd be at it all night.

"How should we handle it?" I asked.

"In the first round, everyone gets one gift," Ceci said. "Once they're all opened, if you want to keep your gift, you're done. You get to keep it. But once you decide to keep it, you can't change your mind. If you don't want to keep it, you go into the swap group. In the swap group, you can swap up to three times. Once you get something you want, you stop. No stealing. We don't want fights. If someone gets stuck with something they really don't want, they can exchange it for a mystery gift, one from the extra gift pile. But if they do that, they are done. No further exchanges. Then we do the next round the same way."

"Isn't the triple swap option a bit much?" I asked.

"You'd think, but it helps make sure that people feel they made a good trade. You'll see."

Ceci got some of the children to help pass out gifts to everyone while she explained the rules. It was interesting to watch people's reactions. Some, like Taquira Showers, Mrs. Joliecoeur, Chaz Warcloud, and Max's niece Betsy, just sat staring, seemingly unaware of the package in their hands. Others, like Max, Nellavon, Lerlene and the children, were feeling, shaking, even smelling their items.

"I bet I got candles. I always get candles," I heard someone say.

"Mine looks like  a to-go bag. I hope this isn't someone's leftovers!"

"Mine is vibrating! Should I be opening this with children present?" Max Jr. asked.

His wife, Olivia, looked at him in disbelief, "What? What are you talking about?" Olivia had brown hair, perfect skin and large soulful eyes. She reminded me of an Italian *giallo* star.

Max Jr. held up a large paper bag that was, in fact, moving.

This created quite a stir as people mentally speculated on what it could be.

When Ceci was satisfied that everyone was ready, she directed, "Okay! You may open your present!"

Enthusiastic ripping, exclaiming, and laughing followed as the contents were revealed. I was still tearing at mine when Olivia let out a shrill scream. This was followed by more screams and laughter. Max Jr. was holding up a fake snake that was gyrating around his arm. Olivia shrieked and bolted away from him, as did Osanna and Clementina.

*"Qué carajo es eso?"* (What the h*** is that?)

*"Me estás tomando el pelo?"* (Are you kidding me?)

Mingo laughed with gusto. Rita shook her head. "Oh, Mingo. *You* did that. For Christmas? Really?"

"Oh, I'm deathly afraid of snakes!" Olivia said, hand on her chest. "Oh, I about died!"

Mingo was leaning back in his chair, head back, chest heaving with laughter. Clementina, now at a safe enough distance from the rubber menace, turned to confront him *"Imbécil!! "Nunca creces*! It never ends with you! What is wrong with you?" She smacked his knee with her hand. She turned to her mother, Aletea, who sat stone-faced beside Dante. "You see what your son does? You see how he is? I hope you are proud, Mama!"

Aletea shot her an accusatory look that asked, "Do you want to challenge me in public?" It was so fierce that I felt like I should be able to see a crackling laser beam between the two women.

Max Jr. found the off button, so the snake went suddenly limp. He tucked it back in the bag. That might have been the end of it, but Rain Warcloud stood up and said, "Mister, could I trade with you? I want that snake and I don't want *this*." He held up a set of nesting plastic measuring cups.

Clementina smacked Mingo one more time and returned to her seat, avoiding her mother's eye. She muttered under her breath in a stage whisper, "You always protect him while he throws snakes!"

Aletea smiled serenely and admired the ceramic angel votive-candle holder she had received. She cocked her head at Clementina with a smug expression as if to say, "You see, I have an angel on my side, and you have the Devil with you."

Meanwhile, Max Jr. did not look like he wanted to part with the snake for a cheap set of measuring cups.

"Hang on, hang on," Ceci interrupted, saving him. "We'll get to the swap in a moment. If you are happy with your gift and do not wish to swap, please move over to this side of the room."

Rain looked panic-stricken that Max Jr. might get up and move over to the "keeping" side of the room. Olivia moving back to sit by her husband said, "You better not keep that thing. Go on and give it to the kid."

"I love this!" Lerlene cooed, squeezing my shoulder as she passed me to the keeping group. She held up a small wreath with a cute Santa sitting in the middle surrounded by plastic gummies, mints, and candy canes. His legs dangled, kicking shiny round boots.

"There's plenty more where that came from!" I said.

Nellavon held up something between two long red false fingernails, "This is utterly dis*gusting*!"

Max leaned over, trying to get a better look at it. "Well quit wavin' it around so I can see the dang thing. What is it?" He snatched it away from her and began laughing. "Oh, I'll swap you for this! Heh-heh! Wish ya had two of 'em! He turned to Urliss and Hollis, "It's a hairy-white-man, beer-gut, belly pouch! Ah-ha-heh! Funny thing is, it ain't half big enough to cover your *real*, fat, white-man, beer gut!" He tossed it over to Urliss. Hollis intercepted it and stood up, holding it up to his

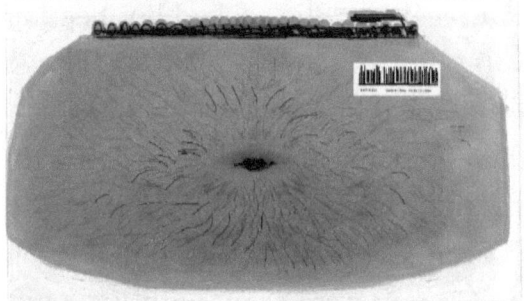

ample belly. It looked like a postage stamp on a beach ball.

"Yep, it's too small! I don't think I could get it to wrap around!" He said laughing, adding some jiggle to his rotund belly. Urliss fumbled to put something in his pocket and yanked the packet away from Hollis to get a better look.

Ceci attempted to bring some order back to the game. She stepped out to the center of the room and said, "So now, remember, if you are on this side of the room, you are keeping your present, no swapping, or at least, not here…you can swap afterwards if you want to, that's on you. And if you are on this side of the room, you want to swap."

I saw the beer-belly pouch fly through the air again, and that's when I noticed that Hollis was taking a discreet sip from a small silver flask. I looked around and wondered who else was enjoying holiday spirits. No wonder the energy in the room seemed a bit overly animated.

Yolanda's mother, Aletea, held up her present and in an accusing tone asked, *"Qué demonios es esto?"*

"Mama, it's not demonic, it's a joke, a cookie jar," said Yolanda, caught between being respectful and earnest of her mother's distress, but amused at the zombies-eating-cookies-in-the-shape-of-brains cookie jar. "Don't worry, you can exchange it."

*"Es asqueroso!"* Aletea exclaimed.

"Mama, it's not disgusting, it's a joke, you know, *broma*. We will get you something else. Look."

"I want that!" cried Cindy, one of the Lamebrains, eyeing the zombie cookie jar. She jumped out of her seat and made her way closer to Aletea.

"Look, Mama, she has one of those pill dispensers so you can keep track of your medications for the week. You can trade her for it."

Aletea shot daggers at Yolanda, "I already have that! That's not a gift, that *es una necesidad*. I want a pretty Christmas gift, not some cheap *pedazo de mierda* or some evil cookie jar!"

"Mama, we will get you something pretty. For now, let's just get rid of the cookie jar, eh? Take the pill box. We'll trade it again, I promise." She handed the cookie jar to Cindy who squealed and happy-danced with it.

"Thank you!" she gushed and dashed over to the keep side of the room.

Aletea watched her go with mistrust as if she were

watching a demon walk away. I thought she might spit at Cindy's back. Yolanda tried to hand the pill box to her mother, but Aletea refused to accept it.

"Hey Max," Buster asked, leaning over Urliss, "you needin' one o'them pill box thangs?"

Max looked over to where Buster was pointing at Aletea. "Yes, as a matter of fact. I lost mine or that new nurse chucked it, 'cause I cain't find the dang thing." He waved his stuffed snowman in the air. "Over here! I need a pill box!" He turned to me and said, "Enjoy your youth, Missy. This is what happens when you get old. You get excited about bowel movements and damn pill organizers." He shook his head. "Merry Christmas, doll face. You enjoy it, ya hear me?" His eyes moved to Buster and back to mine. Hint, hint.

Meanwhile, Aletea's eyes turned to Max. The daggers withdrew and were replaced by relief. She elbowed Yolanda. "That! Like that. Take it, take it to him!" she said, poking at Yolanda.

"Ain'tcha gonna open yours?" Buster asked, pointing at the shopping bag I was clutching.

"Oh yeah, I kinda forgot," I said, opening the bag and pawing through newspaper. The bag had been deceptively large. The object, once freed from its protective wrap was notebook sized, but thick like a hefty book. As it emerged from the paper, it looked at first like a wedding photo album, but no, embossed in gold letters it read,

"Well, I'll be jiggered. What's 'at for?" Buster asked.

"I'm not quite sure," I said, opening it to the preface page:

*You find yourself sitting still,*
*Looks like you've got time to kill.*
*Why not leave a hostess note?*
*Later she'll find what you wrote.*
*Doodle a picture!*
*Compose a song.*
*Write a haiku!*
*You can't go wrong.*
*Make a bucket list! Come! Play along!*

"Well, can't say I have one of these," I said, trying not to sound too disappointed.

"Well, 'at's kinda silly. You gonna use it?" Buster asked, eyeing me with amusement.

"Uh, no. I don't have a lot of people over. What did you get?"

I'd seen Buster opening his present, but he'd stuffed it back in its wrappings before I could see what it was.

"Oh, just this ol' meditating frog statute," he said, pulling out a serene ceramic frog sitting cross-legged.

"That's adorable!"

"Wanna trade?" he asked, grinning.

"You mean you *want* the bathroom guest book? No, be serious. You don't want this."

"Not for me, but I think it'd be a hoot at the Skunk Ape Museum. They got one unisex bathroom. I reckon folks'd get right creative with it. I'll be goin' down thar anyhow..."

"You're serious?"

"Guess we gotta move over to the keepin'-stuff side o' the room."

"Oh, right. Max? Wanna come?"

"Guess so. Don't guess nobody is gonna fight me for the pill box," Max answered, waving the box like a mad orchestra conductor.

As we moved, we heard and saw animated trades of decorations, kitchen wares, soaps, candles, tool kits, phone cases.

"What's Hollis up to?" Buster asked.

Hollis was leaning over Rain who was clutching his prized vibrating snake. Hollis fished out his wallet and flashed some bills at Rain who regarded him warily, then looked to his father, Chaz. Chaz conferred with Rain and in short order, Rain was pocketing the cash and Hollis was skipping towards us waggling the snake.

"What you want that fer?" Urliss asked.

"Porch pirates!" Hollis replied, beaming.

"You just bribed a kid out of his toy?" I asked.

"Hey, he was willin' to take the cash for it."

I shook my head.

"I'm gonna rig me up a special package for them porch

pirates! Oh, they'll be sorry!"

"I don't want to know," I said.

## THE SECOND ROUND

eci rang a jiggling wreath to get our attention. "Now if everyone has settled with the gift from the first round, our little helpers will pass out the second set of gifts." Kate, Angejolie and the twins Oro and Oscar began passing out new gifts.

Max asked, "Hey, when are we gonna do our own gift exchange, Haint? Are we doin' something just us, you know, you, me, Buster, Urliss and Hollis?"

"What about tomorrow after breakfast, Christmas Day?"

Angejolie whooped with glee at opening a pillar candle with the colors of the rainbow. "Look, Momma! Green, blue, and yellow! That's my favorite!" I remembered Gigi had said something about candles on sale. I looked over to see her bumping Aunt Moira and pointing to Angejolie. I lipread, "look—she likes it".

There was a sudden commotion as Essie Jane, the opera singer's personal assistant, squealed, threw something, and scrabbled away from where she'd been sitting. She'd startled several people around her, so some were moving away while others were leaning in to see what had happened.

Aunt Moira picked up what looked like a pile of napkins and asked loudly, "Is someone missing their teeth?" She unfolded the napkins and held the bundle over her head. A set of dentures smiled at the crowd.

Max cussed and covered his face with his hands. Nellavon waved a hand, "They're Mamma Sue's. I'll take them." She got up and retrieved them from Aunt Moira while muttering, "Sorry about that. She's always trying to hide them. Mama! You see what you did?"

Mama Sue sat in her wheelchair with the Santa-suited panda bear she'd won in round one. She stared, unfocused at the ceiling.

Max grumbled, "Don't know why Nellavon even bothers with tryin' to get her to wear them dang thangs. She won't put 'em in her mouth. Look at her over there playin' 'possum. She plays Nellavon all the time and she doesn't catch on."

Mmm. Like mother, like son. This explained a *lot* about Max.

Ceci coaxed Angejolie into getting Essie Jane a new gift. Angejolie skipped over to the leftover table, selected the biggest package, and danced it over to Essie Jane, who had returned to her seat and was regaining her composure. She accepted it with thanks. Angejolie skipped back to her parents, beaming. Such a delightful child. She embraced the better-to-give-than-to-receive concept.

A fight broke out between Oro and Oscar. It seemed one of them had received a gift that they both wanted. Whatever it was, did not appeal to their sisters, Anna and Zelia, who were backing away in disgust, screaming "gross!" and "ewww!"

"I want the scorpion!" one of them yelled.

Yolanda's boy, Vic, interceded giving up his toy. In a flash, the twins were beaming and happy, comparing their gifts with each other.

As the volume in the room increased and the atmosphere became more boisterous, an inflated beach ball bounced up in the air and was kept in motion as it passed over people's heads. Discarded wrapping paper cluttered the floor, Oro and Oscar ran around showing family members their treasures. I caught a glimpse of matching paperweights with creatures embedded in them. One was a scorpion, the other looked like a tarantula.

Benny guffawed and held up his gift over his head like an Oscar. It was an old seventies statue of a cheesy, leering man with a caption that read Dirty Old Men Need Love Too.

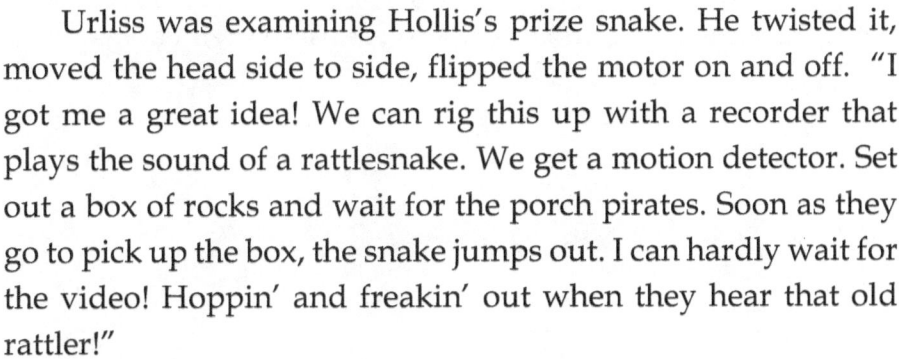

"It's nothing to be proud of!" Olivia exclaimed as Max Jr. tried to shush her.

Max Senior shook his head and covered his eyes. "Insufferable windbag!"

Urliss was examining Hollis's prize snake. He twisted it, moved the head side to side, flipped the motor on and off. "I got me a great idea! We can rig this up with a recorder that plays the sound of a rattlesnake. We get a motion detector. Set out a box of rocks and wait for the porch pirates. Soon as they go to pick up the box, the snake jumps out. I can hardly wait for the video! Hoppin' and freakin' out when they hear that old rattler!"

Swapping continued. Guests eagerly traded jars of pickles, nutcrackers, candles, ugly figurines, kitchen gadgets, soap, ornaments, snow globes, pen sets, sink stoppers, pet toys, etc.

Finally, Ceci called for attention. "Folks, no pun intended but we need to wrap this event up. Please pick up your trash and dispose of it in the bags on your way out. If you want to continue trading, please do it outside."

I was relieved that we'd had no fights, fires or need to call an ambulance. It had been a wildly successful event and a fun way to pass the dreary afternoon. The guests seemed to be in good spirits.

As I was heading out with Buster, Nellavon approached me. "Say, that was a great idea. Thanks! We got rid of a carload of Roberta's junk!" She patted me on the back.

"It was all Ceci's idea," I said.

"Hmm. So those two women run a thrift shop? Maybe they should come look at the shit in the storage unit."

Benny walked by, clutching his Dirty Old Man trophy.

"Can't hurt to ask," I said.

Some of the kids had won bubble-makers. The porch and driveway looked like a wedding reception as guests had to navigate through a bubble battle to return to their cabins.

# Chapter 22

## CHRISTMAS EVE DINNER

Christmas Eve dinner was another crazy blur. We had enough food to feed the county and I didn't want to think about how badly we were exceeding the maximum room capacity mandated by the state. This would be the only time that all my guests were in the dining hall at the same time as they all wanted to see the talent show in the meditation hall afterwards. Thank heavens Yolanda and Paco brought extra tables and chairs from Paco's Restaurant—we needed the extra surfaces for diners as well as for setting out all the food.

My main dishes for the evening were beef tenderloin with mushrooms, roasted potatoes with tarragon, and vegetarian flatbread triangles with pesto and veggies made to look like decorated Christmas trees. My sides were sweet potato biscuits and a beet, pear, and goat-cheese salad. Urliss and Hollis arrived early with two deep fried turkeys and a creamed corn, broccoli, and cheese casserole. Yolanda and Paco concocted a beef birria with chilies, cilantro, onions, and lime.

The Garcias had once again offered up a delicious warm

punch that was being served discretely to those in the know. I was told it was a traditional Mexican Christmas favorite, made with fruit, cinnamon, and dark rum. The predominant flavors were orange, cloves, and cinnamon. The extra cups of cheer further enhanced the already celebratory atmosphere in the room.

Lorraine had gotten help making a gingerbread tower with gingerbread squares with red and green gummies stuck in the icing. She'd found a strand of white mini lights somewhere and surrounded the tower with them. It looked like something from a chic food magazine. The children swarmed around it wanting to touch it. Angejolie was dressed in a frilly red dress with a matching bow in her hair. Entranced by the gingerbread tower, she begged her parents to take lots of photos of her standing next to it. Clover, Dee, and Freddie Jay soon needed their pictures taken with it. Soon there was a line of folks waiting to get their photo opportunity.

Between the decorations, the bright red tablecloths, the bounty of food, you'd have thought we were throwing a wedding feast for royalty. It was all so gorgeous, I started to tear up.

While moving around the room to check on people, clear dishes so we could load the dishwasher and not be up all night cleaning, I overheard snippets of unusual conversation.

Urliss and Hollis were sitting with Clan Max regaling Max Jr., Pike, and Benny about the splendors of EMW — Extreme Midget Wrestling. "They got a show in Lake City — we got season tickets — "

Max shook his head, "Yup. Those guys are buff and fierce. I ain't never seen anything like it."

Benny shook his head, "Isn't it rigged like regular wrestling?"

Urliss said, "Aw, who cares? It's a show."

Pike's wife Betsy shot disapproving looks at them, looking uncomfortable. "Isn't that exploitation? I don't think—"

"No more than any other wrestling is exploitative. These guys are showin' off how ripped and athletic they are. Man, some of the stunts they do on the ropes are crazy!"

Betsy turned to Olivia in a huff. "Honestly."

Hollis was fiddling with his phone, "Here, check this out—this guy's name is Dillinger—watch how he takes down The Mighty Sprout—look a'that!" He turned his phone around to show them all.

Betsy excused herself, "I'll check on Mama Sue."

"Aw, don't fuss at her!" Max grumbled. "If she wants somethin', she'll tell us."

Betsy got up anyway.

Kate and Ceci were sitting with Aunt Moira, Gigi, Amy, and Stuey. It seemed there were multiple conversations happening at the same time. Amy looked like she wanted to teleport to anywhere but there. Stuey's face was frozen in an I-can't-believe-this-is-happening" expression.

Kate was going on about her cats as usual, "...and so I had to give Mr. Whiskers these appetite pills, but he wasn't having any of it, he scratched me up to shreds and barfed them right back up anyway, I *told* the vet that I needed something else —"

Ceci almost spat out her food laughing, "Oh, and then there was the time when we had a rat problem in the storage room. Someone had donated a huge bag of medical stuff — gauze pads, bandages, vitamins, laxative pills, aspirin — you know. Well, wouldn't you know, the rats got into the laxative boxes and ate it all. Oh, my Lord, they had the shits all over the back room! Oh, what a mess, we had to throw away so much stuff. Well, all of the medications had expired anyway, so they'd have gotten thrown out regardless, but —"

Above the din, a shrill voice yelled, "Who *are* you? Leave me alone!"

There was a lull in the cacophony as eyes turned to see Betsy backing away from Mama Sue's wheelchair.

Amy looked at me with a pleading expression as Kate continued, "Have you ever given a cat an enema? Whoa, that's fun, I can tell you —"

Saint Eleanor grabbed my arm, "You've outdone yourself, dear. This is lovely. Look how beautiful the room is and this amazing feast. Just fabulous."

Freddie added, "A far cry from your stint at Lowell Correctional then, eh, Mom?"

Leander, Saint Eleanor's stoic husband, covered his mouth but the amusement was quite visible in his eyes.

Saint Eleanor's cheeks flushed Christmas red as she about levitated out of her chair in indignation, "*Whaaatt?* Oh, Freddie! I never!"

"You dropped your napkin. I'll get it. OH MY! Is that an *ankle bracelet*?"

Lorraine choked on her water. Her father leaned over and pulled the tablecloth up, as if looking for his wife's napkin, but his eyes were on Freddie, not the floor. The tablecloth may have hidden his mouth, but not the muffled chortle.

Lerlene busted out laughing, "Freddie!"

Amy rolled her eyes, "Stuey, your family—"

There was also Freddie joke-sparring with Benny whenever they happened to meet. "Say, Benny. Do ya know what the difference is between an in-law and an outlaw?"

"No, tell me!"

"The outlaw is *wanted*!"

"Yeah, well, ha-ha, everything is relative...especially if you're from West Virginia."

Hollis: "We've been makin' up fake packages for porch pirates and givin' 'em out to our friends."

Urliss: "We've done all kinds o' stuff."

Hollis: "I rigged up this package with rusty old crap we was goin' to chuck anyway, so the box'd feel real heavy, like somethin' excitin'.

Urliss: "We saved up a nasty bag of frozen leftovers—shrimp heads, fish guts, that mystery stuff in the back of the fridge—we poured it all over the metal bits in a thick plastic bag."

Hollis: "We boxed it inside another box, so they'd have really work at gettin' it open."

Aletea, hissing at Clementina: "Are you having sex with that boy?"

Clementina: "Mom! No! Don't embarrass me."

Pedro: "Do you have to have this conversation in public? Maybe we should just take out an ad in the newspaper or call the local news and tell everybody our business."

Aletea: "I've already raised kids; I'm not going to take care of grandbabies! You have them when you are married, and we visit. You don't park them with me."

Clementina: "Mom! What are you talking about? There is no boy! There is no baby! Stop!"

Aletea: "If you end up pregnant, the one who's going to take care of the baby is you. Don't look to me. Uh-uh."

Pedro: "Mom, please. Leave her alone. Let's enjoy dinner."

Dante: "Aletea, *Mi querida*--"

## TACONES VOLADORES

The volume in the dining hall continued to creep higher as the meal progressed. All of a sudden, a harsh female voice broke through the din, "*Oro-lit-to*! *Si valoras tu vida*!" My Spanish is sketchy, but I think it meant 'if you value your life.'

Oro was standing by the gingerbread tower, fingers hovering dangerously close to a frosted cake, about to pick off a square. A chair scraped. Oro froze. In a swift motion, Osanna removed her shoe and held it over her head.

Oro yelped, "Mami, no!" and took off running.

"Don't you move!" she yelled and hurled the shoe with speed and accuracy that would have made a professional quarterback envious.

There was a collective gasp as Oro let out a piercing, desperate shriek of terror and dove behind the window curtain on the far wall. Just as the fabric enveloped him, the shoe struck the outline of his shoulder and bounced off.

"Ow!" he cried and began to wail. The curtain waggled as he stamped his feet and cried.

Osanna got up and walked like a goddess towards the quivering curtain. The dining hall was silent as she crouched down and pulled the curtain away, revealing a red-faced, Oro. She whispered to him for a few, tense moments. Oro looked around the room once in desperation, looking for rescue. There was only Osanna. After gulping air, he pulled it together and emerged from the curtain, holding Osanna's hand. He returned to the table and hid his face in his crossed arms.

After an awkward moment, conversations resumed. Benny's voice boomed out, "Hey, you know how Velcro was invented, dontcha? The shoemaker asked himself, 'Why knot?'!"

# Chapter 23

## The Show

Noni got all the participating kids on the stage with the younger ones bunched like a chorus on the left side and the older ones single file on the right, facing the audience. She nodded to Lerlene who was standing off to the side. Lerlene tapped at her phone and some upbeat instrumental music filled small speakers someone had placed around the stage.

Noni announced, "Ladies and gentlemen, our children have volunteered to entertain you with some holiday cheer. Please keep in mind, we didn't write these jokes, we're just sharing them. If you have any antiacid tablets, you may want to take them now as these jokes are groaners for sure! There's a reason we're in here and not the dining hall, we wouldn't want you throwing food at them!" She turned to the children. "Are we ready?"

They responded with an enthusiastic, collective, "Yeah!"

"Great! Without further ado, please adjust your funny bones and enjoy our show presented to you by the Amazing Guffaws of the Lotus Lodge!" Noni stepped away and nodded to Yolanda's oldest boy, Eliazar, the first child in the line.

Eliazar stepped forward and read out, "What did Rudolph say before he told his best joke?"

The chorus responded, "This one's gonna sleigh you!"

The audience groaned. The identical twins, Oscar and Oro, sitting in the front row of the chorus must have thought they were supposed to groan too, so they did with gusto. This made the other chorus children giggle. The kids were so cute the audience laughed with them.

Eliazar moved to the back of the line and Lerlene's daughter Dee stepped forward, "When a gingerbread man breaks a leg, what does he use?"

The chorus yelled, "A candy cane!"

The audience and chorus groaned again as Dee skipped to the back of the line and Ange-Jolie stepped forward. She put a hand on her hips and cocked her head, "What kind of bike does Santa ride?"

"A Holly Davidson!"

"A Holly Davidson!" she repeated, gesturing with her hands as if revving a motorcycle. She drove the imaginary bike to the back of the line.

Oro clutched at his guts as if in agony, which Oscar immediately imitated. The collective groan was louder than before and Urliss hollered, "Yeah! Good one! Holly Davidson!"

The stoic instrumental music seemed out of place as the atmosphere in the room got more boisterous.

Buster put a hand on my knee and leaned over to whisper in my ear, "This is hi-lare-eous!"

With each joke the chorus got more raucous. Oro and Oscar feigning death throes and falling to the floor, Freddie Jay grabbed at his throat as if choking, the girls giggled and pointed at the boys. Noni tried to encourage order from the stage wings but to no avail; the children were having a grand time hamming it up and the audience egged them on.

"What does a gingerbread man make the bed with?"
"Cookie sheets!"
"Arrrrghh!"

"What did Adam say the day before Christmas?"
"It's Christmas, Eve!"
"Uuugh!"

"What do you get when you cross a vampire and a snowman?"
"Frostbite!"
"Ohhhh!"

Someone behind me yelled, "Oh, it hurts!"
Someone else responded, "This is killing me!"
A saxophone solo which might have been perfect for a romantic holiday dinner for newlyweds, was utterly incongruous with the clown-car mayhem going on with the chorus.

"What did one Christmas tree say to the other?"

273

"Oh, lighten up!"
"Ugh!"

"What do you get if you eat Christmas decorations?"
"Tinsilitis!"
"Ohhh!"

"What do you call it when a Snowman has a hissy fit?"
"He's having a total MELTdown!"
"Noooo!"

"What do you call a bunch of chess masters bragging about their games in a hotel lobby?"
"Chess nuts boasting in an open foyer."
"Uggh!"

Noni turned the music off and stepped forward, waving to the children to join hands and take a bow. This was much like expecting oatmeal to hold together like clay; they were too wound up to focus and act in unison. They switched positions, bowed when the others were upright, and upright when others bowed.

"Ladies and Gentlemen, one more round of applause for The Amazing Guffaws of Lotus Lodge!"

The Amazing Guffaws got whistles, foot stamps, and more applause as they left the stage. When it was cleared, I got up and per Linwood's request, introduced the Lame Brain group with an explanatory note:

"The next performers have asked me to make a disclaimer statement on their behalf. Their act was designed to be performed at a special Christmas party of zombie and zombie-hunter LARPers, that is, live action role players. They have volunteered to perform in full costume for our entertainment and beg that you aren't offended by their warped sense of humor. You've been warned! And so, please welcome, the Lame Brain Zombie Apocalypse Bell Ringers! I moved quickly offstage and returned to my seat next to Buster.

For a moment nothing happened. Then there was a collective gasp as seven zombies lurched and dragged and moaned their way to the makeshift stage. Their makeup was professional and quite scary to tell the truth. They were all

wearing creepy contact lenses, some opaqued, some glowing yellow or red. They'd covered their exposed skin sickly with hues of green. Instead of the crisp white bell gloves, they had monster hands. A few of the children in the audience shrieked and cried as their parents shushed and reassured them.

Kirby—the only one with a beard or I wouldn't have known--lurched forward. His mouth hung open and he remained motionless as if he'd forgotten what he was going to say. His neck moved and a horrendous belch escaped. He groaned, putting his hands to his belly. "It isn't easy being a zombie. You have no idea."

This got laughs, especially from the younger kids in the audience.

Then, abruptly jumping from his zombie persona to an imitation of Groucho Marx , he said, "Well, what else could a *bell choir* play? Of course, we have to do "*Jingle Bells*" right?" He dragged back into line with the others, and they launched into a zombie version, at half tempo with bells with tones that were low and somber, not light and uplifting. Sometimes a player would pull out an extra instrument like a kazoo or an elk horn creating an array of comedic sounds from foghorn to cow bell.

They earned loud applause from the audience, giggles from the younger kids, hoots from the older kids and whistles from Urliss and Hollis.

"They're real good," Buster said in my ear.

"I know! That was great!" I said, clapping.

Linwood, and I only knew it was Linwood by his general shape and height as he was unrecognizable otherwise, stepped forward and announced in a solemn, deep voice, "Our variation on 'O Sacred Head, Now Wounded". I wasn't familiar with the original hymn, but they'd obviously changed the words a *lot*. Their version was funny, punctuated by ringing song, performed with herky-jerky, spasmodic motions. The irreverent song lamenting their zombie lives, their insatiable hunger and the pitiful state of their decaying bodies. There was another collective gasp as a zombie's hand fell off and the bell clanged to the floor. As the song progressed more arms and bells and bodies fell, until the smallest zombie, presumably Wendy, having fallen to her knees, sang the last words "to our eternal rest" and collapsed forward on top of another zombie.

In the silence just before the audience began to clap, Freddie Jay, sitting up front with Lorraine and Lerlene asked "Are they really dead, Mommy?"

As the wave of laughter and applause receded, the group got up, joined their real hands together and bowed.

Buster leaned into me and said, "I ain't sure what I just saw, but it was some kinda different. That was funny."

Kirby stepped forward as the applause died down. (The puns just come on their own, sorry.) "Our next piece is a mangled medley of holiday favorites." The launched into a manic medley with lyrics like "O come, O come Emmanuel, we want your brains and li-ver as well" and "We three zombies, starving are". "All I Want for Christmas is YOU" took on a sinister meaning as they rolled their tongues around. They got a standing ovation as they took their final bows and departed the stage.

As the audience quieted and Noni was just about to introduce the next presentation, Max's mother's voice boomed out, "What in the profane, everlasting fire was *that*? Who were those people?"

# Heavenly Showers

"I have a quick announcement, before our next and final performance," Noni said, "I've just been told that Santa Claus is on his way. He's just parked his reindeer on the roof. Once he gets them some water and snacks, he'll be down to meet the children by the door. So be sure to say hello to Santa Claus as you are leaving."

Buster looked at Urliss and Hollis then asked me, "Who's Santa?"

I shrugged. "No idea." My favorite Polish expression came to mind, "*Nie mój cyrk, nie moje małpy* — not my circus, not my monkeys."

"Ladies and gentlemen, girls and boys, we have an extra treat tonight. The incredibly talented Taquira Showers has graciously volunteered to sing a few Christmas carols for us. From the Metropolitan Opera stage to our little show here, please give a warm welcome to Miss Taquira Showers!"

This was news to me! Last I'd heard, she was going to hide in her cabin. She must have had a change of heart, or someone was exceedingly persuasive. Noni stepped away and the lights went out. Stuart and Stuey shown flashlights in lieu of spotlights as Ms. Showers glided on the stage.

There was a collective intake of breath mingled with "ooh"s and claps. She was utterly gorgeous. She wore a stunning, sparkly red gown that swished as she walked, clinging to her well-proportioned body. The whites of her perfect teeth and warm smile, her pearl earrings, necklace, and

wrist cuffs were accentuated by her dark cocoa skin and black hair.

Noni flipped the lights back on.

"Thank you," Ms. Showers said in a rich, low voice. "I don't know about you, but it seems like every year we get bombarded with the same Christmas music. It kinda loses its meaning when you hear it over and over. You start to hate songs you once loved.

"Well, I grew up listening to my mama's old records, and I'd like to sing a few songs that I bet you haven't heard in a while. My mama had a beautiful voice; she sang in the church choir and she's the reason I took to singing. She used to sing right along with Rosemary Clooney on those old records. I lost Mama this past year, so I'm singing these in her memory. The first one is called Suzy Snowflake."

She launched into the song, elbows up, like she was marching. This brought back long-ago memories of listening to Rosemary Clooney's Christmas album at a friend's house when I was a child. Ms. Showers had quickened the tempo. It was more upbeat than I remembered. Her face was animated, her lips wide as she enunciated each word.

Looking around at the children, they seemed to enjoy the jolly song. Angejolie was imitating her movements, hands on hips, rocking side to side. Her voice was phenomenal despite the less-than-optimal acoustics in the meditation hall. She finished and sank into an elegant curtsey as the place erupted in applause.

"Thank you," she said, putting a hand on her heart. "This next one is a good reminder that we can get wrapped up in holiday craziness, but it's always a good idea that, no matter what stresses or problems you have, you remember to count your blessings."

Once again, the room was filled with her rich resonant voice advising us to count our blessings instead of sheep. Once again, when she finished, she dropped a curtsey, and the audience went nuts with appreciation.

"Thank you. This last one is one of my all-time favorites. Lest we forget what the holiday is really about, it's more than shopping and presents, it's about our Lord. And I could use a little help with this one. Miss Noni? And could I get a bottle of water while you're finding helpers?"

Essie Jane scooted across the stage with a bottle of water as Noni stepped onstage and said, "I've got three tambourines, so I need three children to help."

Angejolie shot up a hand, "ME! Oh, please, ME!"

Noni nodded, and Angejolie sprang up to take a tambourine.

Oscar and Oro jumped up waving their hands.

"Let me see... how about the quiet ones...Clover? You want to help out?"

Clover nodded and stood up.

"And what's your name?" Noni asked, overlooking a histrionic twin.

"Mimi."

"Come on up."

Ms. Showers sipped some water then began clapping out a beat. "Can you do this?"

The kids followed her beat with their tambourines.

"Okay, keep that up. Let's go," she said, then tilted her head back and began singing "C-H-R-I-S-T-M-A-S" a song about what each of the letters of Christmas stands for. Once again, she'd boosted the tempo up, so it was catchier than I remembered. When she got to the refrain, she encouraged everyone to sing along.

I can't adequately describe the harmonious atmosphere in the hall. Even Mama Sue was clapping her hands and swaying a bit in her wheelchair. Stuart and Noni stood off to the side, arm in arm, swaying, Nellavon had an arm around Taylor, Cameron's head rested on Benny's shoulder. The children smiled and clapped, and Grandma Yaya's eyes were shiny with tears.

The applause went on and on until Noni stepped out and did that tamping hand gesture in the air to get people to be quiet. "I'd like to thank all of our performers, particularly Ms. Taquira Showers. If you are interested in buying her CDs, please see her assistant Essie Jane—" she indicated Essie Jane who waved, "and Santa Claus is waiting outside, but please don't block the doorway."

Shrieking pandemonium ensued as excited children

rushed for the door.

Mingo and Rita passed me, "That was so much fun. Thank you."

I nodded dumbly. I hadn't had anything to do with it.

Lorraine worked her way through the crowd to get to me. "That was amazing, Haint. What a great idea. The Lame Brains—hilarious. Ms. Showers—wow. She is incredible. I'm not into opera, but her voice is something else. Hey, who is Santa?"

"I have no idea," I said.

Pedro, who'd been trailing Mingo and Rita leaned towards Lorraine and said, "It's my brother, Rocky. He does it every year. It's the only time you can't see all his tattoos, 'cause he's totally covered with the beard and the gloves and suit. The kids have no idea."

"Interesting," I said. "I wouldn't have guessed."

"He's been doing appearances at the Whatcha Need. He's a big advocate for kids," Pedro said. "He runs the local chapter of bikers for youth. They do all kinds of fundraisers and advocate against child abuse."

Urliss said, "Oh, right! Rocky owns the bar out on the highway towards Fort White, The Bar Hopper. I'm sure you've seen it."

"Strange name for a bar, isn't it?" I asked. "I mean, don't you want your customers to stay and keep drinking?"

Pedro shrugged.

"It's biker slang," Hollis explained. "Fer when you got a bike that's too nice to road trip with, it's just for show, for local bar hoppin'."

Lorraine was having difficulty pulling on her coat.

"May I?" Pedro said, helping her find her sleeve.

"Thanks," she said, shrugging into it properly.

He winked at her and followed Mingo. As she walked with a limp with her foot in the boot, and the crowd pushed against her then, she was blocked while Pedro moved forward away from us.

"Mistletoe on the porch!" I said, elbowing her.

Unfortunately, by the time we got out of the hall and passed the mob of kids getting trinkets from Santa, Pedro was nowhere to be seen.

"So long, Señor Soñador," she said dispiritedly.

"Hey, he helped you with your coat," I said.

Buster patted her back, "Aw, don't despair. What's 'at song? There's always tomorrow?"

"Yeah," she said.

"I need some sleep first. I'm dead on my feet," I said.

The evening was finally over. I'd sent Buster home with Naughty Britches — she wasn't sure she wanted to leave with him, she shot me looks as if she thought he was kidnapping her and wasn't I going to step in? She stared back at me as they drove away. If she'd had a cell phone and the ability to dial, I was sure she'd have dialed an abuse hotline.

I did my final round locking up. The retreat was quiet, the kitchen and meditation hall were clean. Lights out. Time to go home, thank goodness. I dragged myself to the office to get my coat and turn out the light. The bells on the wreath that Angejolie had admired so much jingled as I opened the door.

I froze. In the center of my desk was a lit red candle in a glass holder. Now the obvious explanation was that Buster had lit it somehow as a sweet gesture when he collected Naughty Britches.

- Fact: I'd never seen this candle before.
- Fact: Buster had not gotten this candle in the gift exchange.
- Fact: The candle looked like it had just been lit; there was very little pooled, liquid wax.
- Fact: I got the heebie-jeebies. It just felt uncanny. The room was charged with an expectant energy. The hairs on my neck and arms were tingling with the hinkies.

Part of me wanted to bolt for my truck. The rational part said that I had to blow out the candle as it was a fire hazard. I didn't want to walk into the office.

"It was probably Buster," I said out loud, not believing myself. "I'm going to blow out the candle and take it home. He'll tell me I'm silly. Okay. It's nothing. Here we go. Big girl panties on. And GO!" I dashed in, blew it out, grabbed it, turned out the lights, locked the door and ran down the porch steps. I got in the truck, setting the candle on the passenger floor mat, and cranked up the engine.

# Chapter 24

## PILLOW TALK

It was close to one in the morning before I had brushed my teeth and was getting into bed with Buster. NB was already asleep at the bottom of the bed.

"I'm sorry I didn't call or write. I know things have been bumpy between us since the...incident," he said, holding out his hand. "Come 'ere."

"Me too," I said, settling next to him, my head on his chest. He arranged the covers. I was having an uncomfortable memory of collecting a mysteriously large poop sample with a chewed-up dog collar in it. Buster had been fairly convinced that Poopsie had been done in by a Bigfoot. I didn't buy it. Bear, maybe. Coyote, okay. Bigfoot, no way. But I had dutifully collected it and put the sample in the freezer. And then Saint Eleanor came over and began to fuss about in my kitchen.

"I couldn't believe that Saint Eleanor threw out your poop sample. I'm really sorry. She had no business rooting around in my freezer, I don't know what possessed her—well, I do, actually, she's a control freak. But she's not so bad, really. She did a super job helping put up the decorations at the retreat. She's great with her grandkids."

"Yeah. Well, I got your pictures anyway. Hard to say what it was. Did you tell the woman that her dog—?"

"Yeah. It was awful. But she's got first dibs on Lullabelle's puppies—you remember, Lorraine tripped over Sparky, the Chihuahua and broke her ankle? Sparky was Lullabelle's sire. Mrs. Bunderbridge will console herself with new AKC puppies."

He sighed, "Well, that's good." He moved closer and groaned "*nrr*" and shifted again.

"You sure you don't need medical attention?" I asked.

"Yeah. It'll pass."

"You going to tell me about it?"

He kissed the top of my head. "Not tonight. I'll be fine. I'm just sore, 'at's all."

I hated the not knowing but knew better than to bug him. He'd tell me when he was ready. "So why *didn't* you call?"

"I was fixin' to, but the next thing I knew, I was given this opportunity to go to Africa. Honey, I had no idea what I was getting' myself into. I thought it was just a coupla days, but nothin' over there works on any kind of schedule. I thought I'd call en route, but--" He sighed again, and kissed my forehead. "Then I got to thinkin', if I just get back outta this mess, I'll show up an' surprise you. But nothin' went right. I figured I'd just wait."

"I wasn't sure what to think," I said. "And that time I called, and a strange woman answered, I got all paranoid. Then

you were short on the phone…and then I didn't hear from you-
-"

"I *told* you, she was another cryptozoologist—we were done for the day and stopped in a bar—it was the only joint with food—but yeah, it was a dive, that's for sure. As for the rest," he said shifting, "Do you know that ol' story 'bout the two monks and the woman who wants to cross the river?"

"Uhh-uh."

"Well, see, one day there's these two monks, a senior and novice monk an' they're travelin' in the mountains. Their path is difficult. They walk mindfully without talkin'. The path leads to this big ol' river. Now normally it's not hard to git acrost, but it's the monsoon season, so the water is up and there's this strong current just a whooshin'." Buster ran his hands down my back to indicate fast current.

"Well, they git thar, an' lo and behold, there's this young woman there waitin'. She needs to get to th'other side but she's a little thang and the current might sweep her down river." More hands down my back.

I wondered what this story had to do with anything, but snugged up like this, hearing his voice resonate from his body into my ear, the grudge feelings I'd harbored loosened as if washing away in the imaginary river Buster described.

Buster's voice grew with tension. "She sees the monks comin' and gets excited, 'Oh, please!' she says, 'I have to visit my sick sister. Would you help me get across the river?'"

Buster touched a finger to my forehead, "Now the thang is, monks take a sacred vow that they can't touch or be touched by a woman. But even while the younger monk is shakin' his head, that older monk directs her to put her little arms around his neck and whoop! Just like that, he carries her fireman-style across the river, steady and careful, and he sets her down on the other side.

"Now the young monk, he's just flabbergasted and a bit confused. In his days afore he was a monk, he'd a carried that gal, and he was even a bit conflicted on account of that he was the stronger, younger monk an' he was gettin' showed up by the older monk. So, he's all confused and huffy."

"Figures," I said.

"Now, the young woman thanks him profusely and goes trottin' on her way." I felt fingers walking down my spine. "The old monk rests a moment and waits for the young monk to finish crossin'. The younger monk gets across and his face is all screwed up in confusion. A couple times he starts to say somethin', but the older monk just starts a-walkin' so he shuts up and tags along. But the whole time he's walkin', that young monk is wonderin' about the old monk. Why in the world did he break that vow just like that? Vows are vows, ain't they? What does it mean?"

I was starting to slip into the pre-dream place. I tried to say, "I don't know", but it came out jumbled noise like a sleeping dog dream-barking, "mrr-rrph."

"An hour passes as they travel on. He tries to focus on the path and let his mind be present, but he's strugglin'. More time passes. They climb over rocks and duck under fallen trees. But that young monk is still a strugglin' in his mind." Buster circled my temple with an index finger. "They stop for a break and the older monk looks so serene. And that kinda pisses the younger feller off. Finally, the young monk just can't hold it in no longer, he blurts out, "Why did you carry that woman? We took sacred vows as monks not to touch women! How come you broke the vow?"

"Mmm?"

"The older monk looks surprised and asks, 'What are you still carryin' her for? I set her down hours ago.'"

I frowned. Finding my voice, "What are you saying?"

"Don't dwell on it, Moon Eyes." He kissed the top of my head and whispered in my ear. "*Let her down.*"

"I will."

"Come on, let's get some sleep now," he said, hugging me to him. "Ow. Could you move yer head just a little Moon Eyes? Oh. There. That's better."

*Let it go*, the Inner Critic whispered.

We fell asleep.

# PART SEVEN

# CHRISTMAS DAY

# Chapter 25

## Christmas Morning

By Christmas morning, I was no longer fretting about my guests as I had when they first descended on me two days previously. Preparing three meals a day for this energetic and somewhat chaotic horde felt like I was setting up, hosting, and cleaning up three parties a day. I'd gotten used to Bennie's endless and usually tasteless jokes, Kate talking about puking cats and vet bills, Amy and Stuey's spats, Aletea's queenly manner, and the Garcia women commandeering my kitchen. It was only Mamma Sue who made me truly uncomfortable.

Was she senile or was she manipulating people? Sometimes she looked immobile and half-dead and at other times, I caught her eyes tracking her family members like laser beams. She was alert and engaged when dandling "Baby Vonnie" in her lap. The way everyone seemed to refer to him that way, I began to half-wonder if his birth certificate said Baby Vonnie. Probably not. They were all just pleased to have a new baby in the family.

Mama Sue smiled at Austin and May with love in her eyes.

And somehow, coming in for breakfast, the foot plate on her wheelchair struck Benny in the back of the calf as Nellavon pushed her towards the table. It seemed like an accident, but Mama Sue eyes were alive; her mouth was working to suppress something a bit more than a Mona Lisa smile of satisfaction. I'd always thought of Max as a trickster, but he didn't have the mean edge that his mother seemed to have.

I was contemplating these things as I got dressed that morning. Buster was hugging his pillow and snoring—not an annoying snore, a low steady, rumble. I was pleased that he seemed to be sleeping better—no yelling or thrashing. A few of his bruises had mutated into some hideous colors, but he shrugged it off. "Reckon I got a cracked rib or two. Feels like it. It'll pass with some pain pills and time. " When I asked again what had happened, he kissed me and deflected. "Promise I'll tell you when I'm ready."

O-kay.

I let him sleep. Mischief crept up Buster's leg and was balled up against him in the warm spot that I'd vacated. Naughty Britches was ready for a walk and breakfast.

"Let me get some coffee, little girl," I said, heading to the kitchen. "Come on, let's let them sleep."

I'd love to kick this habit, but I need a cup of coffee even though I have to make coffee when I get to the retreat kitchen. I opened a fresh packet of maple bourbon coffee, delighting in the aroma. As the percolator wheezed to life, I flipped the Word-of-the-Day calendar to the new day. Good thing I wasn't drinking coffee at the time. I laughed out loud!

**Callipygian/callipygous**: *adj.* pronounced cal-i-pi-geon (like the bird in the park) Combining the Greek words for "beauty" and "buttocks": having a shapely backside. Pertaining to a marble statue of Venus Kallipygos…found missing her head, endowed with a well-shaped rear end.

Buster was certainly callipygian! Maybe I'd nickname him Cal.

I opened the fridge for some half and half to find a huge plastic cake tote in the refrigerator with a note on it, **DO NOT TOUCH**. I had a hunch it was the chocolate lava cake for Lorraine's dad.

It was still cold and dark when I got to the dining hall. I unlocked the door and flipped on the lights, mentally going through the checklist of breakfast foods to prepare. Heading to the kitchen, I spotted a long-handled, wooden spoon on the buffet counter. It looked old and primitive, like something out of a pioneer days museum exhibit. I pulled off my gloves and picked it up. I'd never seen it before, and it certainly wasn't there when we left the night before. Where had it come from? Had someone broken in? No, I'd had to unlock the door. And why would someone break in to leave an old spoon on the counter?

"Hello?" I called out, feeling nervous and silly at the same time. "Hello?" I whipped around, feeling as if someone might creep up behind me. There was no one. I strode into the kitchen and flipped on more lights. No one. I patted the spoon in my palm. A chill ran through me.

"Let's just bump up the heat, shall we?" I said aloud, setting down the spoon and moving to the thermostat. "There we go." The air heat kicked on. "And how about some cheery Christmas music because it'll all be over so soon?" I took off my coat, hung it in the alcove at the back of the dining hall, and strode to the radio. Johnny Mathis began crooning about hearts overflowing while I draped a clean apron over my head and tied it snug.

"First up, coffee and hot chocolate."

The spoon on the counter seemed to stare at me, demanding my attention. There was a slim chance that one of the Garcia women had brought it and forgot it, but even as I thought this, I dismissed it. It didn't feel right. I pushed the spoon to the side and focused on making hot drinks. "I can't deal with you right now. Gotta get this show on the road."

Rita, Osanna, and Yolanda arrived, chattering away in Spanish. They greeted me as they donned their aprons and assumed control of the kitchen. They seemed to be fussing as much as ever, which I found a little odd. It was just breakfast, right? As usual, there was music and a high-energy atmosphere. I found myself scrambling eggs to the beat. I focused on my to-do list and blocked out the chatter.

Amy was the first one in for breakfast. I was in the kitchen making grits and happened to see her walking to the back window. In its previous incarnation as part of the Stinkin' Skunk Ape Fish Camp, this building had been a boat house and storage barn. I'd torn out the service door and replaced it with

French doors that led to a tiny flower garden with a bird feeder and bird bath. I'd set up a cozy sitting area, a sort of nook to sit and watch butterflies and songbirds. It was a popular spot mostly in the spring and summer. Currently, there was a candy cane camelia blooming there. The bird feeder attracted cardinals, brown thrashers, chickadees, vireos and my favorite, Carolina wrens.

She sat alone, her back silhouetted in the gray light from the window.

I thought about going over to say something, but she seemed to want the private moment and I had plenty to do. I was relieved when Stuart walked in, looked around and spotted her.

The grits began bubbling, so I focused on stirring and adding butter and a bit of salt. When I next looked up, they were sitting together holding hands.

I poured the grits into the serving pan, covered them with the lid and walked them out to the buffet.

Nellavon barged into the dining hall then, and I could almost feel the energy around her tense up defensively. Taylor followed close behind her, as if hiding in her wake. It was obvious that a "good morning" greeting was inappropriate.

"What's wrong, Nellavon?" I asked.

She leered towards the kitchen and snarled, "Hardly got a wink of sleep last night."

"Oh?" I looked from her to Osanna and Yolanda who were chattering away in rapid-fire Spanish.

"*That family* was up all night. Music booming from their cabin. Fireworks off the dock. Dancing and carrying on!"

*Oh no, surely not all night, she must be exaggerating,* I thought.

"Good thing I was awake! I was out on the porch having a cigarette, when I heard this horrendous scream. Honestly, I thought it was a wild animal in pain, but then I saw this red and purple bomb flying towards me. This lost firework whooshed onto the porch, hitting that family of papier-mâché carolers in their sled. Boof! Kerblooey! They went up in a spectacular shower of purple and pink."

Taylor nodded tenting then released his hands indicating an explosion.

I stared dumbly, beginning to feel like I needed to hold onto something for support.

"Woke most of the rest of us up — Baby Vonnie started wailing, Betsy screamed in her sleep —"

I didn't care about that, I wanted to know if anyone was hurt, if the porch was in cinders, and if I was going to be filing an insurance claim.

"Was anyone hurt?" I asked.

Betsy and Pike came in then and joined us.

"No," Nellavon snarled irritably, "I got hit with a few sparks, but fortunately, you had that fire extinguisher mounted right there on the wall. I got the fire out quick enough."

Pike said, "The carolers didn't make it."

Betsy added, "Scared me silly, that *whoosh-boom*."

Pike said "It's a sludgy mess. I swept what I could into the corner."

"And the porch?" I asked, biting my lip.

Nellavon ignored my question. "Those people were just laughing their asses off over there on the dock. Totally oblivious! Could've killed me dead!" She snarled, actually showing teeth like a rabid wolf. Having vented her grievance to her satisfaction, she grumped her way over to the coffee pot.

Taylor said, "Oh, it's not bad. Nellavon emptied the extinguisher on it to be sure it was out. There's a bit of smoke damage on the ceiling and the floor needs to be cleaned--"

Benny opened the door and Cameron pushed Mama Sue in her wheelchair past him.

Pike said, "Oh here they are. Mama Sue slept through the whole thing."

Taylor trailed behind Nellavon to get some coffee. Betsy turned to Cameron, "We were just telling them about the excitement last night."

"That was something else! I think Mama Sue was the only one who got any sleep."

Mama Sue had a Mona Lisa smile — hard to say if it was one of serenity or mischief.

Cameron glanced toward the kitchen, "I don't know how they do it. Those people are tireless. When they got done with the fireworks, they loaded up into cars and drove off. It was close to midnight!"

*Hadn't Yolanda said something about midnight mass? That was probably it.*

Pike said, "Yeah, it was like one-thirty when I heard them come back."

Benny said, "Hey, speaking of sparks, that reminds me — Did you hear about the explosion at the cheese factory — da brie went everywhere!"

Cameron shook her head and headed toward the juice pitchers.

I'm sure Benny meant to make light of the situation, but it only made me feel more gutted. "Okay, I'll get over there to get it cleaned up right after breakfast." I glanced back to the kitchen to see Yolanda swaying to the beat of the music. Were they aware that they'd almost set my cabin on fire? I hadn't authorized fireworks! I felt powerless and betrayed.

Just then, Angejolie bounded in the door, followed by her parents. Animated, she pointing to the ceiling, saying "But I want to watch the cranes!"

"Good morning, sweetheart," I said, picking up an empty tray of scrambled eggs. "What did you see?"

"Cranes!" she said, jumping, finger still high over her head.

"We heard a flock of them as we came in, but with all the trees, it's almost impossible to see them," her father said.

"Oh, they *are*!" I agreed. "They fly so high up, that by the time the sound travels back to us, they aren't where we think they are."

"I want to see them!" she cried.

"Tell you what," I said. "I think the sun is supposed to come out today. Maybe after breakfast, you can go to the dock or go for a walk to the meditation circle in the woods. You might be able to see them from the dock or the circle."

"Yes! Yes!" she said, jumping.

"Did you know that sandhill cranes can live for a really long time?" I asked.

Angejolie shook her head.

I turned to Duran and Violette. As they seemed like a devoted and happy couple, I blurted, "And they mate for life. In Japan, they are symbolic of good luck at weddings, representing long life and loyalty."

"Nice," Duran said with a side glance to Violette.

"Okay, Angejolie," Violette said, picking up two plates, "Let's focus on breakfast. Would you like some pancakes? Sausage?"

"I'll be back out with more eggs in a few minutes," I said, picking up a serving spoon that had fallen to the floor. I whisked back to the kitchen to fetch another batch of scrambled eggs.

I was considering how to address the fireworks with the Garcias when the remainder of the Garcia family (not already swarming in the kitchen) arrived in a noisy mass, making a big deal out of seating Dante and Aletea at the head of a table. Grandma Yaya was ceremoniously seated next to Aletea. Mingo and Rocky came in last, dressed in mariachi outfits, bearing guitars.

"What's the occasion?" I asked Clementina, who was coming out of the kitchen with a plate of mini cakes.

"It's their fortieth wedding anniversary!" she answered, beaming. She nodded towards Dante and Aletea.

The women presented the couple with heaping plates of food, and soon everyone was singing, clapping and/or clattering silverware to the beat.

Dante and Aletea held hands, eyes filling with tears as various family members hugged and kissed them. The festive atmosphere touched everyone in the dining hall. Several guests got up to shake hands and bestow good wishes on the couple. Many clapped along with the music. As the final song came to an end, cheers rose from family as well as guests:

"Congratulations!"

"Happy Anniversary!"

"*Felicidades!*"

"*Feliz Aniversario!*"

"We love you!"

It seemed to put just about everyone in an especially warm-hearted mood. Nellavon leered at them, understandably, but I had to wonder, did that woman ever smile? Even uptight Saint Eleanor looked misty-eyed. Shortly afterward, when Freddie Jay found it wildly amusing to startle his family members with his prized, petrified-alligator-foot keychain, it was perceived as quaint and amusing, not annoying. Throughout the meal it surfaced here and there: in his mother's lap, by his aunt Amy's plate, and finally, in Aunt Moira's carpetbag of a purse.

"Oh!" She exclaimed, then laughed. "I was reaching for my tissues and thought a monster had me."

Freddie Jay got a wink from his father along with the admonishment, "Okay, son, that's enough, put it away now."

I even laughed after Benny's voice boomed out, "A blonde and a brunette are out shopping. The brunette comments that Christmas will be on a Friday this year. The blonde says, "Oh, I hope it's not on the 13th!"

I happened to catch the gift exchange between Lorraine and her father, Leander: she set a huge gift bag by his seat and kissed his forehead; he pulled an envelope out of his inner jacket pocket and passed it to her. She slipped it into a back pocket. He squeezed her hand.

When I had a moment to talk with her, I mentioned the exchange. Keeping my voice low, I said, "Hey, I'm guessing you gave your dad the lava cake."

"Yup," she said, beaming.

She offered up nothing else, so I prodded, "I saw that he gave you an envelope. What did you get?"

"Oh," she said with a naughty smile, "a coupon for the full spa package — hot rock massage, facial, foot scrub, eyebrows..."

"But..." I looked around, "You lost the bet, right? You bet that Amy and Stuey would break up before Christmas Eve."

"Oh, I know," she said, with a dismissive smirk. "Once when I was a little girl, my father bet me that I could ride my bicycle. That day, I lost the bet. I was shattered. Since then, we bet on stuff all the time, but then we both get each other what we bet anyway. Win-win. Always. It's our thing."

"Aww! That's really sweet," I said, my heart softening.

I was swapping out a pan of sausages when Robin and Rain Warcloud entered the dining hall. Rain looked around the tables, spotted Angejolie and darted over to her. Whatever he said excited her. She became animated with excitement. "I want to see the baby! I want to see the baby!"

Ah-ha! Way to go Mehitabel!

Robin called for Rain to join her in the buffet line, which he did, with difficulty. Violette and Duran had a tough time keeping Angejolie from bolting for the door.

Robin handed Rain a plate and they began their selections.

"Mehitabel had her—oh wait, you told me, oh yes, *cria,* then? Is she okay?"

"Yes, late last night. She's fine. Chaz is bringing them over after breakfast so the children can see them. The cria is so cute. All snowy white. Rain can't wait to show it off."

"Angejolie will lose her mind," I said, nodding to her, still animated and bouncing in her seat.

I glanced over to the buffet line to see Essie Jane and Taquira Showers. After seeing her in the elegant, red performance gown the previous night, it took me a moment to recognize Ms. Showers in blue jeans and a jacket.

I wandered closer. "Thank you again so much for your performance last night. You were amazing. Did you sleep well? Was the cabin comfortable?"

"Yes, thank you, I did," Ms. Showers said as Essie Jane nodded. "I had a strange dream, now that I think about it. I don't usually dream a lot. There was this youngish woman— she was dressed in this loose-fitting outfit, a flowy top and skirt, and a sparkly necklace. She held out her hands to me and said something like 'you are blessed with gifts'. I wish I could remember more. She had such a peculiar expression, kind of earnest and sad, but she was thanking me for something. I felt like I should know who she was, but I don't."

"Well, you certainly are blessed with an amazing voice," I

said.

"Thank you," she said with a warm smile.

"I slept like a baby, better than usual," Essie Jane said. "The bed was so comfortable."

"Glad to hear it," I said, grateful that their cabin was far enough away from the dock and the fireworks.

Ms. Showers said, "I wish we didn't have to get to Sarasota. I'd love to spend more time here. It's beautiful. I'm going to have to sit on the dock for a moment at least before we go. It's so peaceful."

Essie Jane nodded.

I wanted to suggest that they post a review on any of the hotel review pages but thought that would be tacky. I was relieved to know they'd enjoyed their stay.

I was setting out more fresh fruit when Freddy sidled up next to me to get a biscuit. "You've really done a great job, Haint. Mom and Dad really like this place."

"Oh great, happy to hear it," I said.

Just then, we heard Lerlene yell, "*Freddie*! Put it away! If I have to count to three…"

We glanced over to see Freddie Jay pocketing the offending keychain.

Freddie chuckled. "Hey, that reminds me, did you hear about the old alligator who couldn't get it up?"

"No…"

"He suffered from a reptile dysfunction."

"Ouch. Go sit down," I said. "If I have to count to three…"

He smirked, scooping up some fruit.

Buster told me later that Eliazar, Oscar and Oro figured out that Cindy, Kirby, Linwood and the other LARPers had been the zombie bell-ringers of the previous evening. He overheard the children interrogating the adults with questions like:

- "Do zombies sleep?"
- "Do zombies eat anything besides brains?" ("That sounds gross and *boring*.")
- "How do they walk if their legs fall off?"
- "How do they hear if their ears fall off?"
- "If parts fall off, can they be re-attached?"
- "If a boy zombie and a girl zombie have a baby, is it a zombie?"
- "Zombies can't smell, right, because if they could, they would know that they *stink*."
- "Zombies are never happy, are they? They are always groaning and always hungry."

The LARPers were evidently amused by the questions and happy to educate.

Breakfast was winding down when I noticed Pedro and Lorraine having a brief exchange by the coffee machine. She pulled out her wallet and handed him what I guessed was her business card. He nodded, looked around towards his family, and stepped away.

Not long after, Lorraine made her way to me.

"Guess what!"

"He spoke to you, and you gave him your card."

"Yes! He said he really liked my cakes and might want to hire me for an event. But the way he looked at me and pressed my hand, it was like old-fashioned Victorian secret codes…"

"Not surprising. His family is nosier than a pack of bloodhounds on a fresh trail. I *told* you he likes you. Hey, the sun is out. Maybe you could disappear for a walk or something. You know, show him the meditation circle."

"I'll see if I can cut him from the herd. Apparently, they were up all night. Poor guy looks exhausted. They all went to midnight mass, then — did you know they are roasting a pig in a fire pit they made over by their cabin? They're cooking it for Christmas dinner."

I squeezed my eyes shut and forced myself to take a deep breath. "No. I didn't know they were cooking a pig in a pit on my property."

"Oopsie. Well, I didn't tell you."

"Of course, they are. I can hardly get into my own kitchen because it's become a tamale factory." I took another deep breath. They'd be gone tomorrow.

She laughed and waved a hand. "I bet it'll be *delicious.*"

"Well, I sure don't have to worry about feeding everyone, that's for sure. Anyway, good luck with Pedro. You'll have to be stealthy. If they catch you, he won't live it down. They're already telling Clementina that they won't raise her baby. I don't think she even has a boyfriend."

"Gotcha."

My phone rang then. Checking it, the caller was Iggy. I picked up. I trotted outside so I could hear better.

"Merry Christmas, Sis!"

"Merry Christmas, *brat* – miss you. How's it going?"

"Okay, I guess. Apparently, this family sleeps in on Christmas. I'm out on the porch with my coffee for a moment alone."

"And?"

"Oh, all is good…except Louise's uncle had a mini stroke last night just after dinner. We called the ambulance and some of the family spent a good part of the night in the ER with him. Seems to be okay though. He's back with a prescription for blood pressure meds. That was crazy."

"Oh? Well, I don't mean to make light of that, but I'll see your EMTs and raise you bell-ringing zombies, a trailer fire, a porch fire, and a pregnant alpaca."

He laughed. "For real?"

"Could I make that up?"

"Didja ever hear from Buster?"

I smiled as my chest got all warm. "Yes! He surprised me by showing up. Only thing is, with the retreat filled to the max, we haven't had much time together."

"Aw. You've been busy, huh?"

I gave him the truncated version of events ending with, "it's been crazy; I'm exhausted; but this has been a really fun holiday."

Just as I said this, I heard the distinct honking clatter sound of sandhill cranes.

"Oh, Angejolie won't want to miss this–" I said, rushing inside to get her attention.

"What?" I heard Iggy ask.

"Angejolie!" I cried spotting her. "Sandhill cranes! Outside! Come quick!"

She came running, followed by her parents and a few of the other children. They ran to the dock (the best sky-view location) and craned (not my fault, I'm telling you, they just come) their necks upward.

"I gotta go, Iggy—kind of a magical moment here with sandhill cranes. I'll call you back. Love you."

"Okay. You too, Sis."

Soon there was a crowd, mostly made up of children, but some adults too, eyes to the sky tracking the V pattern squadrons of sandhills. There were a lot of them. It was like avian D-day as one after another sets of birds flew overhead.

"I got a picture!" Angejolie yelled in delight.

"You did! Look at that!" Her mother said, patting her back.

"Magic!" she squealed.

Yes, indeed. Magic.

# Chapter 26

## CHRISTMAS GHOSTS

reakfast was over; most of the guests had left the dining hall. As Osanna and Yolanda were having a heated argument in the kitchen, I busied myself wiping tables and sweeping. The LARPers were just about finished at their table. Kirby and Linwood were standing and stretching; Ray was finishing off a pancake. Cindy was downing her juice. Remaining were Buster, Gigi, Aunt Moira, and Lorraine in a cluster by the now empty buffet line, with an uncomfortable-looking Saint Eleanor closer to the door, distancing herself.

"It's all unchristian. I don't understand why you' waste your time with such unwholesome rubbish," she said, wringing her hands.

The others ignored her, engaged in an animated discussion about the nebulous boundaries between mythic, supernatural, and cryptid creatures.

"Have you ever seen a Bigfoot?" Gigi asked Buster.

"Three of 'em. I was in the Himalayas. Up thar, they call

'em *migos*. It was getting' on towards evenin' when I looked up the mountain to this snowy clearin'. Three hairy, bipedal figures was movin' across an open area. Two were full size, one was juvenile. They stopped and looked at me, then hurried on towards the tree line. They was far away, but I cain't think of any animal that'd look like that. They was upright and walkin' but hairy-like."

Lorraine's eyebrows rose. "Interesting."

"Are you a ghost hunter?" Gigi asked.

"Nah, see that's a whole diff-ernt thang. The scope of cryptozoology is the study of hidden or unknown animals. Ghosts, spirits and demons an' all, that's supernatural."

Saint Eleanor, it seemed,  had been growing exponentially uncomfortable. By the time she turned to leave she looked out of sorts and on the verge of paralysis, she was so stiff. Either that, or she was mustering a subconscious impression of Dame Maggie Smith. She sniffed, with an air of haughty virtuosity, "I'll go see what the children are up to. I heard that there was some llama or something…a petting zoo? Show and tell?"

"Okay, Mom," Lorraine called after her, not taking her eyes from Buster. "Okay, but have you ever seen a ghost?"

"I have. Quite a few, actually."

"Oh, where is my brain? I'm *so* glad you said that," Aunt Moira cried, pulling out her phone. "Haint! Come over here! You'll want to see this!"

I set the broom aside, pushed a chair in,  and joined them. "What?"

"Gigi and I are night owls. We were up talking late. It

seemed like the sky cleared a bit and there was a new moon, so it was still real dark. You know, our trailer's parked near your laundry shed. We went to use the little girls' room, there by the parking lot entrance, and on the way back, I thought I heard giggling by where the woods trail starts."

Gigi interrupted. "I didn't hear it, but I got a weird vibe that there was something watching us."

Aunt Moira nodded. "We were curious. We started walking that way."

"Ooh, I'm getting the shivers just thinking about it," Gigi said, rubbing her arms.

"What?" I asked.

"Ah, here it is," Aunt Moira said, holding out her phone, "I'm so glad I had my phone with me. I just had a feeling–and then I saw them, just for a second —"

"I didn't see them, but you can see them plain as day there, on her phone," Gigi said, still rubbing her arms.

"Oh!" Lorraine squealed.

"Well, ain't that somethin'?" Buster said, tugging at his chin. "That's whatsername and her two sons, right?"

Aunt Moira nodded. "Spotted Fawn."

I looked.

My body tingled. It wasn't fear, exactly, but I wasn't prepared for it. Unlike photos on the internet, I couldn't tell myself this was photoshopped. This was real. I stared, then touched the screen carefully to make the image expand to see more detail. "That's really her? Gosh, I've seen her out of the corner of my eye a few times and thought it was my imagination. You took this picture last night?"

"Yep, right near the trail, at the edge of the parking lot."

"Well, let me ask you something. Why are they here? Shouldn't we send her on to the white light or something?"

"She's lonely," Buster said.

"How do you know?" I asked, swiveling my head.

"Well, I mean, Shane said she tried to get in bed with 'im when he was here, an' she never shows up with a man, just her boys, right? Where's Max?" Buster looked around. "Aw, guess he left. He should see this. I don't rightly recall Charlene or Max ever mentioning anyone besides them three."

"That's right," Aunt Moira said.

"Well, what happened? Did you talk with her? Did she say anything?" I asked.

"Couldn't help hearing you talking of ghosts. Don't mean to be nosy, but whatcha got there?" Linwood asked. Kirby, Cindy and Ray were behind him.

Aunt Moira turned her phone so they could see the spooky image.

"Oh, wow!"

"Let me see!"

Aunt Moira let them pass the phone around and turned back to me.

"Well, she communicated, let's say, not in words, but yes. She's here because of you, Haint. She feels like she can relate to you. A lonely woman tied to this place, working hard, isolated...She wasn't from the tribe who lived here. She migrated south from Georgia with her husband, but he was killed. She and her boys made their way here, only to get sick and die among strangers. She felt lost for a long time. She liked Max and Charlene. She loves you. She misses her family terribly but doesn't know how to find them."

"That's so sad," I said. I was also touched by this revelation that Spotted Fawn felt a kinship with me.

"She and the boys love all the decorations and the guests. They think it's a big party. They love all the gifts, the lights, the music."

I got another frisson* at the word "gifts" thinking of the weird things I'd found lately, the feathers, the necklace, the serving spoon. "Is it possible for a ghost to make things appear and then disappear again?"

"When was this taken?" Lloyd asked.

"Last night. Over near the woods by the laundry." Gigi answered.

---

\* one of those Word of the Day words: shiver, goosebumps, chill

"They're *here*?" Kandi asked shuddering.

Gigi nodded enthusiastically.

Aunt Moira nodded, answering me, "Yes. It takes energy to make things move, but they can. Why?"

"I've been finding odd things, but they disappear. I found a necklace — Buster saw it — but then I lost it."

Buster nodded.

I continued, "I took it off that night and put it on the table next to the bed. The next morning, it was gone. Not on the floor, under the bed, nothing. I know I put it there."

Osanna had just come from the kitchen in a huff, but slowed and catching a bit of conversation asked, "What are you talking about?"

"Any feathers?" Aunt Moira asked, cocking her head.

"Yes! How did you know?"

"Ghosts," Lorraine said, answering Osanna.

"I thought so!" Osanna said, eyes wide. "You mean the one here, right? The one that tried to you know, do the nasty with Pedro--?" Her eyes went a bit wild as she jiggled her head.

Aunt Moira tapped the screen to refresh her phone and showed her the picture.

"Oh, no way! Are you serious right now? That's for real? *Here*?" She looked over her shoulder and hollered, Yolanda! Come! You have to see this!" As there was no sign of Yolanda, Osanna trotted back to the kitchen mumbling, "Oh, you aren't even going to believe this."

Gigi turned her gaze from the retreating Osanna to me and continued, "Feathers are signs from the spirit world."

"I've heard about that!" Kandi said.

I looked from Kandi to Aunt Moira, "I've heard that before, but you know, I live in the woods. It's not like I don't have owls and hawks and –"

"But they got your attention, didn't they?" Aunt Moira said.

"Yes. They were right in my path. But then, I'd be more likely to see the ones in my path than the ones in the poison ivy, say—"

"Mmm-hmm," Gigi said. "But somehow you felt like it was a sign, right?"

"Maybe? I don't want to read too much into it."

"And that's smart. What else was there?"

"A necklace… a weird wooden spoon… camellia flowers in strange places."

Ray looked at his watch and shifted his weight.

Aunt Moira grasped my wrist. "She connects with you like a sister she never had. Imagine a lost soul who failed to protect her children, felt abandoned, unloved, frightened. She loves your energy. She loves how you've made this place peaceful and beautiful."

"And she likes some of the men who stay here too," Lorraine said with naughty eyebrow action.

"Oh, *really*?" Linwood asked.

Ray looked decidedly uncomfortable. "Um, guys—"

Several of the LARPers giggled.

Osanna came trotting back, pulling Yolanda by the hand. "Wait 'til you see this."

Ray seemed repelled by the image being passed around on the phone. "Hey guys, we need to hit the road, eh?" He turned to me. "Can we check out with you?"

I was torn. I wanted to know more about Spotted Fawn, but the crowd was too much for me, and the image of a blackened porch with a debris mess nagged at me like a mental tick bite. I needed to see the damage.

"Can we talk about this again later?" I asked Aunt Moira. "They want to check out and I need to go check on a cabin…" I took Buster's hand and slowly pulled him with me.

I turned to Ray. "You can just drop your key cards in the jar in the office if you like — whenever you're ready."

Lorraine shot me a question-mark eyebrow.

"Sure hon," Gigi and Aunt Moira said in unison.

The LARPers mobbed me for a moment with thanks and goodbyes and what a fun time they'd had. We thanked them back for the entertainment and wished them well at their Christmas Day Zombie Hotel Invasion or whatever they'd said that event was called.

I waggled my head to Lorraine, indicating that she could come with us. Finally, the three of us were free. It felt good to be out in the open air again. It had gotten a bit close for me back there. That photo. Not my imagination. Not a quaint little story that Max had cooked up. Spotted Fawn was real.

So was the almost porch fire.

When we got out of earshot of the others, I gave them the rundown of the porch incident. "I'm really not happy about this. I'm dreading what we're going to find."

Buster gave my hand a squeeze, "If she got the extinguisher right on it, it prob'bly ain't too bad."

## PORCH CLEANUP

As we got closer to cabin seven, a truck with a short trailer came into view behind a stand of palmettos. Rocky tossed a shovel onto the trailer bed and turned towards us. His shirt sleeves were rolled up partially revealing his tattooed arms.

"Hey," he said, eyeing a dark mess of debris behind him. "We got it. We're so sorry about your—" his eyes wandered over the mess as he searched for the word and decided on, "--thing."

"Oh—" I said, tongue-tied. I hadn't expected this. Nice of them to help clean up. I regarded the soggy, charry pile. The only recognizable part were the metal runners and a bit of blackened, wood sled. I wasn't entirely sorry to see the demise of the carolers. It meant one less item to put into storage, and they were a bit of the creepy side.

Mingo came around the side of the cabin with a rag mop and a bucket. "So sorry about what happened," he said, with a fearful look. "Okay if I dump the bucket here?" He pointed to the palmettos.

I nodded. Buster tugged me along towards the porch, "Let's have a little ol' look."

May was sitting in a rocking chair with Vonnie in her lap. He was making delightful, happy-baby gurgles.

There was a hint of a smokey taste in the air as we walked

up the steps. To the left was a bare space where the Victorians had been. The floor was clean, wet with mop trails, no sign of damage. The ceiling had a dark spot and some curdling paint.

"Well, that' ain't hardly nothin'," Buster said, squeezing my hand again. "See? All that frettin' –"

"That's not half-bad," Lorraine said, voice filled with relief.

"A bit o' scrapin' and a brush o' paint — be right as rain again," Buster said, smiling.

Rocky and Mingo came up the stairs behind us. Rocky said, "We'll be happy to fix it. Have you got any of that paint?"

"I'm pretty sure I do," I said, feeling relieved and grateful.

The angst and resentment I'd been feeling left me faster than a pizza delivery, replaced by forgiveness and gratitude.

"Got a ladder?" Mingo asked.

"Yeah, sure."

The minor repair job became its own celebratory event as the Garcia and Johnson families stood by watching Mingo scrape and paint the damaged patch. Anna and Zelia had a grand time entertaining Vonnie, as Oscar and Oro did a pantomime recreation of the fireworks and "explosion". Osanna arrived with an industrial-sized cooler of lemonade, and bags of pretzels and cookies. Two hours later, the only evidence that anything had happened, was the wet look of the paint patch and a few empty party cups that had tumbled into the bushes from the porch.

Somewhere in the mix, Ceci, Katie and Clementina had coerced Buster into leading another meditation session. As Christmas day dinner was going to be at three o'clock, and Lord only knew we had plenty of food, I was free to attend.

He *was* amazing.

His hypnotic voice, his gentle direction, his innate knowledge of when to be silent and when to suggest a thought, all made the hour seem way too short. Somewhere between relaxing and deep breathing, I felt like I was almost asleep — deep, deep, away, and yet somehow very present at the same time. Amazing. Honestly, when he guided us back to reality, I had to mentally re-download basic information to get my bearings: I'm in the meditation hall. It's Thursday, Christmas day. These are my guests. That amazing man sitting serenely up there is Buster Shadetree, my boyfriend...

"That was dreamy," Ceci said.

*Yes, it was.*

"I don't know what you did, but that was the first time I've felt relaxed in ages," Lorraine said.

*Me too.*

"He's a keeper, Haint!" Aunt Moira said. "We might stay a

while longer, if that's alright. I could get used to this!"

Buster and I locked eyes and a deep look passed between us. I was proud of him and awed by him. His eyes held unconditional love.

*Oh, yes, he's a keeper,* My Inner Critic whispered.

# PART EIGHT

# SANDHILL CRANE SONG (SWAN SONG)

# Chapter 27

## A Fine Day for Fire Trucks, Motorcycles, And Shooting Stars

Shortly after the meditation, Lorraine got my attention, patting Freddie Jay's head. "This young man has a question for you." A small group of us were milling around outside the meditation hall.

"Could we play with the fire truck? You said if the weather was good. Look—" he spun around in the sunshine.

"Yes, sure, as long as an adult is watching. I don't want you getting hit in the parking lot or anything." I fished a set of keys out of my pocket and passed them to Lorraine. "I've got to run home and get Naughty Britches. The truck is in the shed. Can Freddie get it for you? It's kind of bulky."

"He probably wants to play with it too, right F.J.?"

Freddie Jay furrowed his brow, "He's too big to sit in it."

Lorraine shot me a look that said, "Yeah, when did that ever stop a man from doing something he shouldn't?"

I said, "It usually starts with, 'Y'all what this' or 'hold my beer', right?

She smirked. "Got that right."

I waved goodbye and headed home.

Lorraine told me later that the fire truck was a big hit with the kids. Dee was the designated dispatcher, sending Freddie Jay off to put out fires and rescue Clover who seemed to pop up everywhere in distress. They soon got the attention of Oro, Oscar, Anna, Mimi and Angejolie. Someone found a bucket in the shed, and since you have to have water to put out a fire, they found a spigot and added a bucket of water to the fire engine. In no time, they were slopping water over each other and, as described, became a Keystone Cops adventure with too many children riding on the fire truck at once.

Lorraine reported that in the midst of the fire drills, Urliss, Hollis, Chaz and Rain arrived with the trailer and unloaded the alpacas to exercise them on the walking trail. The children left the fire truck to go see the alpacas.

"Did you know that alpacas hum to each other? Oh, it was insane how cute the baby is, and the mom and the baby humming to each other. I want a baby alpaca."

"Uh-huh."

The excitement drew curious adult guests as well. Chaz and Rain acted as impromptu guides informing their audience of odd facts about alpacas. They advised the children to keep their distance from the baby, as the mother would be very protective of it.

"What's its name?" they asked.

"Well, we need a name," Rain said, "and she's a girl."

"Fido," Freddie offered with a pleased-with-himself smirk.

"Packie!" Crystale said.

"Fluffy!" Clover yelled.

"Marshmallow!" Betsy called out.

Angejolie shot up a hand. "I saw a shooting star last night! I want to name it Shooting Star!"

Rain said, "Ooh, I like Shooting Star. Dad?"

Chaz looked towards Robin. She shrugged, "Works for me."

"YAY!" Angejolie cried, bouncing up and down.

And it was about then that Eliazar asked, "Do you smell smoke?"

People began looking around.

Pedro pointed, "Isn't that smoke coming from that trailer?"

"Whose trailer is that?"

Angejolie was the first to mobilize, leaping to action, running to the fire truck, followed by Oro, Oscar and Freddie Jay.

This was about the time that Clementina came running in to find me, "Excuse me, Ms. Haint—someone's trailer is on fire."

*"What?"*

"Over that way," she said, pointing toward the first parking lot.

Gigi and Aunt Moira had been sitting by the window, bird watching.

"What?" Aunt Moira asked, getting up.

"Whose trailer on fire?" Gigi asked.

"First parking lot? That could be us." Aunt Moira said.

"Oh, shit! I forgot to blow out the candle!" Gigi said, now also rushing towards us.

"Oh, Gigi, no, you didn't! Not again!" Aunt Moira moaned.

We got outside to see gray smoke coming from a trailer surrounded by onlookers, and of all people, Benny taking charge. He'd scooped up the water bucket from the fire truck and rushed inside. He'd taken off his coat to beat at the flames eating the kitchen curtains.

"I'll call 9-1-1," someone said.

"Oh, no!' Aunt Moira said, pushing through the crowd to get to the door of her trailer. "Who said that? Please don't. I'm sure it'll be fine," Aunt Moira said.

I paused, in mid-dial myself. Why wouldn't she want the fire department to come?"

Benny emerged from the trailer, coughing. "I got it. Curtains are toast and the wall will need some repair, but it's not bad, really."

Aunt Moira bustled past him to see for herself.

"Hey, that reminds me… what do an earthquake, tornado, and a redneck divorce have in common?"

No one was paying attention; we were all more concerned about the state of the trailer interior. But that didn't stop Benny.

"Whatever way it goes, someone's going to lose a trailer!" Benny said, laughing, then coughing.

"Thank you so much!" Gigi gushed, grabbing Benny by the

arms. "It's my fault. I forgot to blow out my meditation candle. I'm so bad that way. My nickname in college was Fire Hazard."

"You're welcome. No biggie. I happened to see it, and I used to be a volunteer fireman. It just came natural."

"Well, thanks again!"

Oro and Oscar had gone for another water run and came back with the fire truck blaring its sirens.

"It's okay, boys! The fire is out." Benny announced.

The boys looked crushed. Oro had apparently been looking forward to throwing more water, so even though the side of the trailer was not on fire, he chucked the bucket of water at it anyway. Unfortunately, it was just as Aunt Moira was coming back out. She got a good bit of the backsplash and shrieked.

"The fire and rescue are on the way," someone said.

"Aw, shit," Aunt Moira said, coughing.

I noticed that there was a colorful, fabric handbag over her shoulder that she'd not had with her when she'd gone into the trailer.

*Isn't that curious? What was she guarding? Drugs?*

*Don't jump to conclusions,* the Inner Critic warned. *Could be anything from a bag of doobies, to an inhaler, emergency allergy meds to a mother-of-pearl-handled handgun. Maybe even a pet knitting project.*

Lorraine happened to be in the crowd near me. I wanted to pull her aside and ask her, but that wasn't fair; she wasn't responsible for her aunt. Quite possibly she didn't know. And how would I even ask? Hey, what's in your aunt's handbag? Lyrics from an old blues song came to mind: "Ain't none o' yo bidness." The mystique of Aunt Moira just ratcheted up a notch.

"I'm so sorry, Moira," Gigi said, rubbing Moira's back. "I'll pay for damages."

"Don't sweat it, kid. The insurance'll cover it. You can make some pretty new curtains." She turned to Benny. "Thanks for what you did." She looked like she was going to say something else, but stopped, distracted by something around his head. "Your father was an Eagle Scout, wasn't he?"

Benny's face transformed into something awkward between fear, disbelief, and awe.

"What? My dad? Well…yes, yes, he was. How did —?"

"He's with you," she said, patting his shoulder. "He loves you very much."

All of Benny's bluster and bravado disappeared. He staggered a bit, looking shocked. "Yes, we were close… I need to, I need to, um…" He rubbed his arms and excused himself.

"I'm so sorry," Gigi repeated to no one in particular, "how bad is it really?" She went inside the trailer.

"We'll need a new table and cushions…" Aunt Moira said, following her.

From inside, I could hear Gigi say, "Oh, dear, I'm so sorry, oh, look, what a mess."

The crowd began to disperse. The children went on to play Keystone-cops fire truck around the parking lot with Lerlene tagging along to supervise.

Buster and Max were having a little parley on the office porch.

"Whew. Crisis averted. Small damage, but Benny seems to have saved the day," I reported.

Max snorted.

"Kinda reminds me of a time when my tent caught fire," Buster began with a distant smile. The way he pronounced "fire" was more like "far", so it took me a second to catch up to his story. "I was out in California, back in the early 80's...had been out in the woods on my own for some days, an' hadn't heard about the fires. Woke up chokin' and realized my tent was glowin' orange..."

Before he got too "far" with his story however, the fire and rescue truck arrived. The Keystone-Cop-fire-truck crew met the real fire truck crew with awe.

Gigi and Aunt Moira came out of the trailer to meet the team and assure them that all was well. A uniformed woman asked, "Mind if I just take a look to be sure?"

Aunt Moira stiffened, and I noted that she was clutching that fabric bag tightly between her arm and her side when she said a curt "yes" and stepped aside. Meanwhile, the children swarmed the remaining two firefighters.

"Could we sit in your truck?"

"Can we turn on the hose?"

"Can I put on your hat?"

"Where's the spotted dog, Mister?"

When the brief investigation of the fire was complete, the third firefighter rejoined the others and it was decided that since they didn't have another call at present, they could give the kids a ride around the retreat in the fire truck with the parents' permission. This led to a joyous photo opportunity, as the children posed in hats on the fire truck and got to do one lap with the siren blaring.

Fortunately, Chaz and Violette had walked the alpacas out towards the meditation circle, so they weren't frightened by all the brouhaha. The excitement had drawn everyone else out to see what was going on, even Mama Sue and Grandma Yaya. They smiled, clapped, and cheered as much as the children.

"Well kids, we can't stay, but before we go, we have something for you," said the lead firefighter, ducking into the cab of the truck.

This was met by bouncing cheers, "Yay!" "Yeah!" "Yippee!" Angejolie turned to look at her parents—mouth wide, astonishment and glee all over her face.

"Best Christmas ever!"

"I want to be a fireman when I grow up!"

"Can we turn on the hose?"

He returned with a box of trinkets and began tossing them to the small group of children as if from a Mardi Gras float. Soon the children were putting on red sunglasses, blowing red plastic whistles, rolling red yo-yos or tossing gel stress balls. Eliazar ran over to Mama Yaya and put a pair of red sunglasses on her face. She hugged him hard, he hugged her back.

May was holding Vonnie, who'd been upset by the siren noise. She was bouncing him and trying to make him laugh by squeezing a gel ball for him. She must have noticed Mama Yaya laughing and wearing sunglasses. She grabbed a pair and trotted over to Mama Sue and put them on her face.

Vonnie laughed.

Mama Sue laughed.

Mama Sue hugged May and kissed the baby.

I heard Max gasp like Redd Foxx having a heart attack.

"You okay, Max?" Buster asked.

Max held his chest. "Yeah. Just a flashback. It's nothin'."

And then Benny emerged from the crowd like a moray eel telescoping out of a coral bed (I'd thought he'd gone back to his cabin after his weird encounter with Aunt Moira) and said, "Look out, May, she might be measuring you for the grave!"

May frowning, turned to find him in the assemblage. Once she spotted him, laughing like a fool, she lobbed the gel ball at him like a World Series pitcher, and beaned him right between the eyes.

He blinked and stepped back then shook his head. A bright red spot glowed in the center of his forehead.

Mama Sue laughed so hard her top denture flew out. Between Benny looking like a lost clown and Mama Sue turning red and slapping the arms of her wheelchair, I thought I was going to stroke out laughing. Max was doubled over, holding onto a porch rail for support. Oro and Oscar were rolling on the ground laughing. Cameron was whooping and pointing at Benny.

You know how laughter is contagious — well, this was nuts. There were people all over the parking lot laughing, pointing, tearing up, and gasping for breath. And just when it might have tapered off, Amy got a gel ball and lobbed it at Stuey, beaning him in the head. It so happened that Stuey was close to the children's fire truck that had been restocked with a fresh bucket of water. He picked up the bucket and dumped it over her head.

A great "*Ooooh*" erupted amidst the laughter as Amy stood momentarily stunned, water dripping from the hair in her eyes.

Noni said, "You had *that* coming."

Saint Eleanor stepped forward holding out her hands like a boxing umpire separating two prize fighters, "Amy. Stuey. It's Christmas. How about you call a truce. Everyone's watching."

Freddie Jay said, "I'll get another bucket of water." He said it earnestly, like a scout master fulfilling an obligation.

Stuey laughed, "Thanks, buddy." He picked up the gel ball and tossed it to Amy. "Your turn."

She caught it and lobbed it back, but without much force. It glanced off his chest.

"My turn," he said, walking closer. He waited until they were a foot apart and tapped her on the nose with it. "Tag, you're it."

She popped a kiss on his lips.

Mama Yaya yelled, "You kids need to get a room!"

"Whoa, well, we reckon you don't need us to put out *that* fire," one of the fire fighters said, laughing. "This has been the about the best call we've responded to ever. Y'all have a blessed holiday!" They waved goodbye and got into the fire truck.

The crowd waved and cheered after them.

"Goodbye!"

"Merry Christmas!"

"Blessings to you!"

"Thank you!"

## Peggy Sue

**T**he real fire truck was barely out of view when the *wub-wub-wub* of a motorcycle came up the retreat road. A vintage, cream and crimson motorcycle with matching sidecar came into view.

"Well, my stars," I heard Saint Eleanor exclaim.

"Oh hey, here she is," Urliss said.

The sidecar was loaded with packages. The driver was a hefty woman dressed in a butch rockabilly outfit: heavy black boots, black leather jacket, faded denim knee-length jeans, clingy, low-cut, red-and-white striped blouse, and matching red kerchief wrapped behind a huge roll of silver hair.

Urliss and Hollis went to meet her. "Hey, Sis, glad you could make it."

"How are my favorite brothers?" she asked, flashing a bright red lipstick smile.

"Where's Terry?" Hollis asked.

"Oh, he's having some issues with ulcers and feeling like a homebody. I couldn't just sit there. Not on Christmas! Had to see my twins!"

They hugged.

Hollis turned to me, "You remember Peggy Sue, dontcha?"

I did. Peggy Sue was a warden at the women's correctional facility in Ocala. I liked Peggy, she had a never-ending supply of energy and enthusiasm. I imagined that back in her day, she was the life of the party. She tended to jump eagerly from subject to subject with the enthusiasm of a boxer with a new basket of toys. This one! Wait, no, this one!

"Did I miss all the fun?" she asked, extracting herself from the bike. "Did I just pass a fire truck coming from here?"

*Where do I begin*? I thought. Fortunately, I didn't have to answer as she was getting bear-hugged and smooched by her brothers.

"Mmm, so good to see you," she said. "Superb day for a ride! Sorry I couldn't get here sooner." She looked at me, "Well, hey, Miss Haint! Did you get a new sign? I don't remember it being so, uh, *bright*. Love the colors! Wow, lookee here at all the cars! You must be doin' alright! Merry Christmas, Honey!" She said, enveloping me in a bear-hug. Her black leather coat was thick and supple. She was wearing a spicy perfume — I got hints of cardamom.

"Glad you could make it," I said. "We're doing a big dinner — you're just in time."

Her eyes travelled along the length of the porch, "Oh great! Ooh, look at all your beautiful decorations! I love it!"

"You should see the fronts of the cabins. They all have different themes —" I said, but she had turned back to the sidecar.

"I didn't forget, Urliss, though it's a shame the sun is out today. I've been sucking these down all week. I made you two a big batch of bourbon toddies, just like you like. I'd have heated 'em, but with this weather—" She pulled out two of the largest thermoses I'd ever seen—one green, one red, and handed them over.

"She makes the best drinks," Hollis said, taking his and cradling it like a newborn.

"She really does," Urliss said, eagerly reaching for his. "I've tried making them myself, but she puts some kind of magic into it."

Peggy Sue laughed heartily. "Well. What's doing?"

"We were just going to see the new baby alpaca," I said.

"The what-a?" she said laughing.

Urliss took Hollis's thermos saying, "I'll put these in the truck."

He nodded, parting with his new prize with reluctance.

When Urliss returned, we wandered over to the other parking lot to see Shooting Star.

After so many cold and dreary days, the cool clear day seemed to draw everyone outside. There were guests on the dock, guests paddling about in kayaks, children running and playing hide and go seek around the cabins. In the second parking lot, was a scene from a cordoned petting zoo at the zucchini festival: an audience gathered around the Warclouds and the alpacas, with Shooting Star the main attraction.

Rain was focused and serious as he listed facts about alpacas. Shooting Star, meanwhile, was adorable, goofy, and utterly enchanting. She gazed at the crowd with her warm brown, curious eyes while making funny little trills and coos, mouth going side to side. Mehitabel bumped noses with her, drawing a collective "awwww" from the crowd.

"Well, that's about the cutest thing I ever saw!" Peggy Sue marveled. "*I* want one! Think she'd fit in the sidecar?"

"I got to name her Shooting Star!" Angejolie told Peggy Sue with pride.

"You did? Well, that's a perfect name. Let's all make a wish on Shooting Star—I wish her a long life with excellent health!" As she said this and got cheers as a response, Peggy Sue raised her hand, realizing a bit late that she didn't have a drink to toast with. She looked at me.

"When's this dinner again? I could eat a – " she looked guiltily towards Shooting Star, "I could eat a LOT!"

From somewhere in the crowd, Freddie's voice rang out, "Say, what did the mother alpaca say when the family decided to go on a picnic?"

There was silence for a beat and then Benny guffawed and answered, "Alpaca lunch!"

As the group groaned, Benny asked, "Hey, you know what they call the end of days? The alpaca-lypse!"

I happened to see Max at that moment. He was standing with Urliss, Hollis and Buster. His little body was jiggling with laughter, but his face made me catch my breath—he was smiling, laughing, but with tears in his eyes. He felt me looking at him, turned his head and winked at me. He was having a good time. He was loving being back at his old stomping ground. He was even laughing with Benny. But he missed his Charlene.

I wandered over to him and gave him a long hug. "She's here in spirit, Max."

He didn't answer but hugged me hard back.

# Chapter 28

## WRAPPING IT ALL UP

I'm not sure who brought what, but Christmas dinner was made extra festive as crackers or poppers appeared at each place setting in the dining hall. You know--the pretty rolls things that go bang when you tug them open and silly toys and candies fall out. Red and green balloons had appeared, tied to chairbacks all over the room. I suspected that Mingo and Rita were the elves responsible for that. Midway through the abundant meal, most of the guests were wearing paper crowns and the tables were strewn with trinkets and wadded up paper.

Thanks to Urliss and Hollis and their "ballistic pruning", we had sprigs of real mistletoe in the table arrangements. I've no idea how mistletoe got its romantic mantle. It's actually an invasive, parasitic plant that attaches fairly high up in older trees. How does it get there? Birds eat the berries, fly around, sit in trees, and... It grows in a round clump and saps nutrients from its host. Believe it or not, the easiest way to get it down is with a shotgun, or so I've heard.

The roasted pig was scrumptious. Had I known about it, I wouldn't have planned an apricot glazed ham, but they were seasoned differently enough, so the redundancy wasn't a problem. The rest of the feast included sweet-potato casserole, wild rice pilaf with pistachios and cranberries, red cabbage and apples, succotash, and more tamales than I've ever seen. Lorraine provided a peppermint chocolate layer cake and a German chocolate and coconut cake and a lemon Bundt cake. They were, of course, amazing. (Yes, I paid her, but I suspected she went overboard so she'd have the excuse to avoid family reunion obligations.)

Somewhere in the post-pig-out stupor, Gigi and Aunt Moira thanked me for a lovely Christmas. I kicked myself afterward. I hadn't realized they were saying goodbye. I'd hoped to have another conversation about Spotted Fawn. Shouldn't we send her and her sons to the light or something? I felt so badly that she felt lost. How were we to help her find her true family? I lost my chance to ask Aunt Moira. Lorraine told me later that they'd quietly packed up a heap of leftovers in food storage containers and pulled up their tent stakes, so to speak.

The Warclouds and alpacas had left, with Rain and Angejolie vowing to remain friends and pen pals--well, email or text pals, I guess.

Peggy Sue hugged me and thanked me as she headed out. Her brothers encouraged her to go next door so they could visit some more.

She waved a plastic container of leftovers. "Oh, I wish I could, but I gotta get back to Terry and give him a taste of what he missed. He can hardly fend for himself, you know. Funnily enough, he can find the beer in the fridge, sure, no problem. But ask him to fix a sandwich or a can of soup, *pah*! He has no clue. Not like you boys! I'll come back soon. Promise." She hugged them and was soon heard roaring off on her motorcycle.

The Garcia clan decided to stay over. Made sense. They'd been up all night. Didn't see much of them after dinner; I assumed they were crashed out.

Before Pedro disappeared, however, he and Lorraine managed to find a private corner. She found me a bit later and bubbled, "Haint! It happened! He held the mistletoe over my head and kissed me! He asked me out on a date!"

"Congratulations! Where to?"

"Next Saturday, he suggested we go that horse rescue place in Alachua. We can feed carrots to old and blind horses for a while, then go out to lunch."

I smiled. "Nice."

"I thought so. Hope the weather cooperates."

Buster's words came to mind as I said, "Go anyway. Warm up afterwards with a hot cocoa—that's what it was made for."

"Mmm. I want to warm up with him, that's for sure," she said, twirling a wilting bit of mistletoe.

Once the dining hall was put to order and the kitchen was clean, I too needed a nap.

Early that evening, somewhat refreshed after a power-snooze, I invited Max, Urliss and Hollis over for a little gift exchange of our own.

# JUST US

"Well, I'm guessin' that this one here's mine," Buster said, taking the birch-tree camouflage stocking with a Bigfoot silhouette on the front. He squeezed it and shook it. "Well, that don't tell me much. Guess I'll just dig into it." He pulled out a wrapped bundle and set the rest aside. "Wonder what all we got goin' on here, now?"

"Just something silly," I said.

He ripped it open and unfolded the T-shirt I'd had printed for him. "Attention. Don't eat. Mokèlé-mbèmbé. I'd expected him to laugh out loud. Instead, a dark expression formed on his face. "So, you got that postcard then? Mokèlé-mbèmbé — golly what a mess that was." He ran a hand through his hair and stared at the shirt.

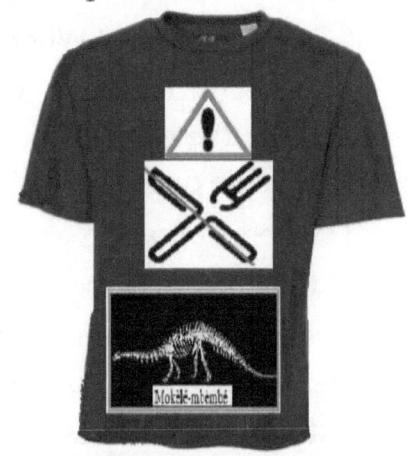

"*Kurwa.*" I muttered. Is there anything quite like the rapid emotional descent from hoping someone will love the gift and realizing that they don't?"

"What?" Buster asked.

"I thought you'd laugh. I looked it up. There was that story, you know, don't cook and eat the meat?"

*Oh yeah, that's it, keep talking…this is going over like a turd in the punch bowl, as Max would say*, groused my Inner Critic.

He nodded, holding it up. "Oh, I love it, Hon, don't worry. This'll be a great little ol' reminder of the most dangerous adventure of my life." He regarded it with the enthusiasm of a new convict being handed his first orange prison outfit.

"I'm sorry," I said again. "It was stupid." I looked away, patting Naughty Britches who was stretched out at my feet.

Buster exhaled and leaned back. "Mo-kè-lé-mbèm-bé," he said, drawing out each syllable. He shook his head. "Mokèlé-mbèmbé almost killed me."

"What?" we all said.

"Was it a big snake or something?" Max said, face all twisted in doubt.

"I shoulda smelled somethin' was off from the git-go," Buster began. "I was talked into goin' there. It was this window of opportunity and they made it sound like I had to jump or lose the chance...got this "invitation" to investigate. They sent me just enough "evidence" and put just enough urgency..."

"Who did?"

"Well, 'at's a question all in itself. SOMEONE heard about me an' got the big idea to get me over there. Don't know if it was the locals or the government... it don't matter."

"I think we need to hear the whole story," I said.

As if he hadn't heard me, Buster kept rambling, "I got in way over my head. And now, well, I've gone an' done somethin' that I didn't think I'd ever do. I'm working up a video an' I'm gonna haveta write an article sayin' that there's strong evidence. That I've seen it. Me. Buster, the Cryptid Buster. I'm gonna say that it's real, but I'm gonna have to word it very carefully so's only some crazy rich fool would think to go lookin' for it."

"*What?*" I asked. "*Why?*"

"It's *so* complicated…but first up, you can't imagine what it's like over there--the poverty and corruption—I, I cain't even hardly talk about it. Don't want to ruin Christmas here. The short of it is, there ain't no monster anything close to a dinosaur hidin' there. Keepin' the mokèlé-mbèmbé legend alive is good for business. A guide can feed his family for years offa one tour. Lead that rich dude to some "evidence", let him get his photo shoot, an' mebbee he survives and gets out, or…maybe not." He rubbed his back.

"Is that what you did?" I asked.

He made a noise like a zombie laugh, lacking humor and heart. "You know what? I've done some dumb things in my life that mighta got me killed. I been in some mighty dangerous situations with some unsavory people. I've been blessed to go to India an' Bhutan--a country most folks haven't even heard of--but the Congo—" he shook his head. "I've never been so scared in my life. Night and day take on new meaning—the officials who are supposed to be keepin' you safe in the daytime will turn into bandits at night. No one travels after dark. And even in the daytime, you don't know who you can trust. I near got killed over a dumb ol' flat tire." He held up his fingers indicating a miniscule space. "I was with a priest and a guide. They were good people, but they explained that other "guides" aren't reputable. An' if someone gets lost in the jungle--" He shrugged. "They'll even take money to investigate the disappearance but they ain't gonna find anythin', right?"

"Wow… more money to investigate. Good scam, huh." I said.

Urliss and Hollis nodded in unison.

Buster continued, "It was gettin' close to dark and we got this flat out in the middle of nowhere. Wouldn'tcha know, the spare was flat too. We found that out the hard way. Spent an uneasy night hidin' out. Heard vehicles drive by and stop. Heard voices and shoutin'. They didn't find us, though they got damn close." He rubbed his neck. "One of 'em almost stepped on me. I thought I'd get caught for sure."

"Jeez," Hollis muttered.

Buster continued, "They picked over the vehicle purty good. Fortunately, our guide had a cell phone signal and was able to reach a friend who came to fetch us in the wee hours o' the dawn. That was a looong night."

"You going to tell me about the bruises?" I asked.

"Let's just say that money usually talks, but sometimes, a security guard just likes roughin' people up for fun, even after they've paid for permission to travel. Some of 'em don't see it like a visa to travel at all. It's more like…grantin' permission to keep living."

"*O, Kurwa…*" I mumbled.

"It wasn't all bad. I got to see a lot of the area and met some good people, but, I'm tellin' ya, I saw a lot of corruption and dire poverty."

"Hey," Urliss said, pushing a huge rectangular something covered in a blanket towards Buster. "Speaking of cryptids, you need to open this."

Naughty Britches leapt up in alarm, eyes wide, and ran towards the bedroom.

"O-kay," Buster said, eyeing it warily. He pulled the blanket back in a swift motion like a magician unveiling a secret compartment. We beheld a dog crate with a motionless, mostly-mauve colored creature in it. The creature had the body of a lemur, the face of a wolf, crazy ears that were lime green inside, and antlers. The legs had two-tone poofs of fabric styled like the puffs they do on poodle legs. The puffs were a non-descript, dusty purple. The glass eyes regarded us with apprehension.

"Didja ever see one o' these before? They're very rare!" laughed Hollis.

"Naw, cain't say as I have," Buster answered, head cocked to one side like a confused Labrador.

"We were sure you didn't already have one!" laughed Urliss.

"Careful! He may look cute, but he bites, trust me! He tried to take my finger off last time I fed him!" Urliss said chuckling, holding up his hand with a bent finger.

The creature jumped and snarled suddenly. Buster and I jumped back. Hollis and Urliss guffawed until tears formed in their eyes. Hollis held up a tiny remote and hit a button. The tail wagged.

"Where in the world did you get that?" I asked. "Did you two make it yourselves?"

"Naw!" Hollis said. "There's a guy in a flea market up in Lake City who has a booth. Makes all kinds of fantastical creatures. The kids love 'em!"

"Ha-ha-ha!" Urliss was trying to talk but was laughing too much. He finally got himself under control, "He used to do proper taxidermy until his kids growed up and didn't like that he was dealin' with dead animals, so he got the bright idea to taxidermy these weird creatures instead using stuffed animals and leftover horns. People bring him stuff like rattles offa rattle snakes and stuff offa roadkill to make into creatures."

"I'm surprised I haven't heard of him before," Buster said, opening the cage door to touch it. "What's his name?"

"That's the best part!" Hollis said. "Deke Skinner. But his initials are D. K. so people call him D.K. like "decay"--ain't that about perfect for a taxidermist? Decay *Skinner*? His business is called D.K.'s Beasties. He's makin' a fortune! Fantasy freaks just love him. We ordered this thang for ya over a year ago."

"This'll be a big hit in the Roamer," Buster said, referring to one of his two massive cryptid research vehicles. "Thanks guys, I love it."

I passed Urliss and Hollis each an identical box wrapped in camouflage paper—one had little deer between leaves, the other had turkeys hiding in trees. The twins got to ripping like eager children.

"I hope you don't already have one, but even if you do, you could always have another, right?"

They laughed and held up their windchimes made of spent shotgun cartridges.

"This'll go on my front porch soon as I get home," Urliss said.

"Oh, Haint, this is great," Hollis said, admiring it while making it clink.

Buster passed me a package wrapped in paper with tiny Santa-suit-wearing UFOs grinning at me. "A little somethin' for you, Moon Eyes."

"Love the paper!" I said, ripping it open. As I pulled the books and documentary videos out, Buster said, "It's all about the Moon Eyed people of Appalachia. Seems like they were Welsh albinos who interbred with the Cherokee…" I guess this was paybacks for the T-shirt. Don't get me wrong, information about a lost colony of Welsh-Cherokee albinos was interesting, but as I was only one of these three, I wasn't as thrilled as perhaps Buster anticipated.

"I was hopin' you might want to go see the moon eye stones," Buster said. "It's a strange little bit o' history."

"Sounds like it. I'm looking forward to it." I said, mustering enthusiasm. Naughty Britches had crept back into the living room, keeping a safe distance from the crate.

I got up and reached behind the sofa, pulling out four wrapped liquor bottles, handing one to Urliss, Hollis, Max and Buster.

"What's this?" Max said, yanking his from the velvet bag. "Haint Blue Bourbon? Where in all of God's green acres did you find this?"

"It wasn't easy. The internet is vast and mysterious. I confess, I haven't tried it, but it sure sounds good. Made by a boutique distillery in Georgia. They put a touch of habanero, honey, and peach in it. It's smooth, a bit sweet but with a kick. If you don't drink it straight, you can put it in a killer marinade.

Wanna try it? I've got an open bottle."

They nodded. I got my bottle and five glasses.

"Cheers!" Urliss said.

"To good friends!" Hollis said.

"Merry Christmas!" Buster said.

Max added, "To Haint! Thanks for the best Christmas in a helluva long time, Sunshine!" His voice faltered over the last three words.

"Aww, Thanks to all of you for helping me get through it. Merry Christmas!" I said.

We clinked glasses and sipped.

"Say, that's mighty tasty," Buster said.

"Works for me," Hollis said, taking another sip.

I noticed that while Max seemed to enjoy his drink, he had tears in his eyes and kept sniffing. His jaw was tight.

"You okay, Max?" I asked.

"Yeah," he said sniffing again. "You did good, Sugar. Even Mama Sue said she enjoyed the get-together. For her to say something—" He shook his head, unable to say anymore."

"You mean it rated higher than *Animal Planet*?" I said, discovering that my voice was betraying emotion as well.

"Yeah," he said, winking through a tear.

"Hey, um," Buster began, tapping my knee with his finger. "Weren't you goin' to run away to the beach for Christmas?"

"Yeah!" I said, letting out an irony-laden laugh. "That was the original plan. What's that expression? Life is what happens while you' re making other plans?"

"Got any people comin' this week or for New Year's?"

"No…"

"And is everyone checking out tomorrow?"

"Yes, thank goodness. Don't get me wrong, you guys, it's been amazing, but I'm a bit whooped."

"No doubt," Max said, taking another sip and smacking with satisfaction.

Buster asked, "How soon can you be ready to hit the road? I made a tentative reservation for the week at the Citrine, isn't that the place you like? Max said it was."

"Yes, it is—you made a reservation? For us?" I asked, realizing that I sounded a bit like one of Benny's dumb-blonde-joke blondes. Here I'd been thinking about cleaning up the retreat, laundry, making beds…Going to the beach with Buster sounded as dreamy as winning a trip to Paris.

"Starting tomorrow night an' goin' through Sunday January 4th… I got that room that you said you like, 2nd floor with the ocean view?"

That's more than a week!" I said, excited.

"We don't have to stay in Flagler… we could go up to St. Augustine, or poke around Gamble Rogers Park, or we could cut it short and head south… I know you're just dyin' to go visit the Skunk Ape Research Center down in the Everglades…"

"Let's start with just the beach for a few days and see how it goes," I said. "Can Naughty Britches go too?"

NB's ears shot up. She took a few steps closer.

"Don't she go everywhere with you? Yeah, she can come too."

"Little girl! We're going to the beach! Pack your treats!"

Max beamed his approval. "You deserve it, kid. You put on quite the show, ya know."

"I dunno. It sort of happened all around me. I mean, I sure didn't plan on an opera singer or zombie bell ringers..."

"That was a hoot," Hollis said. "I'm sorry Peggy Sue missed that. She'd have loved it."

The evening wound down. Urliss and Hollis had to get Max back to the Old Oaks. "I don't think they'd be sorry at all if I croaked. They don't like me. But I don't want 'em filing no Silver Alert on my behalf. They'd take it out on me when I showed up. They hate paperwork."

I suppressed a giggle watching the twins working their way out of their chairs. It required a bit of back and fill.

Still working on the fully-upright position, Urliss said, "You're gonna outlive us all, Max." Finally standing, he gave Max a hearty back slap and bear hug. "Come on. We'll get you back."

After much hugging, and well-wishing, they departed.

Lorraine had discreetly kept to her room so we could have our little gathering.

"You really are amazing, and ya don't even know it," Buster said, hugging me. He eyed the creature in the crate. "Think he'll be okay out here for tonight?"

"Why, do you want to let him out? Give him a water bowl?" I asked.

Buster kissed my forehead. "Naw, Moon Eyes, I was askin' if you minded if he stayed out here tonight, silly."

I let NB outside to piddle. Buster and I stood in the doorway, arm-in-arm, waiting on her. "This was one memorable Christmas, Haint."

"It sure was."

We made our way to the bedroom. Despite being worn out, getting into bed with Buster, well, let's say, last part of that evening was memorable as well.

The following day, my remaining guests checked out with warm goodbyes. I gave the Garcias a hefty discount on the cabins and comped their food — heck, they'd brought as much food as I'd provided. As they were leaving, Aletea caressed Clementina's cheek, "This will be a lovely place to have her wedding reception."

"Mom! What wedding? I don't even have a *boyfriend*!"

"Anytime," I said, and I meant it. Much as they had pushed me out of my comfort zone, I envied their family unity. Iggy and I were tight, but like survivors who clung to each other in wreckage. Let's just say the overwhelming love had been absent in our family dynamic. The Garcia family energy was exhausting and drama-filled, but at the same time, brimmed with heart and celebration of life.

Saint Eleanor hugged me and thanked me for a wonderful time. Amy and Stuart left smiling to each other and holding hands until they had to separate to get into their vehicle.

Lerlene and Freddie said that their kids were still talking about the zombies, the gift exchange, the alpacas, and the fire truck.

"This was the most fun we've had in ages," Lerlene said.

Freddie snickered, "Yeah, about the only thing that could have topped this vacation would have been Saint Eleanor running into a Skunk Ape in the bathroom. You know, I should have bought that costume last Halloween when I had the chance. Boy, would she have been surprised if I'd peeked at her in the shower."

"You would have, too," Lerlene whispered.

His face drained of color. "Yeah, good point."

"She'd have had a heart attack," I said. "She's not so bad really. She was an enormous help with the decorating."

Finally, after more hugging, everyone was gone. Buster and I got some alone time. For once, I turned my worry brain off. It still rankled that Buster had just taken off across the globe without telling me. Did we have a future together? How would we work things out? I had no answers. I was too exhausted to fret about it. He'd made his way back from the jungles in Africa to be with me. We'd made up. I basked in his company, his humor, his love.

Sorry! Closed for much-needed vacation...

I closed up the retreat and put a notice on the web page that we were closed until January 5th. As that was a Monday, I doubted I'd have guests beating down the door to get a cabin. I'd have plenty of time to clean and restock the kitchen. Lorraine was going to stay on at my house while we were gone. No telling how long it would be before her house was habitable again, and Mischief would be grateful for the company. She said she would flip the cabins for me, if Lerlene could give her a ride. And if she wasn't preoccupied with Pedro.

Four hours later, we were heading east to spend a luxurious and decadent week doing anything we wanted or nothing at all. I set up an extra card table and we worked on the thousand-piece puzzle of the basset puppy in a Christmas stocking. We walked the empty beach at sunrise while Naughty Britches chased ghost crabs and sandpipers. We sipped spritzers with our feet on the balcony ledge as the sun set. While Buster went fishing, I dug into my cozy Christmas mystery about a bed and breakfast in snowy Idaho. We slept in. We ate fish tacos and baskets full of fried shrimp. We made love and enjoyed pillow talk.

It was *mostly* idyllic.

Buster told me more about his harrowing trip to Africa.

There were a few times when Buster fell asleep but woke up gasping. It turned out he needed the beach time as much as I did to recover from his trip. On a couple of cold mornings, we meditated together on the bed, propped up by pillows, comfy in our bathrobes.

I guess it would only be fair to mention that dating a fly-fisherman with regular video posts on social media, who also has his own line of flies like the Buster Luster and the Damselfly Dazzler, meant that there was a lot of me waiting around while Buster texted or talked to a client or fan with a fishing question.

"No, Dwayne, any sinkin' fly can be suspended with a "strike indicator" bobber. Any floatin' or neutrally buoyant fly can be sunk with small split shot. The only difference from cane pole or spin fishing is that everything is scaled down –see, the split shot used is as small as No. 6 tin, 0.1 g or about 1/256 of an oz and bobbers are ½" or just a bit of yarn to trap some air bubbles…"

"Was you usin' a Uni Knot, or some folks call it a Duncan Loop? Aw, man, Jerome, you try that now, good an' tight for tyin' the fly to the tippet. The Clinch Knot is for much smaller flies, like hook size twelve or less. Yup, man, I'm tellin' you, just try that Uni, and your problem's solved."

"Oh, no, Brian, you don't gotta get a new reel, that ain't yer problem. Sounds ta me like your reel weight ain't balancin' the rod right. Ya gotta adjust the balance point one inch to one and a half inches down from the top o' the cork, man. Say, if you look, I did a video about that…"

NB and I took a nap while Buster was out on the beach making a how-to-catch-whiting video (on a falling tide, just after high tide).

And yes, my Inner Critic even found me clicking, clicking, clicking to no avail with the remote once or twice.

*You've been through the program options three times. You know it's a sign of mental instability to do the same thing many times and yet expect different results. You aren't really expecting something new to pop up, are you?*

No.

I clicked the television off, tossed the remote on the desk and found something else to do. Make a sandwich. Book. Basset puzzle.

Mostly, it was wonderful.

We brought in New Year's Eve with a fireworks show on the beach and our own fireworks later in bed.

It was the most memorable holiday I'd ever had. I was relaxed and in love. I was living in the moment. And the moment was fine.

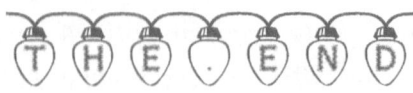

We sure hope you enjoyed this book. If you did, would you do a quick review on Amazon or Goodreads to keep us here in Catfish Springs alive? We'd sure appreciate it!

Stay in touch!

Please visit my blog  at : **https://haintsretreat.com/** It's got some of my recipes, Florida stuff, my favorite movie reviews, and fun basset facts. Please explore!

You can also check in with my publisher at:

**https://hedonistichoundpress.com/**

Until next time, wishing you abundance and peace, and happy holidays--whatever you celebrate, may it be full of joy and love!

--Haint Blue